Moral Hazard

Moral Hazard

J J Eldridge

Published by Iguana Books
720 Bathurst Street, Suite 303
Toronto, Ontario, Canada
M5V 2R4

Publisher: Greg Ioannou
Editor: Vanessa Ricci-Thode
Front cover images: Courtesy of Shutterstock
Front cover design: Ashley James
Book layout design: Kathryn Willms

Library and Archives Canada Cataloguing in Publication

Eldridge, J. J., 1961-, author
Moral hazard / J.J. Eldridge.

Issued in print and electronic formats.
ISBN 978-1-77180-100-3 (pbk.).--ISBN 978-1-77180-101-0 (epub).--
ISBN 978-1-77180-102-7 (kindle).--ISBN 978-1-77180-103-4 (pdf)

I. Title.

PR6105.L47M67 2015 823'.92 C2014-908169-3
C2014-908170-7

This is an original print edition of *Moral Hazard*.

For M&M.

2003, Vienna, The DNA Conscious

Nathan did not know who he worked for. He was bright enough to know that they were apolitical yet instrumental in global decision-making. He knew that their access to scientific research was unprecedented, and that they had unlimited wealth to devote to certain projects that they deemed of exponential importance to the future of mankind's existence. During the two years since his initial engagement, he had never set eyes on any panel member, but discussed concepts with an opaque anonymity that rarely spoke back yet retained a nefarious ubiquity that hung like a shadow across every aspect of his life. He did not believe that he had sold his soul to the devil or anything that dramatic — he was a scientist. However, he did acknowledge that he had consciously chosen a path that had no undoing, and he had therefore long since reconciled himself to embracing it as positive and enlightening.

He remembered the final few words of his second meeting with the panel, when he had agreed to accept the assignment.

"You will be well rewarded," a female voice had confirmed, "but if you start this assignment, you can never leave it. It will personify your life in ways that you can only dream of, or become your nemesis if you choose to behave unwisely."

He had never doubted these words, and had behaved "unwisely" on only one occasion. As a result of a frustrated ego, he had once decided that he wanted to know more, and had hired a private investigator to try ascertaining where the panel might meet by intercepting various communication signals. The attempt had been unsuccessful, but when he visited the bank later that week to put some private papers into his safety deposit box, he found the box empty save for a small, typewritten note.

"Don't do that again," was all it said.

At his third meeting, Nathan concluded that he was being addressed by a single panel member, a Hermes for the others, a woman once again, whose accent fell somewhere in the deep Atlantic between New York and London. She spoke slowly and a number of images were thrown across a screen in front of Nathan.

"As we have previously discussed," she began, "we have employed you on account of your unprecedented research into DNA, brain stem-cell research, and cloning. We also find you egocentric and unscrupulous, traits which suit our purpose."

The woman paused, and Nathan interpreted it as an opportunity to speak, but she cut him off.

"Please, Nathan," she said quickly, "I have lots to get through, so do not interrupt."

Nathan imagined that she had raised a hand from her notes, so he quietly nodded and shifted his weight to the other side of his chair.

"Our preoccupation is population control," she continued. "In 1804, the world's population stood at a mere one billion, and it would be another one hundred and twenty-two years before mankind passed the two billion milestone. What is more alarming is that the world population has doubled since 1950, doubled in the space of forty years, and we expect the seventh billion human to be born in 2011. I will not bore you with all the statistics except to say that this planet can probably sustain five billion souls, and that *Homo sapiens*, this extraordinary cocktail of DNA, are advancing more dramatically than we ever imagined. Put simply, we are losing control, or we will lose control of this special resource unless we act, unless we pre-empt in dramatic fashion. Moreover, we estimate that by 2030, there will be two workers for every retired person, a fact which makes no economic sense in this world; it is simply not sustainable under this financial model and the planet will implode at some point."

The voice paused for a few moments and Nathan wondered if she was sipping from a glass of water.

She cleared her throat and continued, "We have been working on different contingencies for a few years now, we always are. This project has taken priority over all others, a project designed to adjust world population statistics but in a way we can measure accurately, so our focus has not been on war or disease — as you might imagine, it's a complex, tricky subject. Now, you may know that up to the 1970s or so, population increases were calculated based on hyperbolic growth and that hyperbolic growth differs from exponential growth and logistic growth, although the three terms are often confused. Suffice it to say that we had to surmise that calculations based solely on hyperbolic growth were difficult to nail down fifty years into the future, that within these formulae lay too many unknowns. So, we have run many scenarios thus far and they leave us with many unanswered questions, of course, but with one fundamental area of choice as we see it."

A few words appeared on the screen in front of Nathan:

Do you try to control population at the beginning or at the end of life?

"Up to now, Nathan," she continued, "all studies and trials have suggested the beginning of life: fertility studies, birth control plans, look at China's efforts, and so on and so forth. What is most interesting about all this research is that the beginning is not trend proof and never will be, it never has been, and so it's not sustainable. We are only interested in sustainable plans." The woman coughed and cleared her throat.

"Excuse me," she said, "I have a frog in my throat."

Nathan found her apology surreal given what they were discussing.

"So, we looked at options for the end of life, obviously, and we have considered disease, epidemics, et cetera, but as I alluded to earlier, these are short-term solutions that mankind will eventually obviate; we know that, we have experience with such programs."

Nathan's hands became clammy as he clasped them tightly in his lap.

"Furthermore, this solution loads costs disproportionately onto the end of a life, the cost of long life, so to speak, and this simply bears down on those working; remember, the two-to-one ratio of worker to retiree by 2030. If we make people ill, that medical burden will be carried by those working, so we discarded that as an option." The woman paused once again and another set of words appeared in front of Nathan:

> *This is our remit: to reduce the world population by two billion souls over the next fifty years and to sustain a population of less than five billion human souls for the next millennium.*

The woman paused to let the full impact sink in.

"Are you with me so far, Nathan?" she asked quietly.

He nodded without replying, encouraging her to continue.

"You might find the next section of what I have to say fanciful or fantastic," she continued, "but rest assured, we have hundreds of years of experience in manipulating mankind, so we are not interested in what you think about our concept. We simply want to know whether it can be done, scientifically, and if so, how you will do it and how long it will take. Is that clear?"

Nathan nodded once again.

"Good," she said quietly, almost to herself. "Now, you will know from your research that the normal human uses only ten percent of his or her DNA, the remainder being what you referred to last year as junk DNA, but that certain people throughout history — Jesus being the main protagonist — have been able to access their full DNA capacity, which have made them vibrate at a much higher tempo within the universe's electromagnetic spectrum and given them what some perceived to be supernatural powers, powers to heal, for example, in his case. You will know better than I that the healing frequency for damaged DNA is five hundred and twenty-eight Hertz. As a specialist in this field, you will also know that there are many species in nature that retain extraordinary communication abilities, paradoxically because they have yet to become as introspective as *Homo sapiens* — bees, ants, whales, dolphins; the examples in nature are endless.

"What we wish to do is something similar but a little more complicated." She paused. "I can see that I have sparked your imagination," she said.

"You have," Nathan said simply. "Please go on."

"Our intention is to give you access to our work on DNA manipulation, and we want you to create three hybrids, three people who have two unique characteristics. The first is their ability to access their full DNA potential, which will give them certain unique abilities; the second is to close certain areas of their minds to make them less introspective; they will become like the army ant or killer bee, receiving information and instructions subconsciously, *instinctively*, if you prefer that word." The woman paused before adding, "Do you want me to repeat that?"

"No." Nathan shook his head.

“We want to know if it can be done, and if it can, we will then tell you why and what steps to take.”

Nathan sensed that the meeting was drawing to a close.

“We have arranged certain facilities and assistance for you, and, as I said, additional information on DNA manipulation, which you will need. We require your response in twelve months. That should be adequate time.”

The woman did not wait for Nathan to reply; the screen simply went dead.

2005, Vienna,
Nigroque Cygno, A Black Swan

Nathan's research and reports had been approved by the panel, and he had been given control of the program. His anonymous employers would retreat into the shadows where they would weave their spin into the farthest corners of the globe. Nathan recalled his second set of instructions. Their concept seemed incredible at first but no more so than mankind's appetite for religious belief, its enduring dependence on salvation. On this occasion, there were two panel members, a man and a woman, and they took turns delivering his instructions, which Nathan found odd afterward, when he sat in the half-light and considered what he had been instructed to do.

"Do you know what a black swan event is?" the man asked as soon as Nathan sat down.

"Not really, no," Nathan replied. He had a vague idea but had learned that there were no shortcuts when dealing with his employers.

The man sounded a little irritated as he continued, "You are going to implement what we shall call a black swan event, quite simply an event which is a complete surprise, an event which has a major effect across the globe, but an event which, once witnessed and rationalized, mankind will subsequently tell itself could have been expected, that in hindsight there is plausibility, justification even. Let me tell you what you are going to do."

But it was the woman who took up his instructions. "You are going to implement a simple marketing strategy that will be prosecuted through a new set of prophets, the Millennium prophets — three prophets to be precise — two men and one woman who will be born in 2010 with incredible powers, genetically engineered in accordance with your research and reports. They will start their crusades across the globe when they are twenty-five years old, and they will heal through their hands, miracle after miracle — imagine cancer momentarily eradicated, their gift to civilization, and, in tandem, what will they preach, what will they advocate, what will they do themselves at thirty-three years old, the same age as Jesus when he went to the cross? They will self-sacrifice because their unified message throughout their eight-year crusades will be as follows."

A set of words appeared in front of Nathan:

> *Just as God sent his only son to sacrifice himself for the sin of mankind, so mankind must now sacrifice to save mankind, to sustain mankind.*

"Their self-sacrifice will be this black swan event."

Nathan was not sure if he could believe what he was hearing. The speakers went quiet for a while, but a series of slides flashed across the screen in front of him:

> *From Peter's Gospel: "Who his own self bore our sins in his own body on the tree, that we, being dead to sins, should live unto righteousness: by whose stripes you were healed.*
>
> *"Two thousand years ago, the Son of God was born as a man in Bethlehem. So sinful have men become that only a perfect sacrifice could cleanse us of our sins. No man could be a perfect sacrifice because all of us were sinners. Jesus Christ, the Son of God, became the perfect sacrifice to redeem us from death."*

The last slide depicted a single storey building with palatial gardens and a number of water features.

The woman began again, "This is what a self-sacrifice centre might look like, but we have plenty of time to perfect our plans."

Nathan was not really looking at the architecture; he was more flabbergasted by what he had just heard.

As if his thoughts had been read, the woman spoke once again, an icy chill surrounding her tone. "You don't seem convinced," she said quietly. "We have done our homework, philosophically speaking."

"I don't doubt that," Nathan said, almost to himself.

"Let me draw your attention once again to this slide," she responded.

"The *perfect sacrifice*," she said slowly, "let's focus on that word *sacrifice* for a moment. Now, one might argue, philosophically, that Jesus, as the Son of God, set a train of events in motion that were inevitable, almost irreversible, as certain as a man jumping off a bridge, knowing that he will land on whatever is below him with the ensuing consequences. Gravity. And just so, in a similar fashion, Jesus set a train of events in motion that he knew would culminate in his death. So, in his case, Jesus, sacrifice or suicide, which is it?"

Nathan found himself clearing his throat, as if he had something to say.

"And what about Samson?" the man asked simply. The question hung in the silence.

"Sorry, what do you mean?" Nathan asked, suddenly realizing that he was expected to respond.

"I said what about Samson?" the man repeated. "When he destroyed the temple of Dagon, was that sacrifice or suicide?"

"I don't know," Nathan replied. "I have never given it much thought." He paused. "Surely all monotheist religions forbid suicide. Isn't it a mortal sin under the Catholic faith?"

"Yes, quite so," the woman said quickly. "We are not calling it suicide. Philosophically, the Church created divine sanction to allow for Jesus's actions, for his self-sacrifice; our prophets will do the same."

"But will this be credible?" Nathan asked.

"Let me answer your question in two parts," the man said. "These prophets will be healing people throughout their crusades: healing cancer, healing children, healing the rich and influential. Can you imagine such an impact? Furthermore, the three prophets will not be advocating self-sacrifice as their message; they will be receiving messages from God and acting upon them, instructions, just as the queen ant sends instructions to her workers, so the prophets will not question these commands as they will be unable to do so. You will have shut down those parts of their minds responsible for introspection, and, of course, for anyone doubting their credentials, they will lead by example: they will self-sacrifice."

Nathan thought about what he had heard. "Are you suggesting that everyone should do this at thirty-three years old?" he asked, but then he thought about how stupid the question sounded and rubbed his hand across his jaw.

"It will be a choice; it will not be compulsory," the woman added. "We think that some legislation will be likely, that governments will step in. We know that a sixty-five-year-old age threshold will meet our requirements, by way of population reduction over the next forty to fifty years."

A third voice suddenly joined the conversation. It was an older voice, a leader's voice, someone who had been listening, observing.

"Just get the first bit right, Nathan, the laboratory part; the rest will fall into place."

2065, Las Vegas, An Anal Adventure

Brian sat and squinted at the huge screen dominating the conference hall as another set of dentures flashed across the whitewashed canvas, this particular set cradled on a shallow bed of dried sand so that it resembled an amorphous fossil sitting on a remote island, somewhere exotic. Brian had endured three days of dental and periodontal presentations, endless drilling techniques, bridging, caps, floss, and anaesthetics. Each speaker was characterized by an unconvincing earnestness to persuade the drab surroundings and the bored delegates that they were somehow breaking new ground — that teeth were more exciting than Hollywood, that flossing was perhaps, albeit at a stretch, as exciting as masturbation, and that the world's future depended as much on oral health care as it did on global warming and associated self-sacrifice rates.

I am a dentist, Brian thought to himself. *No, that's not quite right*, he corrected himself, *I am a fucking dentist; no, I can do better, I am a fucking bored dentist; in fact, no again, I am forty-eight years old, I have spent most of my adult life looking into peoples' mouths and it must be one of the most ridiculous ways to spend one's short time on this planet.*

Brian seldom travelled, so the Annual Dental Conference did afford some self-indulgence, an opportunity to dwell on his life, to reflect. Well, this was where his mind tended to migrate increasingly but with little positive energy. He was supposed to be researching the latest dental technologies but spent more time thinking, or at least trying to find some clarity of thought, some purpose for his sorry existence. He had stood in front of his hotel mirror for 15 minutes that morning, naked, and had looked at the onset of age, grey hairs covering his chest and more rebellious hairs protruding from his ears and nostrils in eccentric clusters. He had even turned away from the mirror and bent over to examine his backside, the position bringing a rush of blood to his head but not before he had detected a few grey hairs emerging from his anus in a collective and insulting abandon.

He was, in fact, in pretty good shape compared to many of his friends and professional associates. He played squash three times every week, enjoyed the occasional fun run, and could still do 100 sit-ups without pause. He looked along his row of fellow dentists, most of whom sported floppy paunches and uncontrollable jowls. The convention boasted more male than female delegates, and the few women gave little cause for excitement. It was difficult, in fact, to identify a single beautiful member of the human species in the entire room.

Las Vegas must be appalled, he mused. The location was more accustomed to the beautiful set, to youth, to risk, and operated at a faster and more glamorous pace than cavities and gum disease.

ADCs should be held somewhere dull because, let's face it, he smiled to himself, *we are fucking dull! Morbidity has more zip. So what?* Brian asked himself, his mind more focused on an all-life crisis as opposed to a mid-life blip. How the fuck had he ended up looking into perfect strangers' mouths all his life? It was close to self-insulting. Actually not even close, it was just that, degenerating, but, as his sour mother-in-law piped up at every opportunity, such a reliable position, such a stable source of income.

At least I have my Jan, my J, he said to himself, *my childhood sweetheart, my rock.*

"And that concludes Doctor Stankovic's presentation," the podium declared, a short ripple of applause echoing through the dozing throng. "We'll now take a short break before we begin our group workshops, and let's not forget folks, our theme today is floss therapy for the older generation. Should be fascinating, enjoy!"

The thought of another group workshop filled Brian with horror.

I need air, he said to himself and stumbled out of the stuffy conference centre to make his way back toward the hotel's reception, the huge metropolis of the Bellagio buzzing with activity. He felt his telephone vibrate in his inner pocket and pulled it out, a message from his wife, his Jan, sitting in the inbox. He glanced at his watch.

My God, he thought, *it must be one in the morning in the UK.*

Brian opened the message.

> *I loved having you in my mouth and my arse, didn't realize that I could come like that. Kisses, until tomorrow.*

Brian looked at the message and read it over once again, turning the telephone around as if to make sure that it was really his. Was this a joke? The feeling of nausea that swept through him was the only answer he received. He would later reflect on the deluge of thoughts and feelings that bombarded him simultaneously, an onslaught of questions, the past and present colliding in waves of fear, anger, and sorrow; twenty years of friendship and love ripped to shreds in a few seconds, by a few words, words that cut deep furrows into his psyche, that crushed his lungs so that he could barely breathe, that left his heart cascading in limbo and filled his throat with bile, "arse, come, kisses."

He sat down in a chair adjacent to the reception desk and looked at the message again, glancing furtively around him as if his raw angst had somehow spread like a plague across the marble floor. He saw a tiny Pekingese dog pecking like a small bird at its owner's heels and caught the flashy smile of a receptionist as she handed a set of keys to one of her colleagues. It seemed that the rest of the world had not been privy to his message, that the long line of customers were not discussing his personal demise, sniggering at his downfall like naughty children. He felt something scratching around his ankles and looked down to see the small animal pulling at one of his shoelaces. He kicked out with the other foot, catching the animal in its ribs, a high-pitched yelp echoing across the huge ceiling.

But I like dogs, he said to himself. The dog scurried away toward its owner, a tall woman with peroxide blonde hair who fixed Brian with a look of disgust, bending to retrieve the poor creature, her voluminous bosom pulling her toward the floor as if she had dumbbells attached to her chest.

Brian mouthed "stupid bitch" to himself and left his seat, a sudden urge to be alone engulfing him like a cloud, his steps heavy, his feet moving subconsciously as if he had wandered into glutinous clay. He stumbled like a drunk, occasionally bumping into the steady stream of guests who looked at him with a mixture of fear and amusement, the odd parent pulling children a little closer as he staggered by. He bumped into a short woman in a bright red uniform who pushed a glossy pamphlet into his hand — "Sunset over the Grand Canyon, Daily Helicopter Excursions" — that he crushed into his right-hand jacket pocket and sought the security of the elevators, leaning back against the burnished handrail as he was seamlessly delivered to his floor.

Brian kicked his door closed as he cast aside his jacket, moving toward the bed where he threw himself forward, a muffled cry escaping from his mouth as he buried his head in the pillow. He lay there for a few minutes, his body shaking, desperately trying to catch his breath; he turned over and looked at the ceiling, tears running from the corner of his eyes into his shirt collar.

He stood up and retrieved his jacket from the floor, pulling out his telephone once again and looking at the message. He knew that it was not a joke, clearly not, and found it hard to imagine his wife making such a fundamental mistake.

Perhaps her anal lover is also called Brian, he thought sardonically. This fucking Brian had experienced more of his wife than he had in 20 years, it would seem. He could not imagine his wife, his J, screaming "fuck me in the arse" to him.

What happened? he wondered. *What have I missed? Who was the cuckold now?* He giggled, a hint of hysteria brushing across him like a rabid fever. He wondered if she would work it out, when she would work it out, and then what, pretend it was a joke? *I doubt that*, he thought, *even for us, that would be a schizophrenic step too far for anyone's imagination.* Or, he acknowledged, it might get lost in the plethora of messages filling the airways between them, and he would be greeted as normal on return, a peck on the cheek, a squeeze of his arm.

What sort of greeting did he get, Brian wondered. "I loved having you in my mouth" slapped him across his face and sent tears to the corner of his eyes.

He felt wounded, physically beaten, his body moving autonomously around the room, prowling through his despair. He cast his eyes out of the window, the huge fountains in front of the hotel burst into life.

So what? he thought. Nothing would ever look or feel the same now or for a very long time. Every extracted tooth would mock him further, his purpose in life personified by regret and self-indulgent pity.

He opened the small bar that fit neatly into a small cabinet next to the desk, and looked at the array of miniature bottles displayed in rank like a military detachment.

Don't be a cunt, he said. That would be the usual response, the B-movie scene — drunken man lying on his bed, weeping, checking the chamber of his Smith & Wesson. *Do that later*, he told himself, *get drunk, hook up with a whore, never done that, one who is happy to take it up her arse, revenge by proxy, barrel in mouth, brains across the bedstead, remorseful wife.*

But no life insurance, a ridiculous voice piped up, *it would be suicide.*

Jesus Christ, he mused, *I was just in my own little scene for a minute, even then, there, propriety raises her ugly head, conditioning, endless conditioning. So, in conclusion,* he told himself, *get drunk later, wallow in self-pity later, but not right now, right now, do something. Move!*

Brian pulled the glossy brochure from his jacket pocket and glanced at the headlines: Grand Canyon West Rim, Hoover Dam, Champagne Picnic, Low-Level Flight over the Las Vegas Strip.

Why not? he thought. *Do something, keep moving.*

He called the number and booked a place, to the polite message of "the limousine will be in front of the Bellagio at five-thirty sharp, thank you for calling."

He flicked on the television, but the images remained opaque, his mind caught somewhere between continents. Memories kept flashing into his mind like jumbled movie reels, snapshots of his wife, a life he no longer wanted, a life that held bitter betrayal and shavings of anger. His stomach churned in despair, his mind unable to close off the barrage of memories shoving their way through his psyche. Brian changed his clothes quickly and left the room.

Brian spent the next hour wandering through the myriad of pathways that connected the different hotel swimming pools. The ranks of sunbathers were sipping huge cocktails, with glossy magazines thrown over pool chairs, shrieks of laughter from young children jumping into the shallow water, the clear water caught in the bright sunlight. Brian ordered a glass of tonic water and watched the scene from a tangent. His life was so dislocated from this, his pale skin and conservative manner so at odds with the carefree nature of the scene before him.

Life will simply continue, he said. *Your personal demise is irrelevant, as isolated and insignificant as you are, so get used to the fucking concept or you will suffocate.*

But he knew that this would take time, a readjustment, tortuous discussions, separation, the real fallout from a decent blow job or an anal adventure. He liked that, an anal adventure, a good epitaph to their marriage perhaps?

Brian slipped away from the pool like a pale shadow and moved back toward the main building, his limbs heavy, his body moving like a slow train as his mind raced ahead to imaginary scenarios — he and J sitting at their small kitchen table, clutching coffee cups as their dreams slid through their fingers.

Dreams? What were our dreams? he wondered. It had been so long since they had discussed their dreams; they had subconsciously become anonymous, faceless, a blur of mediocrity in a seamless transition to middle age. *Fuck*, he said, *what the fuck was that all about?*

Brian wandered aimlessly into one of the casino halls and stood at the top of a staircase overlooking the huge auditorium. Below were roulette tables and slot machines filling the air with the crackle of excitement, expectation — disappointment, perhaps? He had never been attracted to gambling, an occasional dabble at the lottery the extent of his appetite for risk; a quiet disdain for needless waste hovered around his peripheries as he surveyed the hordes in front of him. Nevertheless, he pulled his wallet out of his pocket and extracted a $100 dollar bill. He changed it for a single token at the cashier's desk before wandering up and down the aisles, trying to select exactly where he would fritter the small, black chip sitting in his palm like a flat pebble.

He had no real knowledge of roulette or black jack, and finally settled on a ridiculous-looking colossus that resembled a time machine, bright lights winking from every corner, the reels occasionally spinning autonomously like a fairground attraction. "Wheel of Fortune" was framed around the head of the beast in golden lights. He felt slightly embarrassed as he pushed his token into the head of the machine and walked away in silent humiliation, his indulgent waste making him blush involuntarily. He could hear the reels humming as he glanced behind him and then the creature vibrated like a washing machine, and a siren shrieked across the ceiling like an approaching train. In an instant, he found himself surrounded by members of staff, an array of red jackets pulling him back in front of the machine, a photographer snapping in front of his face as if he were an instant celebrity, a small crowd of onlookers gathering around him in admiration and quiet envy. Brian's mind remained numb as he was carried through this short carnival before being ushered into a small office behind the cashier's window where casino staff hovered around him like hungry bees. There was a lull in the commotion as a meticulously dressed woman swept into the room and sat down in front of him, a bright smile fixed across her face like a mannequin, her bright fingernails pulling a pen from the inside of her jacket.

"So," she began, "it's Mister…?"

He had literally "hit the jackpot" and was $7.6 million the richer, but, as much as he found this hard to compute, it seemed a little pointless juxtapose to his earlier message. He noticed some of the casino staff whispering amongst themselves, and he could only guess what they must think; that his blank expression is the result of shock; *he was in shock* was what they would tell themselves later as they brushed their teeth before bed.

2065, Las Vegas, The Wallet

Brian's trip to the Grand Canyon passed in a surreal blur, the events of the day jumbled with the pilot's commentary as the helicopter banked over Lake Mead and the Hoover Dam before finally settling in Hualapai Indian land. The guests were served a champagne picnic as the sunset threw colours across the canyon walls in a wash of pastels that superseded nature and drew gasps of delight from his fellow travellers. Brian stood off to one side, his feet shuffling sand between his soles, his mind flicking between his irrelevant life in Salisbury and the small fortune that had been secured in a hotel safety deposit box. One of the guests had tried to engage Brian in small talk and he found himself quietly ashamed when he had admitted to being a dentist, the look of indifference this information elicited lost in the warm breeze that rose from the canyon floor like a distant promise.

But you don't have to be a dentist now, the small voice whispered. *You can do whatever you want: run, disappear, a reinvention, a recalibration?*

What's the point? he wondered. *Everything seems so fucking pointless.*

His personal humiliation dragged him toward the rocky edge where he peered into the abyss, a momentary dizziness causing him to step back as a sudden gust of air caught him off balance. He stepped forward again and kicked a small rock into the space in front of him, glancing over the rim to watch it spit dust as it ricocheted into the dusk. He closed his eyes on the return journey as the helicopter skimmed across the Las Vegas Strip, the bright lights pulsing into the air like a funfair, the extravagance and excess mingling with the thump, thump of the helicopter blades. Before he knew it, Brian found himself back in his hotel room, the dust around his ankles the only reminder of how he had spent the last few hours.

So, now what? he said. *Isn't it time for drama, drinks, whores, that Smith & Wesson?*

But I'm rich, he reminded himself. *I can do whatever I want!*

Instinctive mechanics pulled Brian out of his malaise and pushed him through the shower and into a clean shirt.

I am going to drink now, he decided. *Drink to forget, drink to sleep, drink to get these fucking images out of my head, which make me want to vomit, to scream in misery, to curse my J. My J*, he grunted. *What a fucking joke! Never again my J, perhaps she never was? Was I ever her Brian?* he considered. *Are we ever anyone's but our own? Ownership, possession, and what for, for our own self-importance, our own "up our own arses" sense of belonging, the conforming masses? No more conforming*, he said to himself. *No more stupid drinks and parties where we smile in obsequious abeyance of our fears, our desire for acceptance, our fear of isolation pushing us to small talk, to excessive indulgence. Fuck me*, he said to himself, *go and get a drink and shut up, you pathetic idiot.*

Brian made his way down to the foyer and walked out into the warm night, laughter and the drone of voices tugging at his senses and lightening his step. He walked into the bright array of neon lights, which threw themselves across his path, his eyes darting across the congested traffic until he selected a flashing "Cocktail Lounge" sign as his first port of call. The door swung open automatically, and he found a seat at the far end of the bar, a solitary piano player crooning away to his right side, the place still empty at this relatively early hour.

"Hey, so what can I get you?" asked the girl behind the bar. "You look like you could use a drink," she added, her smile revealing a set of brilliant white teeth, which Brian could not help admiring.

Forget the dentist, he said to himself. *You are not a dentist, be something else for fuck's sake.*

He ordered a glass of red wine and peered at his fingers as the girl slid the glass in front of him. Other customers appeared at the other end of the bar, and he found himself alone, the heavy claret soothing as he drank a first glass and then a second, occasionally popping a peanut into his mouth as the creases in his brow began to wane. He ordered a third glass and subconsciously patted the inside of his jacket, a momentary panic flashing across his features. His wallet was missing.

Fuck, he thought. He knew that he had not touched his jacket in his room so he must have lost it somewhere during the canyon trip. He let out an involuntary groan and patted his pockets once again, the absurdity of the day mocking him from a tangent, a lost love, an amassed fortune, and now this. He couldn't even pay for his wine. Now what?

Keep drinking, he said to himself. *She can always call the hotel.*

His credit was good, his safety deposit box sat like a pregnant cow under lock and key, but what a pain — credit cards, his driving license, a photo of J. He guffawed to himself, a photo of his beloved with someone else's prick up her arse. Good riddance to the wallet! He ordered another glass of wine, the volume of alcohol barely registering as his mind raced.

The bar filled slowly and Brian found himself squeezed into the corner as another customer perched herself on the bar stool next to him, a quick "excuse me" spoken quietly as she settled herself. She ordered a glass of champagne and stared across the bar, her eyes fixed like a hawk on an imaginary spot somewhere across the room. Brian took the opportunity to study her, her age indeterminable, her steel-grey hair pulled back from her forehead, the skin across her face etched by age and sorrow.

Or reflection, he thought. *Perhaps reflection more than sorrow.* She was dressed like someone half her age, a faded leather jacket, jeans, and running shoes. *She must have been incredibly beautiful once. She still is, but old, late fifties, maybe early sixties, impossible to tell.*

The woman drank her first glass quickly and waved toward the girl behind the bar whose smile preceded her as she returned with the bottle of champagne.

"So, ma'am," she said, "how was your day, what have you been doing?"

"Oh, not bad," the woman replied. "I was on one of those sunset trips, you know, the Grand Canyon, the strip, all of that stuff." Her accent was hard to place, eastern European, possibly.

"And did you find my wallet?" Brian asked, the words slipping from his mouth before he had time to think. The woman turned toward Brian, her eyes cast across his face like a wild cat. He found himself unable to hold her gaze and felt the colour rising in his cheeks. After a few moments, during which her eyes did not blink, she reached into her inside pocket and withdrew a wallet, his wallet, and tossed it onto the bar in front of him.

"Yes, I did," she said quietly. "Your photo is on your driving license, I recall. I was going to hand it in to the police in the morning, but, seeing as you are here, you have saved me the trouble."

Brian picked up his wallet in disbelief. "But that's incredible, incredible," he murmured. "That's impossible."

"Clearly not," the woman whispered, and stood up abruptly. "The least you can do is pay for my drinks." And she walked away toward the door, the second glass untouched. Brian's eyes followed the apparition momentarily before he sprung to life. He pulled two hundred dollar bills from his wallet and waved them toward the girl behind the bar before rushing after the woman.

"Wait, wait," Brian called after her as he jogged up the pavement until he was alongside her. The woman stopped abruptly and looked at him, a hint of anger flashing across her eyes.

"What?" she said. "You have your wallet, so please, leave me alone."

Brian attempted a smile, his shoulders dropping momentarily. "But, don't you see," he said with some enthusiasm, "that's just the most impossible coincidence. There are millions of people here, thousands of bars, and yet you end up seated next to me and you have my wallet in your pocket. If you made it up, no one would believe you!"

"What's your point?" she asked simply, and began to walk away from him.

"I don't know," Brian continued unperturbed, and fell in beside her. "My point is that I don't know, but there must be a point, things like that don't happen without a point, surely you can see that?"

"What are you — a damned stalker?" she asked, as her step quickened. "Leave me alone."

"I am a nothing," Brian said quietly, and stopped walking after her.

The woman walked on a few paces and then her pace faltered. She turned back toward Brian. "Sorry, that was uncalled for, the 'damned stalker' bit. I don't mean to be rude but I don't know you. I'm glad you got your wallet back, really I am, but that's it."

"But there must be a reason," Brian added quietly. "Things like that don't happen without a reason?" His question hung in the air between them.

"So what are you?" the woman asked. "If you tell me what you are, there might be a reason."

"A dentist," Brian replied. "I think that a stalker might be more interesting. I am a British dentist who has had the most extraordinary day, and now this, to cap it all."

"Why was it extraordinary?" the woman asked, feigning disinterest.

Brian smiled politely. "Well, I am British, so we don't discuss personal things and some of this is personal."

"Then, we'll never know, will we," she said, waving a dismissive hand in his direction and walked on.

Brian hesitated for a moment and then ran after her once more. "And what are you, then," he asked, "or what were you?"

The woman stopped once more and Brian detected a sense of fear around her, her eyes scanning the street behind him as if she was expecting someone. She caught his arm suddenly and pulled him into an adjacent bar.

"In here, you can buy me a drink."

The woman seemed furtive as she propelled Brian to a booth at the far end of the bar where she sank back into the shadows. Brian sat opposite her and offered his hand over the table.

"By the way, my name is Brian, good to meet you."

"Valeriya," she said, and briefly shook the ends of his fingers.

"What is that?" Brian asked. "Your name, it sounds unusual."

"Russian," she said, her monosyllabic manner amusing to Brian who smiled to himself. Brian ordered drinks and watched Valeriya who still seemed more preoccupied with what was going on outside than with Brian.

"Is there something the matter?" he eventually asked. "You seem distracted."

"Yes, sorry," she said quickly, turning her attention back to Brian. "I am a little preoccupied." She paused. "So, Mister Wallet, tell me about your day."

Brian began hesitantly; he talked about the ADC, how fucking boring it was, how ridiculous it felt to be a dentist, how fed up he was with his petty existence, how irrelevant it all was.

"What is the point?" he asked across the table, but Valeriya said nothing, a simple shrug of her shoulders was all he got. So he continued rambling but eventually got back to the first part of his day, the unwanted message; he didn't go as far as describing the exact text and tried to make light of the fact that his wife's lover might have the same name as him. In fact, he tried to make light of the whole episode, but his words fell heavily across the space between them, tripping in the half-light, caught in the mass of raw uncertainty sitting across his features in deep furrows. Valeriya sensed his discomfort, this confession of confusion, guilt, and blame suddenly pouring from the reticent Englishman.

"I'm sorry," she offered at one point. "I never married, could never understand that nonsense."

"Well," Brian eventually paused, "that was that!" He attempted a smile and gulped at his wine in embarrassment.

"So," Valeriya said quietly, "that was your day, until I found your wallet?"

"No, it gets worse. Well, better — more surreal, actually." So Brian proceeded to tell her about the casino, the ridiculous amount of money, the absurd irony of instant riches in juxtapose to emotional misery, his cynicism surrounding them in a shroud of bitterness.

"And then I found your wallet," Valeriya murmured, twirling her champagne glass between her fingers, seemingly lost in thought. "So, what now, Brian?" she asked. "What will you do, go back and sort things out at home?"

Brian leaned back in the booth and stretched. "I don't know," he said. "All that money, freedom, I might just fuck off somewhere and drop out, disappear, let her come and find me if she feels like it, I really don't care anymore."

Silence descended between them for a few minutes, each lost in thought, both momentarily in another place, lulled by subconscious memories.

"Get another drink, Brian," she said suddenly. "I need to tell you something. I might need your help."

Valeriya left her seat and walked toward the bathroom at the back of the bar. Brian waved toward the bartender who shuffled over with fresh drinks. Valeriya sat back down opposite him and took a sip from her glass.

"So, Brian," she began, smiling hesitantly, "I am going to tell you a story you will find hard to believe, impossible probably, but I am going to take a chance. Why? Because I need help. Why? Because I found your wallet, and I think there must be a point to that, as you said outside. Why? Because you are anonymous here, and now rich and anonymous, which is even more attractive for what I need. And why? Finally, because I will be dead soon, I don't have much time, certainly no time to make a better plan. It is long and complicated," she added. "Do you want to hear or not?"

Brian nodded and smiled across the table.

2065, Las Vegas, The Architect

"Well," Valeriya hesitated, "it's hard to know where to begin, there are so many moving parts." She brushed a strand of hair behind her ear and her eyes appeared to glaze over as the past overtook the present. "I am much older than you think is the first thing. I have had certain work done that makes me look younger for reasons that will become apparent as I unravel the plot."

Brian liked the word "plot" and felt a hint of excitement rising in his throat.

Valeriya continued, "Yes, much older, ninety years old actually. I was born in 1975, in Russia, amongst the privileged, the plutocracy. We always had money, a good education, we were even able to travel before the end of the Cold War. And you must be what, Brian," she asked, "mid-forties?"

“Forty-eight,” Brian said, “a baby.” He smiled.

“Well,” she continued, “as I said, I was lucky, a brilliant education, and I was brilliant, and by ’95 I had already graduated and was deeply entrenched in a program which involved lateralization of brain function, if you know anything about that?”

“Not much,” Brian said, “sorry.”

“That’s okay.” Valeriya smiled over the table. “Not many people do. Well, I will try and give you the layman’s version of events, as you do need to understand some of this. It might come in handy over the coming weeks, if you do decide to help me.”

Brian nodded for her to continue.

“Well, the first bit is a little generic and you’ll have to take my word for some of it.” Brian raised his eyebrows comically. “You see, Brian, not many people really understand how the world works. The world is controlled by money, the big financial institutions, and these are not restricted by borders or governments, they supersede time, presidents, war, race, and religion, but they do control, and they are a club, a club wherein members might compete, but they do depend on each other — mutual programs, mutual concepts — so there is a constant dialogue on the cusp of politics and religion, often complemented by politics or vice versa or both. And let’s not forget religion’s role, which has always been a key aspect to control the herd. Over the centuries, these groups have been referred to as a number of different secret societies; the Illuminati, for example, is probably the best known conspiracy theory but there are many others. The rest of us are their pawns; we follow and they manipulate.”

"That word again," Brian interrupted.

"Oh yes." Valeriya smiled. "That word, just you wait and see. So, to go on, have you heard of a phrase called the moral hazard?" Brian shook his head. "Well, at the turn of the century, world economies were in a state of flux, China and Asia were the emerging superpowers, and the US, or the PBGC to be precise, was starting to pay the price of undercharging employees for retirement pension plans."

"Hang on, PBGC?"

"The Pension Benefit Guaranty Corporation. It's a US public body linked to Social Security, pensions, retirement funds, all that sort of thing. So, by 2010, for example, the PBGC had already worked out that it would have to put 5.4 trillion dollars aside then to cover the shortfall in pension payments over the next seventy-five years. Moral hazard was the term that referred to the PBGC's hitherto tendency to undercharge on its premiums so companies never really paid for future risk to their employees."

"So…?" Brian was struggling.

"So, someone would have to bail them out. This was just the start, you see, Brian. Listen, in 1935, the average American lived to be about sixty-five; by 2010, this number was seventy-five, and now, well, now, as you know, we have the self-sacrifice centres, but I'll come to that later. Let me give you another statistic; in 1960, there were five people working for every one person retired, but it was predicted that this ratio would be two-to-one by 2030. And the western world was not producing enough replacements, people to work to pay for the old. Sub-replacement fertility rates were at an all-time low, and in 2011, the seventh billion person was born on this planet, a planet that many would say can only sustain life for five billion."

"Okay, got that," said Brian, "too many old people, an unbalanced ratio of workers to retirees, in fact too many people for the planet to sustain, go on."

"Well, it was a far bigger problem than just that. I just gave you the tip of the iceberg, probably the primary catalyst that started the 'think tanks.' There were other issues: water, food, energy, the cost of health care, and the pension institutions were creaking and the US government, many governments actually, at least those in the First World, had buried their heads in the sand for too long. Basically, 'think tanks' predicted that large portions of the human race would be unable to work or be paid for, so, what would happen? World wars, anarchy, who knew? But the prognosis was doom and gloom, and the people who really make the world turn, what I was talking about a few minutes ago, they began to talk about this to one another, as did discreet government departments, the ones that plan ahead fifty years, the apolitical parts."

"I had no idea there were departments like that." Brian sighed.

"You are not supposed to know, dummy," said Valeriya. "We are the dummies, remember, the pawns."

"It all sounds like a conspiracy to me," Brian said.

Valeriya shrugged her shoulders. "You have no idea, wait until you hear the next bit."

Brian waved toward the bartender. "Jesus," he said, "think I need another drink if this is going to get any worse."

"Why not?" Valeriya said. "I think that I'll take an espresso, I have reached my limit. But anyway, listen to this next part. The financial institutions began to push, to squeeze, they collaborated across the globe, 'find a solution' they cried at governments, or we will face a breakdown, possibly a war, and we, the living, will be bankrupt by the dying or we, all of us, will destroy the planet anyway through sheer numbers. So, the thinkers, the manipulators began to do just that and now we find ourselves where we are today, with our self-sacrifice centres. Can you imagine what a campaign that was? To convince half the oldies in the world to commit suicide, or self-sacrifice, for the sake of the planet, to remove themselves before they became a burden, voluntarily, yes, but under such peer pressure. A forty year campaign, incredible! But we weren't allowed to use the suicide word; that would have negative connotations."

"Why forty years?" Brian asked.

"Well, they had to agree on a strategy, and then implement one. It has taken that long. They had worked out that there was a high probability of planet implosion, so 'get rid of the old, the dependents' was the cry. 'What, kill them?' the manipulators asked. 'No, get them to do the job themselves, self-sacrifice is the key.' That was the consensus. But how?"

"Yes," Brian murmured, "but hang on, we know that it's the right thing to do, self-sacrifice, the prophets, the miracles, what are you saying to me, that this was all a plan? Don't be ridiculous, now you are becoming fanciful, Miss Ninety-years-old."

"Not so, my dear Brian, not so — let me give you the next bit."

"God." Brian stretched. "My head is about to explode, let me just go to the bathroom."

Brian splashed water across his face and spent a few moments staring at himself in the mirror.

Could this day get any more surreal? I am with a psycho, he mused. *No one is ninety years old anymore.*

He walked back through the bar and sat down opposite the woman.

"So, next chapter?" he asked. "It can't get any crazier, can it?"

Valeriya smiled over the rim of her coffee cup and raised her eyebrows.

"Well, the next part is back to me, do you remember, the brain specialist?"

Brian nodded for her to continue.

"Well, do you know what bicameralism is?"

He shook his head, having never heard of the word.

"Thought not," she continued. "Well, in the 1970s, a certain amount of work had been done on the two sides of the brain, and a man called Julian Jaynes wrote a book called *The Origin of Consciousness in the Breakdown of the Bicameral Mind.* What he believed was that the brain had once, a long time ago, assumed a state in which cognitive functions were divided between the two sides of the brain, basically that one side speaks while the other side listens or obeys, something he called the bicameral mind. It's a metaphor — literally, it means 'two chambers' in Greek. So, in the bicameral mind, man was non-conscious in his ability to reason or articulate, man lacked meta-consciousness, he was unable to mind-wander and was unable to conduct introspection in the way we do today. Modern minds are unicameral. There are still two sides to the brain but they work together in a much more logical way."

"God help me," Brian raised his hands, "in English, please, I am just a dentist!"

"Look, it's not that complicated. According to Jaynes, ancient civilizations in a bicameral state of mind would be unable to interpret the world as we do today. They would, in fact, interpret many things in the way that a schizophrenic might, through voices in their heads, which they would not question but simply listen to and obey. Remember, we are talking about three to four thousand years ago, when gods were more numerous and more anthropomorphic than today. This was, if you like, before the transition from various forms of paganism to what we now understand as the religious beliefs that emerged in pre-modern Europe. It was pretty simple, pre-introspection, if you did not understand something, you explained it by giving it a god-like quality."

Brian nodded.

"So, Jaynes argued that in this bicameral state, man listened to voices that came from the right side of the brain but in a way that was not conscious, in a way that was without introspection, and did what the voices commanded. Everyone had their own internal God or Gods, so to speak. He reckoned that the bicameral state, call it basic instinct if you like, began to break down about 2000 BC, probably as a result of language development and mass migrations in Europe caused by huge earthquakes. The mind had to rationalize, to become more flexible so man had to become self-aware, to question in a way that is second nature for us now. Actually, if you look back, as bicameralism disappeared, divination, prayer, and oracles began to emerge; man was starting to question existence beyond a non-conscious state, you know, all the usual questions, philosophy, our capacity for original thought; man could no longer simply listen to those voices, there needed to be answers, interpretation. Being cynical, you might argue that this was the springboard for modern religion, be it monotheism, henotheism, pantheism, or whatever. We wanted answers to questions, justification for our existence, blah, blah, you get the picture. So, Jesus appeared on the scene, an answer to some of these tricky questions."

"Okay, I see all that," Brian nodded, "I am just having trouble joining the dots, so to speak. What has all this to do with what we're talking about?"

Valeriya leaned forward. "Ah, we are nearly there, Brian. You see, the two sides of the brain are connected by the corpus callosum, so this becomes key, well, it certainly becomes key for a manipulator."

"Sorry," Brian exhaled, "I am still a little lost."

Valeriya ignored him and continued, "Remember where we were? The manipulators need a solution to reduce the number of oldies, to convince them that suicide, or self-sacrifice as we refer to it, is the right thing to do. Well, you can hardly do that over the breakfast table, can you, so you need to change how people think, to change religious context. Look, you were brought up on the fact that people now accept that Jesus committed a suicide of sorts, a self-sacrifice; the Bible tells us so, the prophets tell us so. He, Jesus, consciously manipulated events to ensure that he was crucified, sacrificed, that word again, 'he sacrificed himself for our sins,' yes, a suicide of sorts but we can't call it that. But also as an example for us, not just for our sins, but so that others could live and emulate his actions, more apposite now than it's ever been, don't you think?"

"I am still a little confused, sorry."

"Okay, Brian, listen carefully. If you are going to change religious context, then you need someone to do this, prophets, or something beyond that which the unicameral man can understand or justify. So, the manipulators decided to create them, which is where I come back into the story. I was chosen as the architect for the project."

"A project, at last," Brian whispered to himself. "Okay, tell me about the project."

"I am surprised you can't guess," Valeriya murmured.

"Well, I'm sorry," Brian said. "My head is full of words that I can't pronounce and it's all sounding too ridiculous."

"I did tell you that, didn't I?" she continued. "Now, the project was devised by a few key manipulators per se, those who truly understood how human DNA works, the missing links. Their problem was how to awaken this missing DNA, this junk DNA, to reboot, if you like, the chosen few. How do you produce credible prophets in an age that was already secular, agnostic, or apatheist? Quite a problem, don't you think?"

"I suppose so," Brian acknowledged, "but then anything which you say sounds like an 'I suppose so.' I think I'm getting there, what you are trying to tell me is that the prophets were invented, somehow, by you and your team?"

"Bravo, Brian, bravo!"

"Don't be ridiculous, you are screwing with my brain now!" Brian took a sip from his glass and looked at the woman across the table. "You're not joking, are you?"

He could see the woman's passion and detected huge remorse, her eyes glistening as she fought back her tears. She shook her head.

"What we did, what I did primarily, was to choose a number of human eggs, eggs of brilliant parents, and we worked out how to spark this junk DNA, eventually how to manipulate their minds. We knew that a prophet has to believe, that a simple fraud would be exposed in time. They could not be tutored. So I worked on the corpus callosum, not on the chosen few initially, there were other guinea pigs, but eventually on them. I worked out how we could shut down certain areas of the mind and accelerate others. The aim was to create voices in their heads, voices and abilities that no one would be able to explain or justify, so that when the time arrived for them to preach, it would be done with genuine fervour, with passion, with real belief. We were to take them back to a bicameral state, remember what I said about that? You know these prophets, you were brought up on them, you and the world think that they self-sacrificed. Now, cast your mind back to the miracles, speaking in ancient Hebrew and Arabic, their abilities to preach in ancient tongues although none could write in these texts; do you remember that? The healings? These skills were implanted, accelerated, and we then closed off sections of the brain, those areas that would add logic to the observer, the pawn in waiting, the 'Brians' of this world, the dentists, the followers. Funny, really, it's not that different to how all this religious crap started during round one; we just instigated a twenty-first century version, a version designed to save the planet, to save mankind from its gross overindulgence."

She stopped talking and looked at her hands. "Look, Brian, ninety-year-old hands, I couldn't do much with them."

She lay her hands in front of Brian who touched the thin skin. *Skin like papyrus*, he thought, and could imagine Sanskrit text scratched across her years. He was not sure what to think, it simply sounded too fucking fantastic.

"So," he said quietly after a few moments, "if any of this is true, why are you telling me? The prophets are dead, we are where we are, and self-sacrifice centres are part of our lives. For those who choose, you have done your work; the world seems to be a better place, doesn't it?"

"Perhaps you can't remember the older version," she snapped back at him. "Have you stood outside a self-sacrifice centre? Have you been into one? Might as well be a hideous Nazi gas chamber! And do you know who controls them, who owns them? It's that same club, Brian, that same group of damned manipulators who profit, who design. Do you think that they self-sacrifice, do they? Hell! And people pay for that final step to redemption, a little more advanced than a few bucks into the collection plate. How brilliant is that?"

"So, why have you told me this, now? You talked of my help, but what can I do when I can't even spell half the fucking words you use? What's the point, let's get back to the point, back to my wallet."

"There are three parts to this, Brian…"

"How did I know that there would be more than one?" Brian started laughing but Valeriya remained quiet. "Sorry." He smirked like a small boy. "Continue."

"The first part is that the prophets are not dead, their self-sacrifices were faked, we wanted to keep an eye, in case we needed something else from them."

"Resurrection, maybe?" Brian was unable to contain himself.

"Listen, Brian," Valeriya hissed at him, "am I wasting my time?"

Brian brought his laughter under control. She went on.

"I was against this and fought it, but was overruled, so I left the program. I don't know where the prophets are, they were put somewhere, secret, but subsequently escaped and went into hiding. The second part is that I know too much, I became expendable as would anyone in my position, so I am on the run, hiding, drifting, changing my appearance. But they will find me soon enough, of that there is certainty. I am not that bothered for myself, but they will also kill my daughter; she knows too much."

Brian's manner sobered as he processed her words.

"Where is she?" he asked quietly.

"Hidden, of course. She knows about the program and can access part of her mind where I have hidden all the information, there are no other records. But there is a complication — isn't there always? She had an accident many years ago and suffered brain damage, minor, but I had to realign parts of her corpus callosum so I'm not sure what works, where the information is, even whether it can be retrieved in her current state. I can't see her; it would expose her to danger. Frankly, she has gone a little mad, something I will regret forever, but she has power; she just can't control it."

"Is that where I come in, the third part?" Brian asked. "The anonymous dentist with lots of money, a broken life, a retrieved wallet?"

"Yes, Brian, exactly — exactly that. I will tell you where she is. She will be able to find the prophets; in that sense I aligned their minds many years ago. They will be able to communicate subconsciously, through telepathy, unless the brain damage has affected that too; you will have to find out. Find the prophets and expose them to the world. Put an end to this curse we have inflicted." The woman stood up abruptly. "I need to go now, they are looking for me. I feel that they are close by."

Brian stood up abruptly. "What, you can't just leave, how will I find you?" Brian asked. "How will I give you my answer?"

"So you believe me?" she asked across the table.

"Maybe," he said, shrugging his shoulders, "but I have nothing to do tomorrow and this has been the most incredible day."

"Give me your telephone number," she said. "Quickly, I must go while the streets are still busy. I will get a message to you, it will be encrypted, but still delete it after you have read it."

"Do you have any paper?" he asked.

"Not on paper, just tell me, I'll remember it easily enough."

Brian gave her his number as she turned away from him and headed for the door. She stopped just before the door and walked back toward him.

"I have a sixth sense, and it's not just the wallet. Your name is an anagram of brain. My daughter's name is Alexandra. Goodbye." Valeriya kissed Brian on his forehead and left him alone with his glass of wine.

2065, Las Vegas, Dental Epiphany

Brian sat quietly for some time, occasionally sipping from his glass of wine, voices in his own mind playing with his senses, teasing his feelings.

What was that she had said about voices? he wondered. *Bicameral, unicameral, anthropomorphism? Jesus, what an extraordinary day!*

His mind ran over the extraordinary conspiracy that she had outlined to him, and he found himself asking the same questions that she had alluded to during part of her story: the ability to reason, introspection, justification. He wondered what it was all for, what it was all about. And then fate — the Brian/brain thing was a bit quirky, amusing even, but the wallet coincidence was so incredible that he did find himself wondering whether there might be a purpose to all of this. He marvelled at the idea that a hidden energy was driving events far out of his control, and, were that the case, why not play along, why not jump onto this roller coaster and see where it took him? What else was he going to do, go and listen to another excruciating dental pitch and then wander home to discuss divorce proceedings with Jan?

Thoughts of his wife jumbled in his mind while another possible Brian became embroiled momentarily with Jaynes, pension plans, and prophetic inventions.

Incredible, he thought, *how the mind can jumble so many disparate thoughts together; fuck, my corpus callosum must be in overdrive. I rather wish she was here now, that she could prise open my mind and shut off what I don't want to hear, what I don't want to acknowledge right now.*

He was even mildly surprised that he could remember half of the words she had used that evening, the effects of the alcohol dispersed between a melancholic fascination with potential directions life had suddenly presented.

Children, he said quietly to himself, *thank fuck we could never have children.* Their deepest regret, true, but perhaps a blessing now, now that their lives had taken such different courses.

Anyway, he thought, *I don't need to make any hasty decisions today, I can sleep on it, see Valeriya again, do a bit of research, see if any of this mumbo jumbo is credible. But I do believe her, funny that, but I do.*

It was still before midnight and Brian knew that bed would only bring a torrent of unwelcome images, a cascade of loneliness that he needed to deflect for the time being. He glanced around the room, which was still busy, and his eye caught two women sitting at the bar, their tight blouses and short skirts reminiscent of one of those old films — heavy makeup and blonde hair. Dyed, he suspected. Their slender bodies accentuated by high stilettos. They appeared to be casing the bar, sizing up opportunity, whispering to each other with their painted faces only a few inches apart. Brian peered out the window at the bright lights splashed across car bonnets, the relentless bustle of Las Vegas grinding on into the night. He sensed another presence and looked up to see one of the girls standing by the side of the booth.

"Hey," she said brightly, "I'm Clarissa. Will you buy me a drink? You look lonely, need some company, honey?"

Brian smiled to himself. *Clarissa, you must be fucking joking.*

"Sure," he said, "the day can't get any more surreal." The girl wound herself into the booth, her nylon skirt screeching for attention on the leather covers.

"What's that?" she said. "Surreal, what does that mean?"

Clarissa was from Virginia, she told him, studying to be a hairdresser, had to leave home, dad used to beat her, mother an alcoholic.

Oh, come on, Brian said, *this is ridiculous, this is the B-movie scenario. She's going to tell me that she's just hooking to get by, that she only goes with respectable men, that she'll give it all up as soon as she qualifies as a chartered accountant.*

"I don't want to do this forever." Clarissa drooled toward him, patting his hand across the table. "Anyway, you seem like a nice guy. Where are you from?"

"So, this is what, exactly?" Brian asked innocently. Clarissa giggled over the table and glanced toward her friend who was busy at the bar.

"You are funny," she said, "and cute, you know. This, I'm a call girl, well, you know that, more of an escort, really, a companion for discerning gentlemen of means."

Brian wondered how long it had taken her to rehearse that line.

Well, he thought, *I am not very discerning but certainly of newly acquired means.*

"So, how does this work?" he asked.

"Well, that's easy, honey. We just enjoy our drinks and then enjoy each other, but it's cash only, if that's okay with you?" Brian nodded. Clarissa excused herself briefly and went over to whisper in her friend's ear before returning to her place. "Well, that's settled, then. Do you want to have a drink or should we go?"

Brian paid what was a considerable bill by this stage and they walked out onto the streets, Clarissa hooking an arm under his, leaning into his flank, her heels occasionally catching cracks in the pavement, which accentuated her discomfort but made her giggle into his left ear. They made their way slowly back to the Bellagio and stood in silence as the lift descended. The door opened to a furious conversation, and Brian bumped into one of his fellow dentists, his huge hands gesticulating to a colleague.

"…so, you see, you have to drill into the jawbone or it won't last a lifetime." The man stopped in his tracks momentarily and his voice faltered. Brian was past caring and raised his eyebrows toward the two men before sliding past them into the lift. The door closed with a whisper, and Brian caught a glimpse of mutual disapproval and condescendence skating across their features.

Who fucking cares? he said. *Gum disease seems a million lives away.*

Clarissa threw her bag onto the circular table in the centre of the room and squealed in delight as she caught sight of the fountains in their full splendour in front of the hotel. Her face looked young in the half-light and Brian felt a twinge of remorse, of hesitation.

"I never tire of that sight," she said quietly. "Funny, isn't it? Seen it a million times but it always makes me feel warm and tender."

Brian gave her a quizzical look and opened the small bar. "So, how many rooms in this hotel have you visited? Would you like another drink?" he asked.

"A few, maybe," she giggled. "Sure, thanks, a Scotch for me, straight." Clarissa kicked off her shoes and perched herself on the edge of the bed. "So, to business, can we get that out of the way now so that we can both relax?" Brian smiled at her. "Well, how long shall I stay for and what do you want?"

Brian felt embarrassed. "Well, what's on offer? This is all a bit new to me."

"Well, honey," she giggled, "oral, intercourse, sixty-nine, hand job, pretty much whatever you want, a massage, you tell me, but I don't do anal, I draw the line there."

The irony of this was not lost on Brian.

How discerning, he thought, *here I am with a pro who won't do anal, while Brian-two is getting all of that for nothing.*

"I don't know," Brian said. "Why don't we just see what happens and I'll pay for everything, just in case."

Clarissa seemed very happy with this arrangement and tucked the wad of dollars into her bag. The girl stretched toward the ceiling and began to undress, her bright red bra somehow at odds with her pale torso. Brian watched with interest more than attraction as she peeled off her underwear.

"I'm just going to wash my pussy," she said, almost as if she was ordering a hamburger, and disappeared into the bathroom.

My God, Brian thought, *how romantic, how fucking romantic.* He heard the shower and undressed quickly, pulling back the covers and slipping under the duvet.

Your teeth, teeth, a small voice cried, *clean your teeth.*

Fuck you, Brian responded, *I'm paying, I can do whatever I choose.*

Clarissa returned after a few moments and slid in beside him. Brian noticed a small appendix scar above her bikini line and wondered how many other men had had the same pleasure. Clarissa pulled back the covers and moved her head toward his thighs.

"Let's start here," she said quietly, and Brian felt her warm mouth at the base of his stomach and then her tongue around him, her mouth and fingers suddenly autonomous as she moved her hand to the base of his penis.

Brian glanced down at the girl, her face and mouth obscured by her hair, the dark roots mocking the lighter strands as her head moved backward and forward. Brian felt disengaged, as if he was watching that B movie, now that B porn movie, he told himself, dislocated from reality, a voyeur in the shadows. His mind wandered involuntarily to J, to Valeriya, the day's episodes crashing into his psyche, the movements under the duvet, and his excitement left him instantly, the girl's mouth hesitant around him, her hand stalling in confusion. She raised her head, a question mark poised around her mouth.

"Sorry," Brian said quickly, "I must be tired, sorry, why don't you rest for a while, go to sleep for a bit, I'll wake you up later." Clarissa seemed more than happy with this suggestion and flopped back on the pillow, turning her body away from Brian.

"Night…" she murmured.

He lay there for some time, thinking; her breathing was shallow and she occasionally moaned quietly at the shadows. At one point he touched a small cluster of moles on her left shoulder blade and found a small scar, only about an inch long, at the back of her neck.

How weird, he said. *I have no desire to fuck this girl, anywhere. Today, this day, is simply too bizarre. What the fuck am I doing in bed with a prostitute?*

Brian's mind drifted to Jan and then to children.

My God, how we tried.

It was one of those things that had never really been discussed before marriage, as if it was something that would appear on the horizon at an indefinable point and they would fall happily into its clutches and be washed away by the novelty, awash in a new chapter of their lives. Jan never really told him when she had stopped taking her tiny pills and he had failed to notice the absence of the thin, silver-covered packets in their bathroom cupboard until she had raised the issue late one evening after too much wine when his mind had already switched off for the day.

"Look," she had begun, "I know I should have told you earlier but I stopped taking the pill about four months ago."

She had placed her hand over the back of his and was unconsciously stroking the thin hairs at the base of his wrist. Brian remembered feeling startled yet excited, as if he knew what was coming, its unexpected intrusion into their lives both frightening yet exhilarating. He had raised his eyebrows in a theatrical manner as if to say, "I chastise you for not telling me but at once forgive you because I know what is coming next."

What foolishness. Jan had read all this in an instant, her fingers gently squeezing his in anticipation of disappointment.

"It's not what you think," she had continued. "I'm not pregnant, that's it really, I should be, I had wanted to surprise you, but nothing is happening."

She had leaned back in her chair, a mixture of guilt and pity spreading across her features, acknowledging, perhaps in hindsight, not only her deceit, albeit fairly harmless, but also the clumsy way in which she had broached the subject.

"Look, I'm sorry, it's not how I had planned it, it was supposed to be fun, a surprise," she had murmured, half to herself. "I have been for some tests, the doctor seems to think that everything is in order, he asked if you would be willing to come and talk to him, to do some tests."

Her final few words had ricocheted around their small kitchen like an odious spell before falling in the short space between them, the word “tests” spinning like a coin until it clanked to rest on the hard wooden table top.

“I see…” Brian had begun but stopped abruptly as he had not planned what he had to say; the point was that he didn’t “see” anything.

“Look,” Jan had continued, “it’s no big deal, let’s talk about this another time, give you time to think about it.”

She had left the table and started to busy herself emptying the dishwasher. Brian had felt his disorientation turning to anger, his potential “disability” slapping him in the face, mocking, as if to say, “I have always been in you and you’ve never known, or, more to the point, I have never been in you and you’ve only just found out. Ha ha, poor impotent you!”

He had directed his frustration toward Jan.

“Don’t you think you might have mentioned this when you went for your tests? Christ, I feel like I’ve been ambushed.”

“Look,” she had said as she came back to the table, “please, don’t do this, I was trying to surprise you, it was supposed to be a positive thing.”

“As opposed to a negative result,” Brian had interjected, his sudden cynicism filling the small room like a toxic vapour.

And that had been one of their few rows in so many years, and he had taken the tests, and, yes, it was him all along, poor impotent Brian. Now this, this affair, he wondered how much of this might be connected to that.

“Stop torturing yourself,” he murmured in the half-light.

Brian tried to pull his mind away from his wife and cast it back toward his conversation with Valeriya and her extraordinary role in, if it were true, the most incredible fraud in mankind's history. Brian had been 26 when the first self-sacrifice centres had opened — old enough to reason and to have a view, but young enough for that final decision, the decision on his own mortality, to be sufficiently distant by age to obviate fear. At 26 years old, sixty-five still seemed a lifetime away. It had been harder for his parents and he remembered a stifling Sunday lunch when his father had broached the subject during a family gathering with him and his two sisters. They had gone for a short walk while Brian's mother prepared the meal.

"Your mother and I can't agree," he had blurted out in a mixture of frustration and embarrassment. "We wanted your opinion, you are the next generation after all, the planet will be in your hands in a few short years."

He had been an extremely private man so Brian and his siblings were taken aback by his sudden outburst.

"You see," he had continued, "your mother thinks it's the right thing to do, in fact she insists that she will go through with it. I am not necessarily convinced but can't imagine her doing it alone, it will be an abandonment of sorts."

Brian had remained silent and it had been his eldest sister who had spoken first.

"But Daddy," she had said quietly, "this can only be your decision, this is not about you and Mum, this is your life, your death, your philosophical decision."

"Yes, sweetheart," he had responded, his voice a little softer, "in a sense, that's my point. Don't you see how warped this whole idea is? This whole concept? It should be an individual decision based on philosophy, based on ideology, freedom of expression, religious dogma, and it probably is, in that sense, at the highest levels, even at the divine level, so to speak. But the world doesn't work like that, does it? I mean, my God, certain religious leaders are now castigating anyone who doesn't conform, old age has become a sin. We are encouraged to self-sacrifice as couples, told that it is now the perfect way to celebrate the end of a marriage which is deemed as truly blessed. I mean twenty years ago this would have been unheard of; how has the world turned on its head in such a short period?"

"Well, we've all seen what they did," his sister had added, and then her voice had tailed away. The four had walked on in silence for a while, the sounds of their winter boots echoing down the narrow, country lanes.

"I look at it like war," Brian's other sister had said after a few minutes. Brian had always seen her as left of left field and had almost held his breath in anticipation of what was to come next.

"I know you lot always laugh at me," she had continued, "but my point is actually very simple. We have all learned about the two Great Wars last century, how many died, how many lives were lost. Well, those who went to fight made the ultimate sacrifice for what was termed then as their fellow men, for a collective freedom. Well, I see this as something similar, sure, it's not the same sort of freedom, a freedom from tyranny, but it's still a freedom for others to live without the unsustainable burden of the old, so, perhaps this is our generation's Great War, so to speak, or at least our challenge this century."

"My God, Lizzy," his father had quipped lightly. "Unsustainable burden, God help us."

Brian wondered if he should have said something that day, if it would have made a difference to their ultimate decision.

Brian must have dozed off at some stage but came to his senses when a muted "bleep" woke him from the bedside table. His first thoughts were of Jan, and he groaned internally.

Not another Brian-two message, please, he said to himself, *anything but that.*

He glanced over at Clarissa who was snoring gently. She had moved during the night and thrown the covers off her chest, and he felt momentarily excited by her dark nipples. Lights from the city threw colours across her chest so that her breasts mirrored parts of a rainbow crafted from neon confusion. He scratched around for his telephone and opened the message.

> *They are close, I can feel them, here is Alexandra's address in New York, my address here is at the bottom, there is a spare key hidden under a white stone at the end of the small garden, come in the morning but be careful, V. Remember what I said, delete this.*

Brian rubbed his face, small lines of stubble scraping under his palms, and swung his legs over the side of the bed. He snapped on the bathroom light and peered at his reflection through bleary eyes. He instinctively reached for his toothbrush and began to scrub his mouth, his gums, and even his tongue, which was stained with red wine.

"Beautiful," he murmured, "what a sight. Your mother would be proud of you."

He then took a shower, shaved, and dressed quickly, his movements casting shadows around the room as he fumbled for his watch; half past five in the morning.

God, he thought. His head was throbbing slightly but a surge of adrenaline had kicked in, adding a sense of urgency to his tempo. He opened the small bar and took out three small cans of orange juice, which he drank in quick succession. He glanced at his watch again and then at Clarissa, leaning over her face, her smeared lipstick giving her the appearance of a dishevelled mannequin. He touched a strand of hair by the side of her mouth and she raised a hand, as if to brush away an annoying fly.

Sweet dreams, Clarissa, he thought, *and goodbye.*

Brian gave the address to the taxi driver in front of the hotel and jumped into the back seat.

"How far?" he asked the back of the head in front of him.

"Fifteen, maybe twenty, not far."

Brian spent the next few minutes memorizing the address for Alexandra in New York before deleting the message. He felt like a conspirator, a secret agent embarking on an underground mission. He mused over the last 24 hours.

God, he thought, *this time yesterday dentistry was the highlight of my life and now this. I wonder where it will all end?*

By the time the taxi drifted off the main drag onto the side streets, dawn was reaching through the high-rise buildings and bouncing off the few trees lining the streets. A warm wind from the desert swirled in the streets as the taxi moved into the little part of Las Vegas that could be called suburbia before eventually pulling to a stop at a small junction.

"Well, this is the street, what number did you say?" the driver asked.

"I'll get out here," Brian said quickly and thrust a few notes into the front of the car.

"Shall I wait, it's early, not much traffic about?" the driver enquired.

"No thanks, I'll be fine," Brian said and closed the door behind him, stamping his feet on the pavement to generate some blood flow. He glanced at the house numbers and walked tentatively along a small row of houses, one or two with small children's toys thrown across the lawns, the odd vehicle perched on blocks in disrepair. It was a far cry from twenty minutes ago and a scene that could have been replicated across half the country. He took his time to check for passengers in vehicles parked on the street before stepping down a short driveway and opening a small wooden gate that led to the back garden.

A slow start, he thought, *but I guess it's Las Vegas. Half these houses will be owned by people who are nocturnal, casino staff, bartenders, hookers even,* he reminded himself.

Brian had not really considered his next move but assumed, perhaps subconsciously, that he would have another discussion with Valeriya and then decide if he would help. In that respect, he was unprepared for the sight of her body hanging from the central rafters on the back veranda, the heavy knot twisting her head to one side, strands of her silver hair blowing across her face in the light breeze. His first instinct was to rush forward to lift up her legs, to relieve the weight, but he quickly drew back, the full impact of what he had found smashing into his mind amid the jumble of their conversation of the previous evening, "manipulators, conspiracy, they will find me." He drew back a few paces, a compelling instinct to distance himself from the macabre scene competing with what he knew he had to do. This was his epiphany, he knew that; whatever he did over the next few minutes might determine his fate, not just his, but the fate of so many others if any of what she had said was true.

Brian took a tentative step onto the veranda and edged around the body, half expecting a hand to reach out and touch him on the shoulder. The house was shrouded in darkness, pockets of early morning sunlight squeezing through the blinds and winking through the rafters. The back door was open and Brian edged inside, pulling the door closed behind him. Inside, the house was as he had expected, a bolthole, a temporary staging post, bare, anonymous, soulless. He walked through the living area and glanced around the kitchen, opening and closing the fridge door and peering into a few cupboards, most of which were empty. It looked as if the place had never been occupied, but then he found a small bedroom at the back of the house where a bed had been slept in and a few clothes were thrown over the back of a chair next to a worn leather bag, what appeared to be her only possession of any value.

How many years on the run, he pondered, *maybe twenty, thirty?*

He poked his head around the corner of the adjoining bathroom, a few cosmetics strewn next to the side of the basin, a hairbrush and a solitary headband, a single strand of her hair still tangled like a bare root. He noticed some dental floss next to her toothbrush.

She had been flossing her teeth, he thought. *Who flosses their teeth before jumping off the small veranda wall into thin air? But why hanging?* he asked. *It seems so crude. Surely there are clever drugs these days, surely these people have their methods, it seems such a cruel and barbaric epitaph.*

But effective, he told himself. *If you are going to kill someone who has implanted the future in people's minds, get the job done; a broken neck is as conclusive as any solution, and it passes for suicide.*

Brian felt exposed; he knew that remaining in the house any longer was already a risk, that he should get out as quickly as possible. There was also a nagging concern pulling him around the room, and he began to look through the few belongings she had to her name. It took his mind a few moments to realize what his subconscious already knew: he needed more than an address, that if he turned up in New York to convince Alexandra of her mother's story and her subsequent murder, her initial reaction would be distrust, his story as implausible as the one he had heard the evening before. He needed something, she would have left something somewhere; she was simply too smart not to have thought about that. But what, where? Her executioners would have thought the same, would have searched for clues of her daughter's whereabouts.

He cast his mind back to their meeting, what they had discussed, there might be a clue somewhere in their extraordinary exchange. He rifled through her leather bag but found nothing and then spent the next few minutes walking through the house, checking in cupboards, running his fingers above pelmets: nothing. He glanced at his watch and realized that he had been in the house for over 30 minutes.

Run, his mind told him, *run quickly!*

A few more minutes, he said to himself. *She was too smart not to have been ahead of them, of me.*

Brian's desperate search revealed no clues, and he began to panic to the point that he knew that his efforts were becoming counterproductive.

Perhaps I should take a photo of the body, he said, *to prove that I was here?*

He was wasting his time now and feeling increasingly vulnerable. He moved toward the veranda door, glancing back into the room, one last look. He noticed a small pile of dust-covered books propped against the kitchen door, a makeshift doorstop. He walked back into the room and kicked the pile, three books, old books. He blew dust off the covers and scanned the titles. He had found what he needed; the second book in the pile was *The Origin of Consciousness in the Breakdown of the Bicameral Mind*, and he was certain that somewhere in those pages or in the binding, he would find his clue.

Brian moved back out onto the veranda and past Valeriya, a last glance at her face.

"I found it," he said to her lifeless body, keeping his voice at the barest whisper. "You knew I would, clever woman."

2065, Las Vegas, A Temporary Filling

It was still relatively early for Las Vegas when Brian got back to the hotel, which was just starting to come to life. He passed quickly through the foyer and made his way up to his room, half wondering if Clarissa would still be stretched out across his bed. The room was empty but she had left a small note, "honey, call me, I still owe ya!" with her telephone number scrawled across the bathroom mirror in bright lipstick.

Fuck, Brian said, *this is increasingly surreal.*

Brian ordered room service but found that he could barely touch the tray when it arrived, his mind grappling with images and ideas, a jumble of facts running amok, completely without form or purpose.

I need some fresh air, he told himself, and went back downstairs where he wandered the maze of walkways that joined different sections of the hotel to one another.

He paused in a small boutique to buy some shorts and a pair of light sandals. After a half-hour of wandering, Brian found a place next to the pool where he felt he might hide from reality or at least get the bones of a plan together. He felt conspicuous, as if he did not belong, and uncomfortable in his new shorts, the creases synonymous with their packaging, his white legs glaring back at him in sharp defiance, and in stark contrast to the array of golden bodies that floated around the pool in pockets of sunlight and laughter.

He was unable to focus with any clarity, repetitious images pushing to the front of his mind only to be jostled aside by other competitors. He seemed to be compromised by three images; the first was another man with his hands wrapped around his wife's waist, the head of his penis pushing into her arse, her face pushed hard into the mattress. He tried to imagine the look on her face; was it lust, pain, humour? The second was the image of Valeriya's body, buffeted by the early morning breeze, her silver hair falling across her face like strands from a spider's webs. And the third image was less invasive: Clarissa's dark nipples caught in a neon frame of colours. He kept asking himself why he had not touched her.

As confusion cornered Brian by the pool, so these contingent images crashed against one another — lust, despair, abject jealousy, fear, pity, self-pity, self-loathing — even hate emerged for the unknown man who was fucking his wife.

Who are you, when have you found the time, where have you been fucking her? he wondered. *In our bed, in a spare bedroom, across the kitchen table?*

Calm down, Brian told himself, but he felt like an idiot, the original Shakespearean cuckold, the cross-gartered Malvolio in yellow stockings. *Do you really care?* he asked himself. *Does it really matter?*

Yes, he answered himself, *I do care. I wish desperately that I did not but seem as predictable as the next man, controlled by ego, restricted by others' perceptions; I am defined by what I have, by what I do, by my reputation. I care what people think of me, however hard I wish this were not the case.*

So, is that why you have been drilling holes in people's mouths for twenty-five years, you boring fuckwit?

Very probably, he smiled to himself. *No, not probably*, he corrected himself, *most definitely*. *So*, he asked himself, *now what? What are my choices? There are two, perhaps three, fundamentally: go home and sort things out with Jan; go and find Alexandra and see if there's any truth in all of this madness; or just go and hide, take the money and run*, Brian pondered, *literally — buy a car, drive down to Peru, buy a beach hut, drop out, find some peace, make some sense of it all. Time will assuage the pain, time will become a poultice, a mucous of protection, a contiguous ally.*

But as much as Brian knew that he could sit and dramatize his petty existence, he also knew that running away was not an option, that the mucous was just that, a straw trap door.

It's a temporary filling, he told himself, *and we know how short-lived they are, four to six weeks at the most. So, the Jan question first, what to do about that?* he asked himself.

He was due on a flight home that evening. Surely she deserved an explanation, after all these years of marriage?

Trouble is, he reminded himself, *if I go back, then I'll become embroiled in "us," tortuous discussions, separation, remorse, resentment, reconciliation?* Brian mused. *Do I want reconciliation? What am I feeling now?* he asked himself.

That's easy, jealousy, Brian thought. What an incredible feeling, what an exponential rush of angst, an instantaneous well of nausea crouching like bile in his gut.

He had heard of people with open marriages but had never imagined just how that worked, how the respective other felt when their partner crawled into bed having shared another's, perhaps, the evening before. He tried to drag his mind away from the sordid images that jumped through his psyche.

So, in an open marriage, his mind prompted him, *how would you feel about kissing your wife when someone else had come there the day before? Or...* but he stopped himself in mid-flow, such images were as much corrosive as explosive. *So, back to jealousy*, he told himself. *What might it be not to feel jealousy, to give complete freedom to another, to push the ownership issue into the background?*

I would like to be there, Brian told himself, *but I am not big enough for that, not yet.*

So, come on, he urged himself, *think, Brian, think, for fuck's sake! Are you going home to face the music, and, if not, when will you?*

Although Brian knew that he was conducting his own internal debate, he also acknowledged that it was all rather ridiculous, that he knew where his mind sat with his theoretical questions. He was afraid to go back, to sit in front of his wife and open the debate, to sit in their familiar spaces and discuss unfamiliar images, to sleep in his own bed not quite knowing if Brian-two had been using his toothpaste or exercising his toothbrush as much as he had been exercising his wife.

Fuck, this is unhealthy, he told himself. These were torturous thoughts that he knew would keep him awake for many weeks to come. *So, run away for a little while*, he told himself, *but not to Peru, that's too cowardly.*

So, Valeriya and her daughter, is that the option, is that your compromise for now, Brian? he asked.

He looked up to see a small child gazing intently at him, a smudge of chocolate smeared across her cheeks, an ice cream cone clutched in her right hand, the dark chocolate dripping down the side of the cone and through her fingers. The child's face was without expression, but her eyes seemed to see through him, to pass through him as if he were not there.

"What would you do?" he asked quietly, breaking the spell between them.

The child looked down at the ice cream cone and her sticky fingers, and then once more at Brian, fear and misgiving clouding her features like a difficult puzzle. The small girl turned away quickly and ran off toward a group of children, small spots of chocolate ice cream following her like a paper trail. Brian picked up his telephone, a sudden resolve prodding him from behind.

Keep moving, he told himself, *but try and be fair, try and find some compassion, try and be something bigger, something better, you do actually have a chance to do that, here and now, to change your life, to be something, at least to be honest with yourself and your feelings. This might be a long message*, he told himself, *but it needs to be sent, and I can't face hearing her voice, not just yet.*

> *Jan…*

He began the text. He paused and then continued.

> *I will not be coming home today but will come home in a few weeks. I need some space and time to think. I think that you do, too, about us, as you are clearly not happy with us.*

Would she get that, he wondered, *or do I need to spell it all out?*

He knew that she would get it, that these simple words would cause her heart to leap into her mouth, for her guts to creak with despair as his had such a short time ago, that she would interrogate herself and check the obvious places, well, the obvious space, her telephone. He could imagine her calling Brian-two, her voice creased with trepidation, "An odd question, darling…" Would she call him darling or might she have a nickname for him? Anyway, "An odd question, darling, but did you get a text from me yesterday, after you left or maybe after I left, you know, it was a bit crude but playful? I deleted it but I just wanted to check." And then her precarious world might begin to topple as her worst fears are realized, as she thinks of what she wrote and what effect those words had on her dear husband.

Is that what will happen? Brian asked. *Or should I be more aggressive, more direct?*

I don't know what will happen, he told himself, *but it will be awful for her, in any and all ways.*

He continued with his message.

> *You sent me a message by mistake, yesterday, it hurt me. I am going to go on a drive to clear my mind, and will come home when things are a bit clearer. I will send a note to the practice to let them know. Please don't call, I am going to turn this number off for a while but please don't worry, I am simply going to drive and then fly home when ready. I will tell you when. Bx.*

He wondered, *Is that enough, is that fair? What could be fair, in these circumstances? Is there any kindness or compassion in this message? Should there be, could there be?*

Brian read through the message once again, pausing to digest his own words, to reflect on their external combustion. He flicked to the message he had received the previous day, the words shredding his internal organs into rashers of despair, instant nausea rising in his throat.

It will have to do for now, he told himself, and pressed the "send" button. He waited for a few moments and then switched off his telephone.

Keep moving, he told himself.

2065, Vienna, Nathan

Nathan looked at his hands, which sat in his lap like old parchment scrolls, the skin as thin as a lettuce leaf, his veins bulging like birthmarks through the skin.

The tapestry of my life, he thought, *my tangled roots of time.*

It was difficult for Nathan to be seen in public, his one hundred and seven years caught in blemishes across his skin despite the many hours of plastic surgery.

The job is not finished, he said to himself, looking out of the window. *We are still vulnerable, I have not fully delivered, not yet, but I will, so help me, I will, before I go, I will finish what I started.*

"That stupid bitch," he murmured, another fair-weather sailor, take the money and run, just like so many other freeloaders, no integrity, no staying power, no vision.

Twenty-two years to find you, my darling Valeriya, but finally, perhaps, we can retrieve the scent and find these bastards, put an end to this saga. My epitaph, he thought, *or perhaps my eulogy, let's not rush things.*

His mind slipped into the past like silk floating on a light breeze, images of their intertwined lives throwing memories back at him. Odd, he reminded himself, how the mind works, an event or sometimes a song stirring the past like shifting silt. He could remember their collective excitement as the program took shape, shaping lives, shaping the very future together. And their tangential love affair, stolen moments on a deserted beach, sitting across a chess board, reading poetry to each other in the early hours, wind gusting against frozen windowpanes in the mountain lodge they had hired over one particular Easter break.

Her hair, yes, he had always loved her hair, and she had always murmured in excitement as he wound it into his fist as they made love, pushing his knuckles into the nape of her neck as they moved together. He asked himself if he had been in love. He snorted, his age mocking his memory. Perhaps, or as in love as he was capable of at that time, a time when the world needed to be saved, when building blocks, the very foundation, needed to be recalibrated. He looked into the garden, a light drizzle obscuring the orchard that sat on a small hillock at the bottom of his modest estate. He could see his gardener sweeping leaves into piles, a trail of cigarette smoke following him like a spider's web through the late afternoon.

He took a sip of herbal tea and glanced at his watch. "Come on, come on," he murmured, "hurry up." As if on cue, the telephone rang and he snatched it greedily from its cradle. He said nothing, but just waited, it was his private line after all.

"It's me," the voice said simply.

"Well," he sighed, "impress me."

"It's done, finally," the voice continued, "she is dead, suicide, and the trail has been set, we think, but we will know in twenty-four hours."

"Don't lose it, then, and keep me posted." The line went dead.

Nathan set the receiver back in its cradle and rubbed his fingers across his forehead, concern and adrenaline mingling in a toxic storm of anxiety.

"So, my dear Valeriya," he whispered toward the garden, "our paths have crossed for the final time. Your death will bring me new life, new energy to finish what we started together. Silly girl," he sighed, "why did that have to be so difficult, so wasteful, so fucking stupid?" He slumped into a heavy armchair and closed his eyes. "Keep going," he told himself, "the hardest part is over, we found her, finally, she is dead, and this oddball will show us the way now."

2035, Vienna, Pending Papal Approval

Valeriya continued to stare down at the magazine in her hands, but her eyes were not focused on the page before her; her senses instead stretched across the room to Nathan as she detected the intensity and eagerness in his voice as he spoke to the caller.

"I have some interesting news for you," the voice said quietly, with a hint of excitement. "I would say good news but that might be construed as disingenuous."

"Go on," he said calmly.

"It's been confirmed as cancer, so we can consider this as an addition to the list. I just need to arrange an audience, which might take a little time, but we will have some statistics by then or that's what you've promised me, is that correct?"

"Yes, we are starting slowly, as we discussed, but we have started already, the campaign is under way."

"Good, let's agree a date soon, as his condition will deteriorate quickly. Who will do it?"

"Francisco, he is our prominent and foremost link to Christianity. I understand the urgency," Nathan replied and the line went dead.

There had been an increasingly heated debate amongst the DNA conscious as to just how to prepare the world for the introduction of the three prodigies. Some preferred to closet the three until they "came of age" and then launch them across the planet in a fanfare of hype and marketing. Others, Nathan and Valeriya included, lobbied for a more transparent upbringing, worried that closeting would only engender suspicion and that a clandestine approach would be nigh on impossible in a world where it was increasingly difficult to keep a secret. There must be no question of skulduggery, Nathan insisted, the skulduggery takes place during the cloning process and through surgery directly after birth, thereafter they must develop like any other children, just as Jesus grew up in a simple household.

So the three were initially developed under laboratory conditions, their genetics prescribed secretly by a select group before they were handed on to Valeriya at birth to allow her to create a bicameral brain that would make them genuine believers in what they themselves would eventually preach. With the exception of one of the cells dividing to create monozygotic twins — the other twin, Alexandra, who Valeriya removed but who was presumed destroyed — the program went according to plan.

Following surgery, the three were passed on to foster parents in different locations and were monitored from a distance, their regular medical checkups predicated on allergies that did not exist; none of the three ever suffered from a single day of illness during their formative years. All three were mentored by their foster parents to ensure that they realized that they were special from an early age. They were assured that their voices were normal for special people; that they had certain gifts they should care for and cherish; that some things they were unable to explain, such as their abilities to interpret ancient languages and texts, were causes for wonder as opposed to worry; that a time would come when they would be able to share their gifts with those around them, but that those gifts should be nourished privately while they grow up. They were told those same voices would tell them what to do when the time was right.

What their mentors did not know, however, was that the three children began to communicate with each other from an early age, their extraordinary telepathic abilities an unexpected string to their genetic lineage, an ability that would one day return to haunt their creators. This remained a secret between Francisco, Parvati, and Ibrahim.

Nathan closed his telephone and took a deep breath. He glanced across the room toward Valeriya who was back to reading a magazine, her feet propped up on a coffee table, her beauty and intensity still beguiling despite the fact that she would be 60 later this year.

"You won't believe this," he said, a hint of a smile crossing his features.

"Try me," she said, unwinding her legs momentarily and stretching toward the ceiling. The pair had been up for most of the night; in fact, they had been working 20-hour days for most of the year as the program began to creep toward its birth on the world stage.

"That was our man in the Vatican. It's confirmed, terribly confidential of course, but the Pope has cancer, pancreatic cancer apparently."

"Well then his chances are not good." Valeriya sighed. "If my memory serves me, about a twenty-five percent survival rate in year one and the numbers get worse after that."

"Well, either way, it plays into our hands. What a prize, what a bonus."

Valeriya glanced across the room at Nathan. He looked like a small schoolboy, a schoolboy excited because someone has just been diagnosed with cancer.

Fuck, she said to herself. She sometimes wondered what she had become embroiled in. The plan had seemed so brilliant, so apposite when she first became involved, but she had her doubts now.

She had real moral misgivings over manipulation predicated on illness, but then she was hardly a saint. What about the numerous children who had died under her hands as she experimented with creating the bicameral brain? What of her crucial role in this project that she increasingly saw as…? Well, she was not sure how she saw it anymore. She had changed, but she did know how she regarded its architect, its driving force. Nathan was studying a list of names, and she saw that same sheen that had started to emerge a few years ago, a sheen she interpreted as madness, a growing insanity, a megalomania, which had developed unabated as the project neared its launch.

"You see," Nathan continued, "it's brilliant. Did I tell you what we discussed yesterday? What these fucking pricks have been arguing about for two years but which they finally agreed to yesterday?"

Valeriya shook her head. Whether she had nodded or shaken her head was irrelevant, it was quite clear that she would be hearing it anyway. She looked at his hands fluttering across the list of names in front of him.

Those hands used to touch me, she thought for a moment. *They used to excite me as much as his mind, but something has become twisted, diseased; megalomania is as much of an illness as cancer*, she thought. She had separated from Nathan emotionally many years before, partly because he had become claustrophobic and possessive, partly because he had grown old sexually, older than her anyway.

"Can you believe this shit?" he continued. "We launch next year and these imbeciles give me the green light yesterday after months, not months, after years of debate. Some of them have no idea what we are trying to achieve here, that it's not just a question of turning a switch on and the world's population agrees that self-sacrifice is suddenly a good idea. So now we are under real pressure to deliver." Nathan sighed deeply, he was exhausted. "But we will, it's still possible."

"What's the hiccup now?" Valeriya asked innocently, although she knew exactly what he was talking about. Nathan threw the list of names down on his desk and walked over to the window. He turned toward her and attempted a smile.

"Oh, you know, strategy as usual. I told them last year, and the year before, that if this is going to work, the dissemination of a new philosophy will take time. It needs to gestate, it needs to become familiar, and it needs sponsors — that's key — and what better sponsor than mortality herself? What better advocate for this than those pilgrims who have actually completed the pilgrimage between life and death, who have faced the curse of death with all her false faces, who have faced death prematurely but been given a second chance, a second bite. Those are our sponsors because their appetite for life is ten times that of their fellow man. It is one of the biggest truisms in life. What did Oscar Wilde say, 'to live is the rarest thing in the world, most people exist, that is all.' And that's my point! Only those who have nearly lost life can really appreciate life, and Wilde was right, most of us simply exist."

Nathan walked around the room like a prowling cat.

"Anyway, some of my colleagues wanted this fanfare launch, a Hollywood-style extravaganza, a celebrity event — what clowns," he said with some disgust. "I have been telling them bottom up, top down for months, years. The bottom up is easy, it's low-key, it's subtle, it's gradual, I'm talking about hospital wards, children's hospitals to be precise, that slow eradication of disease, but without the preaching. Let the people ask for an opinion, when actions have spoken louder than words, that's my point. Let them ask!"

Valeriya nodded slowly. "And the top down?" she asked.

"The top down is where we market unobtrusively, to start with anyway. This list is how we get those who are already in the spotlight to market for us. Imagine this," he said, snatching the list from the table. "Listen to this — the eldest son of the Chinese president has leukemia, did you know that?" Valeriya shook her head. Nathan flicked to the second page. "The wife of the Colombian president has been in and out of hospital for the last two years, the doctors can do no more, and she has been given six to nine months to live. Then there is the financial sector. Here, what about this — the head of the World Bank resigned last year to give himself time to care for his wife who has a brain tumour. And now, today, the icing on the cake, so to speak, the Pope himself will die of cancer, but he won't, because a miracle will take place, a miracle that will shake the world by its foundations, a very public miracle."

Nathan threw the list back onto the table. "Yes, bottom up is important, sure, but no one really gives a fuck if some Indian beggar dies of cancer in a slum in Mumbai. Why? Very simple, because he is not a celebrity, and this world is obsessed with celebrities. We all want to be one irrespective of any natural talent, no one cares what that talent might be. So, as the incoming tide slowly gathers credibility from the cheap seats, those in the state boxes, those in the royal boxes will become our champions, our tsunami. Think about it — our ambassadors, religious leaders, politicians, rock stars, they are all on my list and they are all expecting to die soon, sooner than they would wish. These are our sponsors!"

Valeriya smiled across the room, Nathan had done his homework, there was no doubting that, but then his capacity for hard work had never been in doubt.

"So, my dear Valeriya, guess what will happen in a few days? A most scurrilous act, a most heinous act of betrayal."

Valeriya was familiar with Nathan's theatrics. She raised her eyebrows in anticipation.

"I have been told by a source who wishes to remain anonymous, an anonymous source, can one say that?" Nathan laughed quietly. "Anyway, where was I? Yes, I have been told that someone will leak a critical piece of information to the media in Rome, that the Pope has been diagnosed with cancer and that he has but a number of months to live. Then, watch this space!"

2043, The SS, "Greater Love Has No One than This, that One Lay Down His Life for His Friends. You Are My Friends If You Do What I Command You"

As might have been expected, the emergence of the three prophets into an increasingly agnostic world had a profound effect on humanity. In accordance with Nathan's plans, Francisco, Parvati, and Ibrahim began their work in as low-key a manner as was possible so that they were seen as reluctant celebrities, reserved, shunning media attention. Their profiles and behaviour were cast in the tradition of a Mahatma Gandhi or a Nelson Mandela — humility and service to their fellows at the forefront of their campaigns. They began their work silently, that is to say that they did not preach during the first three years of their missions. They simply healed the sick and dying, their focus on children and the select list of rich and famous who were pushed innocuously in front of them by Nathan and his team, so much so that by the end of their third year in circulation, they had unconsciously earned a hugely influential band of sponsors from all walks of life — politicians, religious leaders, celebrities, the old and the young, particularly the latter.

Nathan's plans had some subtle, psychological twists, and he insisted early on that the prophets charge a fee when curing those of means and that this money be invested in foundations that would eventually take the lead and build a number of self-sacrifice centres. This topic was not mentioned in the early days, rather these foundations were seen as philanthropic by nature, reinvesting donations in projects that related to the imbalances between the rich and poor, the haves and the have-nots. The most crucial parts of the campaign in the early days were twofold; firstly, the prophets had no opinions of their own because they listened to voices in their heads, voices from a God of no specific monotheist tradition; and secondly, they behaved and conducted themselves without ego and unilaterally. The fact that their actions and brief messages were identical would become a decisive factor later when their collective message to the world at large would focus on self-sacrifice.

By the beginning of 2039, just over three years after their launch, the three prophets began to take more active roles, holding mass gatherings in huge venues all over the globe where hundreds of thousands could gather simultaneously. Venues where they could lay their hands on the sick and stun the audience with ancient tongues, their followers increasing in number day by day, the world finally rescued from its cynical and shallow trajectory.

Their early messages were predicated on tolerance, justice, and equality, but their focus quickly moved toward mankind's place and role on the planet, that the planet was not inanimate, that the planet was as much a gift from God as life itself. These two ideas were not merely contiguous; they were one and the same. Their message was pantheist in that God was the whole, the universe, but also panentheist in that the divine is synonymous with the universe, that God interpenetrates all living things, that divine energy is present in everything. They also spoke about their source of energy, their healing energy, their ability to raise their level of vibration to 528 Hz, a frequency that resonates throughout nature, one of the six Solfeggio frequencies, the specific frequency that relates to transformation and miracles, most notably that which relates to DNA repair. Throughout this process, their actions spoke as loud as their words and a bow wave of expectation preceded their daily appearances.

And so in early 2039, as their internal voices sharpened in focus, so their collective message turned toward mankind's steady but consistent destruction of the planet, mankind's focus on accumulation, greed, excessive consumption, and chaotic reproduction. They spoke of sustainment, collective responsibility, demographic trends, that the planet was as much the sum of its moving parts as it was a cog in the universal balance that superseded individual preference. They spoke of nature's ability to adjust imbalances subconsciously but warned that mankind had lost that ability, our scientific platforms so advanced that our evolution had become conscious, perhaps even controllable. And they predicted the demise of mankind unless such conscious adjustments were considered, that they had been sent in one way or another to deliver that message, that the world would only survive if mankind became mindful of its rapacious trends, of its destructive legacy. And so they crept toward population control and finally a solution, the right solution, the right to self-sacrifice, to sacrifice those later years in life for the next generations, for the young, just as nature regenerates through the seasons, so mankind should re-explore its own roots, should exercise its ability to consciously regulate.

Not surprisingly, the dogma surrounding suicide for all mainstream religious groups was well recorded, from Aristotle to Plato, from Socrates in "Phaedo" to the philosopher Seneca, from St. Augustine to Freud. The prophets did not attempt to argue on the basis of hundreds of years of philosophy; they focused on a number of themes. Firstly, that self-sacrifice for the common good was not suicide, and that self-sacrifice was a common theme throughout history, not just in the case of Jesus, but in many other examples across all cultures. Secondly, that mankind's historical and philosophical precedence was simply that, mankind's interpretation of mankind's actions, and therein flawed, influenced by evolution, by politics, by tribal affiliations, by religious dogmas, a philosophy determined by time and space. Their message was unique in that it was not "their" message, not a man-made message, it was a message from another source, the same source that afforded their ability to heal, to project energy from that other source. They were simply the energy conductors of a mind-based cosmos.

It was hardly surprising that most main religious groups sat on the fence for some time, the legalities of self-sacrifice as contentious as the euthanasia debate had been toward the end of the 20th century. However, what was not in contention was the physical abilities of the prophets and their extraordinary powers, which they continued to demonstrate during the years that followed and became the primary catalysts for change.

By early 2043, three self-sacrifice centres were approved for construction and financed by the foundations the prophets themselves had sponsored. Nathan's team had a discreet hand in their design and construction. Months later, the prophets' decision to self-sacrifice themselves was met with dismay and horror, and stimulated mass pilgrimages to the three sites that the prophets had stipulated as their respective locations to undergo the ultimate sacrifice. Their mutual and complementary decisions started an avalanche, the floodgates opened as those wishing to self-sacrifice with the prophets, on the very same day, started a bidding war, as if vying for tickets to the Super Bowl or the Olympics 100-metre final. Salvation had never been so hotly contested. This avalanche prompted action from governments and religious organizations alike, urgent discussions, secret meetings, where they determined the age of 65 to be the minimum age at which self-sacrifice could be considered as both propitiate yet still *humanized*, a word the US government used in its campaign to force legislation through Congress.

The three prophets, Francisco, Parvati, and Ibrahim, thought little of their own mortality — they were simply listening to voices and following instructions. In that sense, their impulse to self-sacrifice was as natural as any other bodily function, and they did not necessarily associate an impending mortality with their chosen course of action. It was simply another step, whether that step was forward or backward in time and space was irrelevant. They instinctively knew that this dimension, mankind's current dimension, was the only place in the universe where time and space seemed to move in anything less than ten or eleven dimensions and that their energy would be sustained in one of the others. Given their beliefs and total lack of fear, their composure and balance added yet another dimension, a serenity, a godliness.

The internal designs of the self-sacrifice centres were a closely guarded secret. The experience, or the "ultimate" as it became known, would of course be painless and dignified, but, unlike buying a house, those who elected the ultimate were not shown the facilities before the appointed day. Those who had chosen to self-sacrifice were asked to bid farewell to loved ones and relatives in a preparation area where they were given a small sedative and where they shed their belongings, so that they could enter their own respective eye of the needle.

Francisco's self-sacrifice centre had been built in Brazil, Parvati's in India, and Ibrahim's in Iraq. They would lead by example on the day the centres opened and entered the preparation areas with the same serenity and dignity that had surrounded them during the preceding months. The world stopped in its tracks as it witnessed what many believed was the dawn of a New Age, which, for many, it was.

When Francisco, Parvati, and Ibrahim all awoke from their sedatives to find themselves alive, confused, and in confinement, they began to communicate with one another.

2044, Vatican III

It was in the middle of the night, once again, when Pope Francis II left his bed and made his way into the small dressing room that adjoined his sleeping quarters. At the back of his dressing room was a curtain that he pulled to one side to reveal a small, makeshift altar — a simple cross and three flat pebbles, which he had been given by a teenager on his recent visit to San Paulo, his birthplace. The child, Gabriel, had recounted the tale of how he had been diagnosed with cerebral palsy at an early age and had been undergoing further tests in the San Paolo Maternidade Hospital in 2035 when a young man had been ushered into the ward, a gaggle of medical staff hovering around him like a swarm of bees. The man had seemed oblivious to the commotion around him and had asked for privacy as he spoke with

Gabriel's mother. Gabriel could see his mother's hands shaking in front of her as the man spoke quietly with her. At one point, the young man took her hands within his, and, even at such a young age, Gabriel could still remember his mother buckling under his touch as if a beam of intense light had struck her to her core. The young man had guided his mother to a chair in the corner and had then asked the hospital staff to leave the room, leaving him alone with Gabriel who sat scrunched in his wheelchair like a broken toy. The man came and sat on his haunches in front of Gabriel.

"Hi," he said, "my name is Francisco, who are you?"

"Gabriel."

"Do you like soccer?" the man asked simply, rising from his haunches and dribbling an imaginary football around Gabriel's wheelchair. "I do, love it, but I was never fast enough, a bit of a failure at sports, I'm afraid."

Gabriel found himself giggling at the man's antics, hospital visits were usually boring and often painful. He glanced toward his mother to see what she was making of all this to find her sleeping in the chair where the man had left her, a glow covering her cheeks as if she had been kissed by a summer breeze.

"Oh, don't worry about Mum." Francisco smiled. "She's taking a quick nap, she's exhausted. It's you I came to see today." The man stopped moving around the room and picked up the imaginary football. "Now," he said quietly, raising his eyes toward the far side of the room, "we've been awarded a penalty. What do you reckon, low and hard in the corner or shall I just blast it?"

Gabriel looked a little embarrassed as the man took a few steps back from the imaginary ball and then ran forward, striking the ball with his left leg, his arm immediately raised in a gesture of celebration. Francisco stopped pirouetting and returned to face Gabriel once again, crouching on his haunches, this time a few inches from the boy's face.

"Okay, I need to work," he said quietly, "and you need a little physiotherapy today, Gabriel, so I am going to move you up onto the bed and get some of this circulation going. Is that okay, pal?"

Gabriel nodded without speaking, transfixed by the man's eyes, which held a raw but kind intent. Francisco lifted Gabriel onto the bed in a seamless movement and the boy remembered closing his eyes, drifting away from the hospital ward with its hard floors and opaque disinfectants. And that, he had told the Pope, was all that he remembers, that he awoke whenever he did to find his mother's face above his, tears flowing freely from her eyes, his body dancing like pools of mercury.

"I play football now," had been his first words.

Gabriel had passed Francis the three flat pebbles now sitting on the small altar in front of him. Francis knelt down and looked at the pebbles, equally spaced in front of the crucifix. The boy had painted a name on each pebble, Francisco, Parvati, and Ibrahim.

Francis cast his mind back to his own encounter with Francisco a few months after this incident, the debate surrounding his illness, whether he should abdicate his position, whether the Vatican should go public, the fact that rumours were creeping into pulpits around the world concerning his health, his inability to fulfill his spiritual leadership. There had been no soccer when he met Francisco under a veil of secrecy, but he knew instinctively that he was encountering something or someone with an additional dimension, a force that transcended any mortal he had ever met. Francisco had agreed to meet with the Pope and had even undergone a series of psychological tests and interviews, a pre-screening before he was ushered into the very bedchamber that Francis had just left. Rather like Gabriel, Francis did not remember much, he had been in such excruciating pain at the time, but woke to find his body at peace, a hitherto unknown energy dancing across his skin.

Francis picked up a small file that sat to the right side of the altar and glanced through the few pages, which he knew by heart. They were his medical records concerning his pancreatic cancer, the before and after, quite simply, the oncologist had remarked at the time, a miracle, Holy Father, there is no other way to describe what had happened.

The Vatican had retained its veil of secrecy over the affair, a fact that drove Francis from his bed at all hours to where he found himself now, crouched in prayer, desperately trying to untangle his beliefs. The two thousand years since Christ had been blown open by events around the globe, events culminating in what he had witnessed the year before, the three prophets disappearing into the self-sacrifice centres under the intense scrutiny of the world's media. The subsequent debates, dogma, and doctrine had been strewn across the tabloids; the Church was crying out for leadership, for a stance, and Francis found himself hamstrung by precedence but personified by his own personal miracle.

This personal torment was not restricted to Francis alone, as it had become ubiquitous throughout the Church, and Francis knew that the Vatican could not sit on the fence for much longer. What he struggled the most with, however, was to find real clarity, his mind clouded by two overriding preoccupations: one that he knew to be fear, the other a tingle of destiny, which he also knew to be ego, something at odds with his holy office but a reality nevertheless. The fear issue was simple: if the Church condoned self-sacrifice, then should or would he lead by example? The ego matter was more elusive; he knew that if he led by example, he would become the most famous Pope in history, that his name would eclipse even Constantine the Great. It would be an unprecedented epiphany but also his eulogy, and, as much as he hated to admit his weaknesses, he was afraid of death, his brush with cancer an ever-present reminder of the precarious thread that bound all humans to their short tenure on Earth.

Francis also recognized that his burdens were ordained by a force greater than mortality, so, after much internal and subsequent public debate, he gave instructions to convene Vatican III, some 82 years after Pope John XXIII had formally opened Vatican II, a Vatican Council that addressed the role of the Church in the modern era. Vatican III would address one simple topic, whether self-sacrifice was suicide, and, therefore, whether self-sacrifice was a mortal sin.

In the same vein as Vatican II, Francis was determined to open the debate to as many beliefs as possible, so the gathering included leaders from all faiths, including, most significantly, the Ecumenical

Patriarch of Constantinople, his attendance unprecedented since the Great Schism between the Latin and Greek Churches in 1045. At the core lay the fundamental question: Is self-sacrifice suicide or a justifiable act within the paradigm presented by the prophets? Did mankind's jeopardous tenure on Earth warrant a conscious, divine sanction on a collective scale? In part, this had been St. Augustine's position on suicide, that it was unlawful, that it disobeyed the Sixth Commandment, "Thou Shalt Not Kill," but Augustine had introduced divine sanction as an exception, that this exception was necessary to allow for the self-sacrifice of Christ. So, could such an exception be applied to more than a singular or individual case?

As Francis had expected, the debate was elusive. Council members had drawn on historical precedence: Aristotle who had condemned suicide on political grounds, stating that an individual's allegiance to the state precluded them from taking their own lives, a view expanded on and supported by Thomas Aquinas in his *Summa Theologiae*; Socrates, in "Phaedo," who argued against prolonging life at any cost. The 18th century philosophers such as Voltaire had rallied against absolutism in the name of freedom, citing Cicero, Seneca, and Lucretius as enlightened heroes in their time. The philosophical debate had been inconclusive, as might have been expected, aside from one fundamental agreement within the Council, which was simply this: the Council acknowledged and reconfirmed that Christ had performed the ultimate act of self-sacrifice, so the Church had to provide guidance on whether this was any different to an individual's decision to self-sacrifice for another human being. In other words, self-sacrifice should not be viewed as a reflection of a general will, but each individual case should be judged as just that, as isolated and unique in time and space *individually* as much as any birth or death had ever been.

This was, in a sense, a loophole, "as long as we have a get-out-of-jail-free card" Nathan had insisted, and this was just that. The Council's ruling did not abjure self-sacrifice, neither did it endorse it. Significantly, it did decree that self-sacrifice was not a mortal sin, differentiating the act from suicide, and, as such, left the final decision within an individual's interpretation of divine sanction. This was more than Nathan could have hoped for; it left the world's population at the mercy of his marketing machine, the prophets' brand far more intoxicating and relevant than traditional churches. Collective guilt in relation to the state of the planet was far more marketable than individual principles.

On January 6th, 2045, Francis resigned as Pope and returned to live quietly in his beloved San Paulo. Twelve months later to the day, the Pope Emeritus walked through the very same doors that Francisco had three years earlier, three flat pebbles clutched in his right hand.

2065, Broadway, New York, A Night Shift

"I simply don't understand," murmured the Chief Pediatric Consultant at the Morgan Stanley Children's Hospital on Broadway, half to himself, half to the female radiologist who was peering over his shoulder at the latest computerized tomography scan she had prepared. "This is the third case this month, which beggars belief, which confounds everything we know or knew about these children. Two leukemia cases and now this, stomach cancer, terminal last week, invisible this week, no trace, it's just not possible."

Samuel Kozinski glanced at his colleague and noticed a few grey hairs appearing around her temples.

"Look, I know that the scanner rarely lies but can we do another one before I talk to the boy's parents, just in case? This is all too weird." Samuel took another long look at the woman next to him, her half-moon spectacles sitting toward the end of her angular nose, her dark eyes shrouded in concentration.

"It never lies," Ruth said, raising her eyebrows. "There are interpretive errors, pods of uncertainty, sometimes, but never death one week, life the next, not at these extremes. It's as if a miracle has taken place."

Ruth scratched absentmindedly at the side of her face where a stray hair tickled her cheek. She tucked the hair behind her ear and stretched for a few seconds, her head and neck angled toward the ceiling, a movement that made her spectacles move autonomously, a barely tangible shift toward the bridge of her nose.

The two colleagues were discussing these cases in Samuel's office situated on the third floor of the Cohen's Children Emergency Department, a palatial addition to the hospital made possible by a huge grant from the Cohen Foundation in 2011. It had been an obvious choice for Ruth Cohen, the granddaughter of the Foundation's founder, who now headed up the radiology department. Samuel noticed the spectacles shift once again as Ruth focused on the scan in front of them before she snapped them from her face with a sweep of her hand and tucked them into the breast pocket of her hospital uniform.

"Okay, Sammy," she said, raising her eyebrows in mock bewilderment, "I'll get him in again this afternoon and we can see what happens. We can then chat to his parents this evening. How does that sound?"

"Perfect." He smiled back at her. "Thanks for coming up, and sorry about the cold coffee, again!"

"Oh, I'm used to your coffee." She grinned a little sheepishly. "It would be a shock if it ever arrived on time or even tepid." Ruth picked up her copy of the scan and waved over her shoulder as she left the office. "See you later!"

Samuel watched her float out of his small office as a small hand squeezed the pit of his stomach.

She must know how I feel, he mused. *How I blush uncontrollably every time I see her, how my hands shake just a little when she is standing next to me, how every line on her face is carved in my memory like stone.*

Samuel glanced at the photograph on the wall behind his desk, his three children arrayed around his wife, their arms draped over each other like comfortable clothing, their collective features merging across time and gender like cirrus clouds, their shared lineage denoted by thick, dark hair and prominent, strong noses. He thought about his wife now, a few years on from the shot in the photograph — her unbending will, her tenacious energy, driving the small unit around her with remorseless love and an iron will. Her life seemed to be in straight lines, one-dimensional — grades, scholarships, grandparents, Thanksgiving, bar and bat mitzvahs, bridge clubs, racquetball. There was nothing wrong with any of this, he reminded himself. Traditional values, the family stalwart, sensible, responsible living, blah, blah. It was all good and solid, he told himself.

Who am I trying to convince? he wondered.

He glanced toward the faint hint of perfume Ruth had left in his office and wondered what her personal space was like. He had never been to her home but knew that she lived in an expensive apartment on the Upper East

Side, that money was not an issue but that she lived a somewhat alternative, bohemian lifestyle. He could only judge from her office, her motorcycle jacket thrown across the back of her chair, poetry books piled on the window sills and various artifacts from her many travels strewn along the bookshelves behind her desk; hardly the traditional senior radiologist's profile, but she was elusive, enigmatically so, and therein, he told himself, was the attraction. She was probably everything which his wife was not and everything he thought that he might want but knew that he would never have. But then perhaps that was just an age thing, he told himself.

Ruth returned to her office on the second floor and arranged the three mysterious cases in front of her.

"Two leukemia, one stomach cancer," she said out loud, "all this month, straight out of the blue."

She tapped her pen on the cover of a medical journal that lay beside her computer and had remained unopened despite an article on DNA mutation she intended to read. Ruth picked up the files for the two leukemia patients, the first a seven-year-old girl who had been diagnosed with T-cell prolymphocytic leukemia, the first such case in a child that the hospital had ever encountered. The disease had shrugged off the monoclonal antibody treatment with relative ease, the child withering like a vine before the bloodshot eyes of her parents. The 11-year-old boy's case had been more protracted; his juvenile myelomonocytic leukemia had been treated with chemotherapy and a bone marrow transplantation, neither of which seemed to affect the remorseless advance of the disease. The stomach cancer victim had been a more rapid evolution and had been caught too late, the symptoms first confused with dietary complications by the child's mother. In all cases, it was as clear as day that something extraordinary had occurred. Ruth leaned back in her chair and unconsciously tapped out the beat of one of her favourite rock songs on her desktop, a classic from the 1980s, which had recently resurged with a cult following.

And then a thought skipped to the front of her mind that made the skin across her forehead scrunch momentarily like an old floor mat. She pulled her telephone toward her, perched her spectacles on the bridge of her nose, and tapped in the number for the head of security. She tried to keep her tone light as she made enquiries relating to activities in a number of rooms, feigning conducting a survey of nurse routines as her excuse to examine a random selection of CCTV images across the hospital floors.

"But what's that got to do with radiology?" the voice queried.

"Nothing, Frank," she said as flatly as possible, "I'm just the poor sod saddled with the project."

"Okay, you can come down whenever you want, I'll let the others know to expect you."

Late that afternoon, having been shown the ropes by the duty security manager, Ruth flicked through the rows of CCTV discs until she found the private rooms she was looking for, flicking the images back and forth so the frames sped forward like an old, silent movie. She manoeuvred the joystick on the controls to pause images here and there as staff entered and left the wards, most of the staff well-known to her after her many years walking the corridors. After about 15 minutes, she felt as if someone had walked over her grave as the small hairs on the back of her neck began to twitch uncontrollably. She paused her search on the image of a slim nurse whom she did not recognize, her hands extended over a patient, the seven-year-old girl in this case.

The nurse appeared to start at the girl's feet and slowly move her hands up the full length of the body, a process that took more than 20 minutes to complete. Ruth noted the time at which the process started, a few minutes before 3 a.m. and also made a note of the date. She noticed that her hands were shaking as she slipped another disc into the recorder and ran images for the second leukemia victim. She had picked up the scent by this stage and it did not take her long to find what she was looking for: the same diminutive figure, a second night shift, the same ritual, the process taking 30 minutes on this occasion before the shadow slipped out of the room.

Ruth did not recognize the nurse who had kept her chin low enough to deceive the CCTV image so that all she could make out was the shadow of a nose and reflective spectacles. She made further notes of dates and times for the third patient and then returned to her office. Ruth then spent the next hour checking staff manifests and schedules until two names sat in isolation on the notepad in front of her, one of which was well-known to her, a vast woman who clutched small children to her huge chest in compassionate bear hugs and sang Irish ballads as she pushed tiny patients in and out of operating theatres. The second name, Sophia Levy, was unknown to her.

A good Jewish name, she thought, *but never heard of her.*

She called a contact in the personnel department and asked about the nurse.

"Been here for six weeks, I think," said the voice. "Wait, let me double-check. Yes, Sophia Levy, aged twenty-four, recently qualified. We are still waiting for her permanent address. That seems odd, so, not much on file. Why, what's the problem?"

"Oh, nothing," Ruth replied innocently. "A relative just asked me to look out for her, that's all, you know, Jewish mafia and all that," she paused, "but thanks, sweetie," and she rang off. "Sophia Levy," she said aloud to the tip of her pencil. "Who are you, what are you?"

2065, New York, Something Extra

The following morning, as the night shift gave way to the day, Ruth pulled on her heavy jacket and wandered nonchalantly out of the hospital double doors to join the bustle on Broadway, her pace aligned to the slim nurse who was picking her way through the crowd ahead of her, moving northward. It was a grey morning and the sky hinted at rain, the clouds heavy and cumbersome like pregnant elephants. The nurse, Sophia Levy, appeared to be in no hurry and occasionally paused to glance up at the sky, the morning light competing with shadows as the night gave way to a blustery autumn morning. After a few hundred metres, Sophia turned east and ducked inside a small Italian coffee shop. She eased into a booth, casually waving to the waitress who waved back with a "hey honey" and instinctively retrieved a menu from the pile on the counter and slid it in front of Sophia. Ruth followed her into the small restaurant and pretended to look at a copy of the menu beside the till. The place had just opened so the two women were the only customers, but it would not remain that way for long. Ruth glanced toward Sophia but the young woman had opened a paperback novel and appeared to be unaware of any movement around her. Ruth took a deep breath and walked over to the window table.

"What are you reading?" she asked, her tone as friendly and unthreatening as she could make it. Sophia looked up, the unexpected intrusion throwing a scowl across her forehead.

"I beg your pardon?" she asked, her irritation casting a shadow between them. "What do you care?"

"Sorry." Ruth smiled. "I love books, you hardly ever see people reading these days, a real book that is."

Sophia looked at the cover of the book that she then lifted toward Ruth as if to say, "I don't want to talk, read the title and then fuck off and leave me in peace."

"Ah, Murakami," Ruth sighed, "love his stuff, what a genius!"

Sophia attempted a smile and lowered her eyes to the book once again. Ruth slid into the booth opposite her and tugged at the scarf around her neck.

"What's your favourite?" she asked. "*Kafka on the Shore* must be mine, love that book."

Sophia placed the thick paperback face down between them and looked at the woman opposite her.

"Do you mind?" she said quietly. "I've just finished work, and I'm tired. I normally come here to have my breakfast, to be calm, to read alone before going home to sleep." Sophia paused. "So I like to be alone. Are you trying to pick me up, isn't it a bit early for that?"

Ruth smiled as warmly as she could. "No, no," she said quickly, "we work in the same place, the hospital." A look of suspicion left a small crease across Sophia's brow. "I'm the chief radiologist," Ruth continued and then extended her arm across the table, offering her hand to Sophia. "My name is Ruth Cohen."

Sophia took her hand briefly and muttered, "Sophia," and then glanced toward the waitress, her discomfort rising in her cheeks as she sought a distraction. The waitress moved quickly to the side of the table and flipped her small notebook with a dramatic flourish.

"So, ladies?" She smiled, her newly applied lipstick glistening under the strip lighting.

"Let me have a quick coffee with you," Ruth said quickly, "ten minutes, then I'll leave you in peace."

Sophia looked at Ruth, openly assessing her, and then seemed to come to a decision.

"Okay," she said quietly, "ten minutes. I'll have an espresso and an orange juice," she said to the waitress.

"Me too," added Ruth, keen to dispense with formalities and distractions, and to regain their privacy.

The waitress nodded, smiled, and then moved toward the counter, their order passed to her colleague who snapped on the coffee bean grinder as if he was directing a small orchestra. He winked at the waitress who pursed her lips toward him as if to say, "Yes, you do that every day, and yes, I have been working here for ten years, and no, you are still not getting into my pants." Ruth and Sophia were unaware of this daily ritual and eyed each other with some distrust as the small pantomime played out behind them.

"So," Ruth began, "how long have you been at the hospital, Sophia?" She tried to gauge Sophia's eyes but the nurse was wearing heavy spectacles with dark orchid lenses that threw a haze across the upper part of her face and gave her eyes an opaque facade. Sophia attempted a smile but her distrust distorted her attempt, so much so that her mouth curled into a grimace.

"I think that you know that, don't you?" she said with some aggression. "So why don't you stop fucking around and get to whatever point you have to make, and then leave me in peace."

"I was trying to be friendly," Ruth said quietly, an edge creeping into her voice, which was not lost on Sophia.

An uneasy silence settled between the two women as the waitress returned with the espressos and glasses of orange juice. Sophia emptied a small sachet of sugar into her cup and stirred the dark, thick coffee before looking up at Ruth, her eyebrows raised in a gesture for her to continue. Ruth reached into her satchel and pulled out a still photograph from the CCTV footage and placed it in the space between them. Sophia barely glanced down at the picture before raising her eyes once again. She sipped from her orange juice but said nothing. Ruth cleared her throat and glanced out at the sidewalk where small drops of rain had started to mingle with the grime and membrane of embedded filth.

"Look, Sophia…" she attempted, but then looked away once more, shaking her head slowly. "Listen, my grandparents donated fifty million dollars to get this hospital wing going, I have given a decade plus of my life, it's in my blood, part of me, so I get very protective and territorial when weird things start happening in the early hours—"

"What weird things?" Sophia interrupted. "A nurse checking on a patient?"

Ruth smiled in quiet contemplation. "Sure, Sophia," she said quietly, "we can patronize each other for the next thirty minutes if you like or we can level with each other and have a discussion. Three patients, three children to be precise, three terminal cases, and you, visiting each, healing hands or something extraordinary. I am not stupid so please don't treat me like a cunt."

The final word was spat across the table and seemed to rouse Sophia as if she had been stung by a wasp. She looked hard at Ruth who imagined for a moment that the woman in front of her might attack her like a wild animal, but she did not. Instead, Sophia removed her spectacles and raised her eyes toward Ruth. This unexpected movement caught Ruth off guard and she found herself staring at an enigma. It had not been the dark orchid lenses that had given Sophia an opaque anonymity; her eyes themselves were dark orchid and slightly different colours, the thick lenses were in a sense refractive, but clear, a simple prop to obscure an almost supernatural abnormality. Sophia replaced her spectacles and the illusion disappeared.

"Is that supposed to frighten me?" Ruth asked.

"So," Sophia said slowly, "if what you say is true, so what, how can good be bad?"

"It's not that," Ruth said quickly, "of course, it's good, in a sense, but you can't imagine that these things remain hidden, that recurrent miracles, as such, will go unnoticed. And then what? What happens to the hospital? A media circus, who knows what. It's not something I can keep hidden, that you can keep hidden. Surely you know that?"

"It has to remain hidden," Sophia said quietly, "or it will be very dangerous for me, and others." Her tone was flat and layered like a memory.

"How so?" Ruth asked. "I need more than that to stop me going to the authorities."

Sophia scoffed across the table and tapped her teaspoon against the side of her cup.

"Oh dear," she murmured, "I thought that you had a little something extra, that 'cunt' was spontaneous, that you had a twist of the bohemian in you, but no, you seem just like the rest, another fucking pen-pusher, a box ticker."

The tempo between the two women had risen exponentially and Ruth attempted to smile through her anger.

"Listen," she said with a grimace, "I came here to make friends, but you seem too fucking special to need a friend or any help for that matter, and I don't want some freak fucking up my hospital." She regretted the word "freak" as soon as it left her mouth and so it hovered between them, in limbo.

"Why don't you leave now?" Sophia said quietly.

Ruth began to gather her jacket and scarf and shuffle her backside toward the edge of the booth.

"I'm sorry," she said, her tone starched and businesslike, but the words aimed at something she was about to do as opposed to an apology for their exchange. Her intent was not lost on Sophia.

"By the way," Sophia said quietly, "what I said, about you having something extra?"

Ruth was standing up by now and had begun to pull on her jacket. She glanced down at Sophia, her frustration and anger still bubbling under her skin. "What?"

"You do have something extra," Sophia said calmly. "I can feel it from here. I can see it, if you like, that's the sort of fucking freak I am. It will cost you your right breast over the coming months, maybe more. But don't take my word for it, go and check before you sound alarm bells about me with your supervisors, with your fellow administrators. Go away and check."

Sophia turned away from Ruth and picked up her book, her eyes cast toward the pages. Ruth hesitated, confusion gathering around her like a fog. She had unconsciously raised one hand to her chest and had covered her right breast.

She walked away from the table.

2065, New York, An Elephant Hair

Ruth stood naked in front of the full-length mirror that hung behind her bathroom door. She had her right breast cupped in the palm of her left hand and was methodically working across her pale skin to see if there were any signs of a lump. She was still smarting from her encounter with Sophia, and she kept asking herself how their conversation, their meeting, had got quite so out of hand quite so quickly. Had she, Ruth herself, been clumsy and insensitive? Perhaps, but how else does one broach the subject of miracles to an orchid-eyed weirdo or freak as she had so tactlessly referred to her. So, they had got off to a bad start, to put it lightly, and she had to figure out a next step, quite what to present to Sammy and what effect she hoped to achieve. It would certainly put an end to any more late-night healings, which was a negative.

But we are running a hospital, not a circus for freaks. Her mind ran over their encounter once more. *Those orchid eyes*, she said to the mirror, *what the hell is going on there?*

Ruth released her right breast and placed her hands on her hips. She looked at her breasts, almost anticipating a short conversation between the two areas of flesh, as if they might strike up a short debate, the pros and cons of large or small, breastfeeding, and, what every breast no doubt feared most in life, the dreaded mastectomy. At 38, she was still in good shape, although she had started to notice a slight sag here and there that seemed immune to any amount of pounding in the gym.

At least my tummy is flat and hard, and I have not had any complaints from the few men who have crossed my sexual threshold. Although some of them could have done with a few hours with her personal trainer. Ruth stepped closer to the mirror and cupped both breasts together so that the nipples brushed against each other.

That's weird, she said to herself. They were different sizes, not that noticeable but different nevertheless. She looked at the areola around her nipples, the darker shade of skin emphasized by her alabaster skin. Her mind wandered to a time when her breasts had just matured, a little after her 18th birthday, when a solitary hair had emerged from the areola of her right breast — a thick, dark hair that seemed to belong to another being, to an elephant she had felt at the time.

This is certainly not me, of me, she had said at the time. *I have auburn hair, on my head and between my thighs, the hair on my forearms is wispy at best, barely visible, and yet this oaf of a hair has emerged from within me, on the most delicate part of my breast, and why only one breast, what about the other?*

This intruding hair, this "elephant invader," intrigued her for over two years; she began by snipping it away with a pair of nail scissors, but the hair grew faster and thicker so that she could wrap it around her little finger and pull gently, the areola stretching under the pressure.

My God. She remembered how she even started to gather her clippings week by week until she had a small collection of the thick hair in a jewellery box that she kept in her bedside locker.

She dreamt one night of lying on the beach with her girlfriends, what beach or where, she had no idea, but she was dozing under the bright sunlight, the light chatter of her friends surrounding her in a warm glow until she heard giggling, which she assumed was as a result of some mindless gossip until she felt a tickle across her cheek, as if someone was teasing her with a feather. She was too drowsy to pull herself back from the sunlight but was increasingly aware of a gathering, a commotion, so she sat up abruptly to find a small crowd around her towel, perfectly shaped boys and girls in tight swimsuits, their faces set in bemusement, an odd finger pointing down toward her. Having sat up, and still aware of a tickling sensation across her face, she found the source of their amusement, the dark hair twisting out of the top of her bikini like a grapevine, rising across her upper chest and chin to where it tickled her cheek now. She had pulled frantically at the hair but it was as strong as a guitar string, so she had grabbed for her towel and pushed through the small group of onlookers, running … and then she woke up.

She grimaced at herself in the mirror momentarily, her hands running across her breasts, prodding here and there. She remembered the morning after the dream with such clarity, the meticulous precision with which she engaged the hair with tweezers, the tweezers and areola fighting for possession until the latter gave way, almost as if a tug-of-war had ended, the hair popping out between the tweezers, the areola slumping back into place, in submission, a tiny dot of bright red blood emerging in its place. She remembered looking at what had emerged, the hair's sheath and papilla intact.

No wonder there is a drop of blood, she had said. The hair never reappeared.

Ruth pushed the memory away and lay down on the floor, lifting one arm behind her head so that she could push her fingers up toward her armpit, toward the "axillary tail" of her right breast. Her mobile telephone began to ring in the bedroom, and she cursed quietly to herself and glanced quickly at her watch.

Shit, she thought, *I need to get on.* And then her heart leapt into her mouth spontaneously as a rush of adrenaline slammed through her body. She pushed her middle three fingers a little higher once more and felt a slight nausea, the tips of her fingers pushing as high as her armpit.

"Fuck," she whispered, "fuck, there is something there, not very big, but it's there."

She felt tears gathering in her eyes as fear washed over her like an icy wind, and she sat up abruptly, the sudden movement throwing teardrops onto her breasts. She stood up and leaned over the sink, bile rising in her throat that she spat into the basin. She wiped her forearm across her eyes, her tears smearing across the auburn down and scattered freckles. Ruth lifted her head and stared at herself in the mirror, lifting her arm to brush her hair behind her ears.

"Fuck," she said to the mirror, "fuck, fuck!" Her telephone started to ring once more. "Fuck off," she cried, "leave me in peace."

"I am supposed to be invincible," she whispered at her reflection.

Ruth remained where she was for a few minutes, a strange paralysis anchoring her to the bathroom tiles, an occasional tear creeping down her cheeks, which she no longer bothered to brush away. She had had one similar experience, at 21, when she had stared in disbelief at the pregnancy tester, the obstinate blob of colour mocking her, mocking her stupidity, her moment of recklessness. This was far worse, she knew; that episode had been dealt with quickly and quietly. She still bore psychological scars, she probably always would, and housed a deep regret that she had still not had a child, that she had subconsciously always opted for career, for independence, even solitude. She harboured a deep mistrust for the male species, their egos synonymous with their outward image as opposed to inner strength, well, most men anyway; she had yet to meet the exception. The telephone had stopped ringing, but no sooner had Ruth pulled herself away from the mirror than it started once again. She muttered under her breath and walked through to her bedroom, snatching the phone in frustration from where she had tossed it onto the bed.

"Yes?" she said, anger and fear still hovering within her tone.

"It's Sophia," the voice said quietly. "How are you, Ruth?"

Ruth was taken by surprise by the underlying compassion in the way Sophia asked the question, so much so that she sat down on the edge of the bed.

"Oh, okay," she said mechanically. "How did you get this number?"

"From the hospital," Sophia said, as if the question was rather unnecessary.

"Why are you calling?" Ruth asked, a little more abruptly, an inexplicable desire to gain control of the conversation pulling her to her senses.

"To see how you are. We got off to a bad start, and I know that you found something, so I want to see if you are okay."

Ruth paused and looked at the number on the front of the telephone.

"Can I call you back, five minutes?"

"Okay," and the line went dead.

For some bizarre reason, Ruth dressed quickly, scrubbing at her face and arranging her makeup as if the call might go better if she were presentable, even composed, despite her recent shock. She felt completely out of her depth with this extraordinary woman and was grappling with her thoughts and ideas, scrambling for traction on a crumbling rock face. She walked out of her bedroom and into the kitchen, pulling a bottle of white wine from the fridge and pouring herself a glass. She gulped at the crisp, dry wine, set the glass to one side, and then picked up her telephone. The call was answered immediately.

"What do you want, Sophia?" Ruth asked quietly. "I thought our respective positions were clear?"

"I can help you," Sophia said quietly, "and then let me disappear, to another hospital. No more freaks, no more late-night stuff. I disappear, you get well, we never see each other again, but you say nothing, not a word, that's what I want."

The line went quiet, and Ruth tried to imagine where Sophia was, the spiritual intensity of the young woman bristling at the other end of the line.

"How do you know that you can help?" she asked softly.

"Do you really need to ask that? Why don't you go and do a formal check first, if you are not certain, and then we can chat?"

"I don't need to," Ruth said, her voice a little flat. "There is something there, that I know, how bad it might be is another story."

"So…?" Sophia asked.

"What do you suggest?" Ruth asked.

"Why don't we meet after the day shift, on Friday? We'll go to my place, thirty minutes, that's all, you can meet my mother, it might help you to understand."

"It's hard to believe," Ruth said, more to herself than to Sophia.

"Not really," Sophia said, "if you knew a little more, it's not really that hard to believe. So, Friday, yes or no?"

"Yes," Ruth said quietly, her voice weak with emotion, "Friday."

"Please, don't worry," Sophia said, and the line went dead.

2065, Salisbury, England, Jan

> *Jan, I will not be coming home today but will come home in a few weeks. I need some space and time to think. I think that you do, too, about us, as you are clearly not happy with us. You sent me a message by mistake, yesterday, it hurt me.*

Brian had been right in his assessment of his wife's reaction to his text message but incorrect in some of his assumptions. Nausea engulfed her as soon as her mind managed to piece together what might have happened, her fingers prodding at her phone, frantically searching for the text he alluded to. She could not find it and reminded herself that she deleted anything sensitive. She opened up her address book and paged down her list of contacts until she found the number for her husband, groaning inwardly as she acknowledged the name sitting above his, Brenda, the exponential effect of what had happened crashing around inside her skull like a mad bull.

What did I write? My God, something about having an orgasm, something about mouths, something about my arse?

She could only imagine his face when he read the text; in fact, no, she had no idea how to even imagine what he must have thought, what hurt she had inflicted, what tortuous and toxic thoughts must be running through his head. Tears gathered in the wrinkles that framed her eyes, and she rubbed at her nose unconsciously, sitting down quickly to steady herself. A million consecutive thoughts subsumed her with fear and a deep sadness.

"Oh my God," she whispered quietly. "What have I done?"

Her mind slipped back over recent weeks, the extraordinary set of events that had led her to this moment. Well, perhaps they were not extraordinary per se, but they had been for her, a genesis. Jan had met Brenda over a series of visits to her local supermarket, Brenda being the woman whom she gravitated toward when she needed to check out. There was something serene about the woman, Jan had said to herself one day, an innate compassion that sat across her skin like a coat of paint, a gentleness that exuded contentment even when performing such a seemingly dull task as running goods across the small conveyor belt to ensure that they bleeped in acknowledgment. Jan knew her name was Brenda as she wore a small name badge pinned to her uniform, and she always took the time to ask how she was and to thank her as she hauled her shopping into her trolley before leaving the store.

On one occasion, Brenda glanced down at one of Jan's purchases, some hand cream, and murmured, "You don't need that, love, you have beautiful hands."

The two women had smiled at each other despite, in some ways, being the apparent antithesis of one another.

Jan pursed her lips as she recollected their next unexpected meeting, bumping into each other at a cash dispenser in the pouring rain. Brenda had been soaked to the skin with no umbrella.

There had been a quick "Oh, I know you" from Jan. "You are going to freeze to death, let me give you a lift," she had said.

"No, don't worry, there is a bus," Brenda replied, but Jan insisted, and moments later the two women were shivering in the warmth of Jan's car.

She manoeuvred the car gingerly through the heavy rain to the outskirts of town where Brenda indicated toward a small apartment building with a "that's me!" She pulled her heavy frame from the car and squeezed Jan's arm in a gesture of thanks when, for no apparent reason, Jan simply asked, "Can I come in?" a question that made Brenda pause for a moment.

Finally she said, "Of course, love, park over there, those slots are allocated to our apartments."

Brenda's apartment was a small, two bedroom space where she lived alone, and which she seemed to share with a huge collection of books and music. Jan could see no sign of a television or any modern electrical appliance with the exception of the music player sitting on a small sideboard in one corner of the room.

On entering the apartment, Brenda muttered, “I need to get out of these wet things. Why don’t you put the kettle on?” And she disappeared into one of the bedrooms from which Jan could hear her opening cupboards, the muffled thud of her throwing her soaking shoes into a corner and the rustle of coat hangers as she hummed a melody to herself.

“Where’s the tea?” Jan called through the open door.

“Second cupboard to the right of the fridge,” was shouted back from the bedroom, and seconds later Brenda emerged, her hair tied up in a bundle and a heavy, towelled robe tied at her waist.

“That’s better,” she said. “Now, tea or something stronger?”

“Oh, I better stick with tea,” Jan said with a smile. “I’m not used to drinking this early.”

“Nor am I, love,” Brenda replied, as she pulled open the fridge to inspect its contents. “Now,” she said, almost to herself, “what have we in here?” She pulled a chilled bottle of white wine from the top shelf and thrust the bottle under Jan’s nose. “Italian,” she said, “very dry and very cold, but maybe not your scene, seeing as you seem a bit posh and all.”

Jan smirked back at Brenda.

“Okay then, why not, thank you.”

The two women talked their way through the crisp white wine, after which Brenda opened a bottle of equally good red wine and laid some cheese and biscuits between them to nullify some of the wine’s effects. It turned out that Brenda was far better read than Jan and there was nothing that she seemed not to know about opera.

"I don't get it," Jan said, "why the job at the supermarket? You're obviously far more intelligent than anyone else there — all this literature, the music. Why the job? It must be so boring."

Brenda twirled the stem of her glass for a while, her eyes cast downward in quiet contemplation.

"Funny, really," she said quietly. "I like it, simple, lots of people, gets me out and about, so, it could have been anything really, by way of its simplicity, frees my mind for writing, that's my passion."

"Really?" Jan said, leaning forward. "What do you write?"

"Poems," Brenda replied.

"Well?" Jan said, raising her eyebrows. "Don't be shy, what sort of poems?"

"Oh, I don't know, all sorts." Brenda left the table and walked over to the bookshelf from which she extracted a slim, hard-backed volume that she passed to Jan. "There," she said, "see for yourself."

"You've been published?" Jan shrieked, snatching the book from Brenda and turning it over to examine the back cover. There was a short piece on the nature of the poems and a small picture of Brenda tucked into the top, right-hand corner. She shook her head slowly and, turning to the front of the book, opened the cover and scrolled down the list of 30 or so poems.

"Can I read one?" she asked across the table. Brenda smiled and nodded, and then topped up their glasses as Jan examined the titles before selecting a first poem that was called "Yesterday's Cloak." She read aloud:

What a life if we could shed despair as
The snake shrugs off yesterday's cloak,
Deflect grief in an abundance of autumnal release
Sacrifice pity at the altar of forbearance
Eclipse jealousy in fiery passion
Dispel fear through embracing light,
The human spirit trips on her longevous denials
Stutters within her egoistic flight,
A lisp of insecurity tangled in her tresses
A brambled epitaph of retrospective regret,
The echoes of mortality mocking from the shadows,
The curse of ignorance pulled across bloodshot eyes
An unwelcome poultice of our savage failure

To live our truth

To embrace the fragility of our very raw, such
Preening arrogance framed under hope's mannequin

"That's beautiful," Jan said quietly when she had finished, almost to herself as she turned a few more pages and cast her eyes across another few verses, her attention drawn by the word "clot." The poem was entitled, "For Whom the Clot Tolls."

"Oh God," she said, giggling, "I am too embarrassed to read this aloud, but oh well, what the heck!"

Clotted, you are a clot and you have clotted me,
I am be-clotted by a fucking clot,
But the clot was like raw skin branded by fire,

Personified by depth, a breaking wave,
I wanted to fuck the clot, this clot,
A clotted hood of lust, a metaphorical clot of hope,
And the clot looked through me,
The clot could see the other side of her mirror, me,

You can't look at me like that, I said,
Your clot is an analogous energy, clot nemesis,
How can a clot be so pervasive, persuasive,
I thought about a word, clotsuasive, fuck,
The clot had me fucked, the clot was a filibuster,
The clot was rearranging my universe,
So, get a fucking grip I said, but I rather knew
Which clot was the clot, my clotarical damage

Is that what you have become, a clotgential
Voice asked me as I scrubbed at my emotions,
As the clot of Damocles hovered ominously above
A clotted sky, boiling my soul, squeezing my aorta
In to a clot of despair, a wandering clot,
Bumping in to space, bruised by emptiness,
Compromised by a stagnating clot of loss,
Lost love clotted under skin, trapped in my veins

You are the fucking clot, the clot said to himself,
And there you will fester, another clot in limbo

"Gosh, Brenda," Jan said quietly, "I suppose I always thought that there was something special about you. I can see it on your skin, you have a sort of aura about you, it's as if you are shining, literally."

"Now you are a little tipsy, Jan," Brenda said with a smile, ignoring the compliment.

For no apparent reason, Jan found tears welling up behind her eyes and she tried to brush them away before Brenda had the chance to notice, but the woman opposite her was far too wise to miss such a thing. Still, she said nothing, she simply took one of Jan's hands in hers and held it lightly, occasionally squeezing the fingertips by way of reassurance. After a minute or so, Jan regained her composure and smiled through her tears across the table.

"I'm so sorry," she said, barely audibly. "Not quite sure what happened there. I feel a little silly now, I barely know you. I must go." Jan paused before adding, "I don't seem to be very happy with so many things these days…" and her voice tailed away.

"Now you are being silly," said Brenda, her tone gentle, her hands still moving over Jan's fingertips. "You can't drive like this anyway, come."

Jan found herself being led by her hand into Brenda's bedroom where Brenda pulled back the duvet and tucked Jan under the covers.

"Where are you going?" Jan whispered into the shadows.

"I'm coming back," Brenda called from the kitchen. "Have a little sleep."

Jan felt her mind wandering into the strains of opera drifting into the bedroom, and she pulled her knees up under her torso like a fetus, a faint smell of Brenda hovering across the pillow like the smell of wet grass after an April shower. She must have dozed off and woke with a start in the half-light, the bedroom consumed by shadows, an aria playing to itself from the other room. She sat up in bed and then realized that Brenda was next to her, her dark hair thrown across the pillow like a heavy cape, her steady breathing breaking the oncoming dusk. Her sudden movement must have roused Brenda who also sat up in bed, the covers falling away from her shoulders, her heavy breasts eclipsed in the half-light.

"Oh," she said quietly, "sorry."

"What for?" Brenda asked simply, making no effort to cover her nakedness.

"For waking you," Jan added. "I better go, it's late." Jan felt embarrassed by Brenda's nakedness and looked away into the corner of the room. "I am not sure what I'm doing here," she said quietly. "I am not a lesbian, you know."

"Nor am I, love," Brenda giggled softly, "but I am very fucking turned on by you, look."

Jan cast her eyes back toward Brenda, whose hands had encircled one of her breasts, the nipple huge and erect, much bigger than anything Jan had ever seen. Brenda took one of Jan's hands and placed it over her other breast, the nipple jumping to life between her fingers. Jan felt a sudden pulse between her thighs and found her hand moving automatically, encircling the area around the nipple, her fingers occasionally brushing across the hard tip. Brenda turned toward Jan and ran her mouth across her cheek, her tongue occasionally slipping from between her lips to brush against the side of Jan's mouth before kissing her fully on the mouth, traces of wine and toothpaste sending Jan into a giddy spin. She could feel her own excitement mounting and pushed her tongue into

Brenda's mouth, her fingers squeezing her nipples as hard as she could. An unexpected lust rose through her body, so much so that she began pulling at her clothes, desperate to rub her skin against Brenda's nakedness, to rub her thighs against her nipples, to feel a part of Brenda's body inside her, any part.

That had been six weeks ago, Jan reminded herself, and since then the two women had met three times per week, their lovemaking as frantic as ever, Brenda more erotic and generous in bed than anything that Jan had ever imagined. She was totally at ease with her body, with their bodies, and had urged Jan to break some subconscious taboos, to do whatever she pleased and to be honest about what pleased her.

"So, back to my fateful message," Jan whispered. "Brian will think it's another man, not this voluptuous creature, this Amazon of smooth curves and heavy breasts who pushes her erect clitoris into my mouth and pushes her tongue into my arse, and who then reads a poem to me. My God, what a change, what a metamorphosis. In just a few weeks, I have literally become another woman, happy, loved in a simple and honest way."

But now what? she asked. *Now what do I say to my disappearing husband? I wonder where he is, going for a drive, for fuck's sake, what the hell does he mean by that?*

She felt a sudden urge to confront the situation and called his number, the automatic response service confirming what he had said that he would do, switch off, literally.

You coward — lightweight! Where are you, stupid man?

2065, New York, The Cat's Paw

Brian thought long and hard about crossing the USA by car, effectively taking a road trip. He could remember old movies from the late 1970s and 1980s, long-haired drifters in leather jackets driving extraordinary motorbikes. "Choppers" he thought they were called. They were reminiscent of crazy stories about long distance races across the desert plains, Route 66 across New Mexico, Highway 50, which straddled Nevada. They had been huge, gas-guzzling machines that engulfed the audience with dust and screeching metal in a manner that resonated excess and "devil may care" in a tone that would not be tolerated these days. He also felt that he should not take too long, that his domestic affairs could not simply fester in a dark corner of his mind even though there was an overwhelming temptation to leave them just there, to run away, as simple as that.

So, Brian took the flight to New York where he settled into the Carlyle Hotel on Upper East Side Manhattan, a rare treat under the trappings of his newly acquired wealth. The hotel was just as he had imagined, a retreat into a residential refinement, a subtle line between exquisite taste and simple comfort, the staff blending in and out of the art deco with seamless ease. Brian arrived in the evening and opted for a small snack in his room before falling into a restless sleep. He had the most extraordinary dream that he was surprised he could recall and equally bemused by its content.

The dream concerned a certain cat, and Brian was allergic to cats, but nevertheless, by some dint of fortune, Brian had been saddled with a cat that appeared holding a severed paw. The creature hopped along on three feet but was still able to carry its fourth paw in its other front paw. The wound looked as precise as if the cat had in fact undergone a surgical procedure to remove the paw, and the flesh was a healthy, bright red. Brian's recollection of the dream was hazy at best, but he did remember finding a vet who was prepared to sew the paw back on but who, en route to the operating theatre, popped the severed paw into his mouth, exclaiming that human saliva would create a hygienic seal around the stump of the severed limb and ensure a successful operation.

Brian awoke with a confusion of images in his mind, the most stark being the aftermath of the operation, when he and the cat were doing the rounds at a cocktail party at which the cat was displaying his bandaged and recently re-attached paw, which, on closer inspection, revealed that the surgeon had sewn on a human index finger instead of his paw. They bumped into the vet at the party, who seemed pleased with his handiwork and admitted, rather sheepishly, that he had swallowed the cat's paw by mistake, hence the human replacement. The vet's hand was heavily bandaged and Brian suspected that he had amputated his own index finger, which the cat now waggled with such aplomb.

Brian was unable to link any recent event in his life to such a dream but was left wondering about the integrity of the vet. Had he really swallowed the paw by accident or had it been his plan all along to eat the furry morsel?

Brian left the hotel mid-morning, the copy of *The Origin of Consciousness in the Breakdown of the Bicameral Mind* tucked under his arm. He had chatted to the concierge at the hotel after breakfast and was torn between visits to the Guggenheim and Museum of Modern Art, and the pressing business of establishing contact with Alexandra. He wondered what sort of woman he might find. Valeriya had not seen her daughter for many years and had mentioned her state of mind, or, more accurately, had said that there might be a problem.

He remembered her words: "But there is a complication; she had an accident a few years ago and suffered brain damage, minor, but I had to realign parts of her corpus callosum so I'm not sure what works, where the information is, even whether it can be retrieved in her current state."

So, what of her state of mind, what of her ability to contact the prophets, how might she react to news of her mother's murder? For reasons that he was unable to explain, Brian expected hostility and resentment, and suspected that the mother-to-daughter relationship had not been healthy even when they had been together. So, these drifting thoughts teased Brian like an elusive song title — it was akin to finding himself humming a tune to which he knew the melody backward, but could not put his finger on the actual song title or coax the melody into the chorus line, which would surely produce the answer. Unease sat under his skin like a predatory virus and shook his general feeling of well-being from him, like shaking apples from a tree. By the time Brian found himself adjacent to Central Park, he had descended into a mood of melancholic foreboding. Thoughts of his life in England pounced at him from behind bushes, and he marvelled that it was only four days earlier that he had been sitting in a dentist's forum in Las Vegas.

I wonder how the conference finished?

Did he care? At least that was easy to answer.

Brian moved north along the heavy stone wall bordering Central Park, the shades of autumn throwing copper reflections against the sides of high-rise buildings in spectacular fashion. He caught sight of cyclists and joggers within the park, all shapes and sizes, all ages and creeds, those struggling under heavy excess, those in perfect harmony with the music they had plugged into their ears. Brian glanced at the map that the concierge had given to him and decided to cross the park on the 86th Street Transverse that would take him on to Upper West Side and then Broadway. He also wanted to take his time on Museum Mile and indulge in some of the timeless architecture.

Brian had, subconsciously, already decided to stop for coffee, for some reason finding every excuse he could to delay his encounter with Alexandra. Unease sat like a lead weight behind his eyes. He selected a table on the edge of a small restaurant from which he could spend a few moments to gather his thoughts, to prepare a small soliloquy for Alexandra, a synopsis of his encounter with her mother. He marvelled at the high-rise buildings towering on the other side of the park — the glitz, the glamour. He pondered what incredible achievements humans had managed at all ends of every spectrum — good and evil, war and peace, breathtaking beauty, even greater ugliness, the ability to send satellites to Mars matched by the inability to cure some disease. Life was somehow disjointed, so prone to dislocation, so often recalibrated in history only to be undone by sustaining traits in humankind's behaviour.

Must be our genes, our DNA.

And that whole time thing, he mused, *that's all a bit odd, as if time sometimes speeds up for different people in different life zones depending on what they are or were doing, depending on their levels of stimulation.*

He was not sure exactly what he meant by this but knew, for example, that his life seemed to be running at two speeds. The first was at the Valeriya speed, the "corpus callosum" speed, which rushed ahead and behind him in more dimensions than he could fathom, pinching him with excitement and expectation in an elusive game of hide-and-seek. The second was his "personal life" speed, which he could feel like a long, heavy tail behind him, an additional limb with which he had been lumbered, as debilitating as it was cumbersome, so much so that he felt he was dragging these thoughts through thick glue, a line of slime trailing behind him like a slug.

In this time zone, I am a new species, Homo sapiens, *with a fucking slug stapled to my arse, a slug covered in fifty coats of slime, just for good measure.*

Brian ordered an espresso from the waitress, who delivered an obsequious smile as she jotted down his order. He pondered whether it had been obsequious or friendly as she floated between the chairs, her trim figure accentuated by her tight uniform.

That's quite something, Brian thought, *and she has beautiful, white teeth.* The waitress came back with Brian's espresso and he tried to engage her in a light conversation.

"First time here?" she asked, her accent slapping him across his face.

"Yes," Brian responded. "How long will it take me to walk to Broadway from here?"

"How fast do you walk, honey? Broadway does not sit still," she smiled back at him, raising her eyebrows theatrically. She leaned forward to adjust the window blinds and Brian found his face adjacent to her ears, which were small and elegant, and he had time to quickly count the nine studs contouring the cartilage. He tried desperately not to lower his eyes toward her cleavage.

She glanced at him as she stood up.

"You know, my mother is always on the lookout for a date, if you need a local guide," she said and, with perfect timing, "sassied" away from Brian's open mouth.

He shook his head gently and smiled toward the busy pavement. A few minutes later, Brian left some notes on the table and slipped out quietly while the waitress was not visible. He worked his way through the park adjacent to the 86th Street Transverse, pausing occasionally to look at the burnished reflections of autumn shimmering in the Jacqueline Kennedy Onassis Reservoir or casting his eyes north and south, particularly south where the huge buildings framed the southern end of Central Park. There were hints of winter whispering through the trees and a chill in the air that brushed the fallen leaves into makeshift piles of decay, their frail edges still gilded by the night's frost.

Brian emerged on Central Park West and paused to collect his bearings. He could either go a further three blocks and then turn north on Broadway or work his way northwest in a more indirect manner. What he had failed to appreciate, however, was that he still had 82 blocks to walk to get to Alexandra's address at West 168th Street and Broadway. Brian glanced at his watch and looked at the map once again. Perhaps it would be better to grab a taxi?

The two people following Brian had not expected this sudden change in tempo and were catapulted into a frenzy as he tucked his map into his inside pocket and pulled open the door of the nearest yellow cab. They found themselves jogging across Central Park West and waving toward another cab that had just deposited its fare. They settled into the back of their cab with one of the two shaking her head in disbelief as if to say, "Fuck, we were switching off there; if we lose him now, we'll become another Nathan sacrifice, switch on!"

Thankfully, and rather ironically, it seemed that Brian's preoccupations would have kept him oblivious to a herd of buffalo scrambling for cabs behind him, his mind tripping over images and ideas from the last few days as if he was playing solitaire, each card meticulously placed in front of him, scrutinized, weighted by value, by exponential mystery.

The two agents in the taxi behind Brian had picked up his scent as he left the small house in the Las Vegas suburbs, the tracking device embedded in the spine of the book that now sat on the seat beside Brian, no more than four cars ahead of them. The pair had been together for over ten years, their remit and purpose in life as simple as it had proved nigh on impossible, with the exception of their most recent break in Las Vegas when they had finally honed in on Valeriya and disposed of the first link in the chain.

Nathan had recruited the two from a pool of operatives who had worked all over the world in various guises and whose patience and resilience had been tested in many scenarios. Their remit was simple: find the woman Valeriya, then find her daughter, then find the prophets and dispose of them all, no traces — kill everything associated with them, anything near them and everything remotely dear to them. Despite such clear terms of reference, their start point, Valeriya, had eluded them for over a decade and their predecessors for almost as protracted a period. But they were professionals, remorseless, dedicated, extremely well rewarded, and they were like bloodhounds now, fresh from a hard-earned kill and eager to inflict more pain, final justification for the hours spent pursuing dead ends, the days of waiting in hotel lobbies, the months on standby in derelict corners of the globe where glimpses of their prey had teased them to the point of insane frustration. They were in their zone now, however, spurred by potential success, ruthlessness purring in the void between them in the rear of the taxi.

Ultimately, Nathan had chosen them well, not only on the grounds of basic skill sets such as languages, a capacity for violence, patience, and reliability, but also because they were compatible in a way that engendered longevity in their relationship. He had chosen one man and one woman, their different sexes and physiology synonymous with access, role play, and, most importantly, an absence of ego when they worked juxtapose. He had also chosen flawed goods. Not flawed in terms of any propensity for error or miscalculation, but intentionally flawed, something Nathan had learned from historical precedence, events that had produced hybrid killing machines. But these killing machines had many layers — Nathan knew that psychological layers of friction spawned resilient determination, a de facto, inbuilt payback setting for events that sat deep within them but not on them, their internal stimuli as sharp as yesterday's memories.

Neither knew the other's real name or very much about the other despite their decade together in so many corners of the globe, and neither displayed any inherent interest in the other's past. They only discussed an event in the past if it had a bearing on the mission looking forward, nor did they discuss their employer, their motives, or their private lives. In truth, neither had much interest in a private life but were driven by internal scarring, wounds that dribbled internally, a steady stream of controllable madness dripping into the bloodstream, almost as if their controller was adjusting an intravenous drip.

The woman, who was referred to as K, which the real world understood to be her name, Kay, but it was not, looked as if she might have been trained to be a high jumper. Now in her early forties, she stood at over six feet tall, her natural elegance tripped by a slight limp she had developed as a teenager after an internal infection following one of the many operations she had undergone to repair her uterus. Her uterus had been repeatedly ripped to shreds in a commune that had sprung from the many religious cults that had developed in tandem to and as a result of the emergence of the prophets.

Nathan and his team had pre-empted these tangential groups and had extinguished each as quickly as they arose but not without fallout. One such victim, K, was rescued from a commune in Mexico where male dominants had right of passage, literally, over younger inmates, vaginal and anal rights of passage that resulted in physical and psychological mayhem. Nathan became her mentor by proxy before eventually recognizing that some scars would never heal, that such cruelties in life were better served through tacit recognition and subsequent manipulation rather than through endless counselling. So she had matured into a bespoke assassin, the perfect foil for the freaks who emerged from the early days of the prophets, a perfect closure for the fakes who threatened to derail the purity of the movement during those early years. As the movement stabilized, it seemed natural that she should play a role in its sustainment, a key instrument to snuff out the final threats to Nathan's concept, the very prophets themselves.

The man, whose name was Kazuo, was a few years older than K but was also a product of the prophetic revolution, which, like any religious birth, gave rise to distortion and misinterpretation. Physically, he was the antithesis of K — oriental and squat, he resembled the flat end of a shovel, square and hard-edged. He maintained a relentless fitness regime that had taken its toll on his body, with the exception of his face, which still had the appearance of someone half his age. Kazuo was harder to characterize than K; he barely moved unless he had to and could easily be mistaken for a mannequin if observed on a plane or in a hotel lobby. He could sit for many hours without making a single movement, as if in a trance, his eyes occasionally blinking behind thick spectacles that served as a prop to hide a continuous tic pouncing from eye to eye like a tennis ball being struck from one side of the court to the other. This restless tic was Kazuo's nemesis.

Unlike K, Kazuo had been a neophyte in a cult that had emerged in Southeast Asia as a result of the prophetic revolution. Predicated on Buddhism, the cult appeared harmless at first, but its leader began to adopt his own interpretation of self-sacrifice and assumed the right to impose such a penalty in extremis when cult members transgressed. One such victim was a beautiful boy from Cambodia who had become Kazuo's lover in the early days of what he, Kazuo, sincerely believed to be their Utopia. When Nathan's roving team finally focused their attention on the abnormalities within the cult and cut them down like wheat, Kazuo requested permission to track down the leader.

The task took over three years, but it was a task he performed with such single-minded focus that Nathan decided to recruit him on a permanent basis. Kazuo's relentless pursuit had given him great personal satisfaction, and his tic would pause its own relentless migration from eye to eye when he occasionally recalled dismembering his victim — his fingers and toes clipped away, one by one, until the erstwhile leader bled to death during a hot summer evening in Bali, his muffled cries lost between the heavy rag pushed to the back of his throat and the remnants of his upper jaw, which Kazuo had broken into many asymmetrical parts, the hard sides of his hands raining down like blows from a cleaver.

Ahead of the two bloodhounds, Brian sat back in the warmth of the cab and let his mind drift back to the conversation with Valeriya — the incredible project she had described, the intermittent years, the prophets, the manipulation of so many by so few, and where the world found itself now, a population under some control, the world's resources and capacity in tandem with its rapacious inhabitants. Was that so wrong? Was he about to embark on a crusade to redress a wrong, and with what repercussions? Was the sum of mankind responsible enough to manage the planet or did it need visionary manipulators? A fine line, he reflected, between a visionary and a lunatic. She was right in a sense; he had never been inside a self-sacrifice centre and had not given it that much thought, that seemingly inevitable step or choice still some 17 years away in his case.

Brian's thoughts were interrupted as the cab pulled over to the corner of West 168th Street, and he pushed some notes between the sliding window separating the front seat from the rear. The cab pulled away from the curb, and Brian scanned the numbers above the doorways until he found what he was looking for. Brian walked purposefully along the street and up to a red front door, an assortment of apartments listed next to a line of buzzers adjacent to the doorway. Brian pressed repeatedly on the buzzer, the chime echoing up the stairs inside the four-storey building but without a response. He stamped his feet on the entrance mat a few times to get his circulation going and glanced up and down the street in frustration. Oddly enough, it had not occurred to him that there might not be anyone home.

Now what? he said to himself. He glanced back across Broadway and saw the entrance to the 168th Street subway station, his mind subconsciously flicking across Central Park to the cluster of tall buildings across the Manhattan skyline. He had a sudden desire to be rid of this burden, of this mission that had suddenly become such an unenviable cross to bear.

I could be in Times Square in no time at all, he said to himself. *Why not, why not come back later? It was stupid to call at this time of the day anyway, she is probably out, working or shopping.*

The weaker option prevailed in Brian's mind, the "my heart's not really in this anymore," and he headed for the subway, a tinge of regret stroking the back of his collar as he rushed across the busy street.

2065, New York, Alexandra

Unbeknown to Brian, as he descended the steps into the subway, the sound from his finger on the door buzzer did reverberate around the small third-floor apartment but fell on ears already besieged by strange sounds and voices, so much so that the woman sitting with a blanket around her shoulders barely registered this additional intrusion. At 55 years old, Alexandra resembled a patchwork quilt, two people seemingly stapled together like an old rag doll that had been passed between excited children over decades of use, threadbare, restored, a patch here or there, an ad hoc piece of tapestry woven into the base fabric. This duality, by way of appearance, was asymmetrical, so that it was hard to define what was real by way of origin, where the past aligned with the present and vice versa, and which was the more plausible, if either.

Had her physical appearance at least followed some symmetrical lines, it might have been possible to explain her development by way of a one-dimensional illness, that a stroke or a paralysis had driven a firebreak through her anatomy, but this was not the case. Her hair grew rapidly in waves of thick chestnut in some areas, yet on other areas of her scalp, it turned into clumps of ashen grey and fell around her in piles of cinders. Her skin and limbs defied her internal organs, a tapestry of old and new covering her in a harlequin of confusion. A soft and supple forearm distinguished by a withered bicep, the fingers on her hands confusing life and mortality despite their juxtaposition — a gnarled, arthritic index finger sitting aside a smooth middle finger, unblemished, sculptured for precision. Her one breast heavy and withered like a prune, the other firm, pushing against her blouse in a delicate raw. Decay and rejuvenation lived in the same space.

This external paradigm of physiological disarray was mirrored internally, but even more acutely. What had been an engineered specimen, a hybrid of advanced DNA cloning, had become a cauldron of confusion. The highs and lows of evolution crashed into each other, a million pieces of brilliance plunged into muddy darkness, their original orientation transcended by mutation and then compounded by a motorcycle accident that Alexandra had when her daughter, Sophia, was only five years old. Since then, this deterioration into her present state had been gradual but consistent. To fully understand this half beautiful Frankenstein, one had to have witnessed the creation of one of the three prophets, the moment when one zygote divided into two embryos to create monozygotic twins, one of which was believed to have been destroyed, until it emerged that Valeriya had squirrelled the child away, eventually raising her as her own, as Alexandra. What was unknown then was quite what such an experiment would create, when a foreign, highly advanced DNA was cloned to cells that subsequently divided; would the replica be as enriched, as spiritually pure? Theoretically, this should have been the case.

In limbo, was how Sophia regarded her mother, apposite, she felt, as it was what the Catholic Church used to refer to as that intermediate place for the unbaptized, literally between heaven and hell. What Sophia could not know was that her mother was more in hell than anywhere else, her sanity compromised by a torrent of voices that attacked her from all angles, a maelstrom of past and present crashing into her psyche such that she was left utterly immobilized by information that could no longer be rationalized. What had been a discreet but functional unicameral mind where her voices and linguistic abilities could be negotiated with introspectively was now, in her post-accident state, more bicameral but, significantly, missing the golden threads of neural connectivity in her corpus callosum that connected the two sides of the brain and made sense of all the noise. And so the noise prevailed, Sumerian texts bouncing backward and forward, Vedic Sanskrit competing with ancient Chinese, Mayan with Hittite, Akkadian with Greek, Latin with Hebrew.

When she did move from her trance-like position, it was only to scoop up a heavy felt pen and frantically scribble hieroglyphics across the walls, bizarre texts or diagrams of solar systems, which Sophia tried not to read too closely as she painted over the evidence every few days. Somewhere else, within this confusion, she heard more recent voices, the living, snatches of telepathic conversations that seemed to include her but that she was unable to unravel, her exhaustion compounded by the heavy sleeping tablets Sophia had eventually resorted to giving her, the only weapon against her incurable insomnia.

On seeing Brian's departure for the subway, Kazuo and K had quickly agreed to divide their efforts, K following Brian into the subway while Kazuo investigated the empty apartment. He crossed the road, his gait as nimble as a ballerina despite the folds of muscle and raw power that sat like bunching herds of buffalo under his skin. He quickly slipped the latch on the main entrance and took the steps in twos until he reached the third floor where there were two apartments. The front doors were in marked contrast: one a pine door, typically anonymous and standard, the second unusual, a steel door protected by a code pad as if the door was the entrance to a bank vault. There was no number on the steel door, but Kazuo knew that he was in the right place and his pulse slipped up a notch as he began to smell his prey, a potential victim. He slipped a small gadget out of his coat pocket and ran a scanner across the keypad. There was a slight delay for a few seconds before a code appeared across the small screen, after which he tucked the gadget away and punched in the four digit number to access the steel door. There was a loud click as the heavy latch opened and Kazuo pushed gently against the door, which swung open before him. He grunted in satisfaction and stepped across the threshold.

The apartment was shrouded in semi-darkness, although small pockets of light crept in between gaps in the curtains, the day trying to force its way in through the heavy material. Kazuo wrinkled his nose slightly as he inched forward on the balls of his feet, an enigmatic odour clinging to the walls like lichen, a smell with which Kazuo was unfamiliar, as if death lived alongside birth and the two had competed to spread their scents within the confined space. The small hallway gave way to two doors, one to a small kitchen and dining area, and the second, Kazuo imagined, to a living room from which one could probably access the bedrooms. The kitchen area was empty and deserted, the soft hum of electrical appliances the only sign of life. He moved through to the living area and was confronted by a wall of texts and hieroglyphics, sketches of what looked, to Kazuo, like alien creatures, mathematical formulae, and a myriad of other symbols, which meant nothing to him. He pulled a small camera from his jacket and flipped open the lens. As he did so, a small alarm sounded in Nathan's boardroom and the image appeared across a huge screen in a discreet corner of Vienna. The alarm also vibrated in K's pocket and she opened her telephone to allow her to follow the conversation between Kazuo and Nathan.

"Well?" Nathan asked, typically monosyllabic.

"I am in," Kazuo said quietly. "Thought you might like to copy these images, looks like we are in the right place."

The shrouded images floated like ghosts across the screen in front of Nathan's eyes, some of the images and texts familiar to him, others more obscure and unknown. The images were automatically stored as they relayed across the Atlantic.

"Yes," Nathan said quickly, "you are in the right place. If you find anyone there, make sure you cover this evidence before you leave the scene, don't want anyone poking around these images. Burn the place down if need be."

Kazuo bit down on the corner of his mouth; he did not like someone trying to tell him his profession, but he kept his voice steady.

"Yes, Nathan," he said quietly, "of course."

K smirked to herself as she closed her telephone, knowing full well that such instructions would burrow under Kazuo's skin like a tick. Kazuo also flicked off his camera and turned away from the main wall. He pulled one of the heavy curtains a few inches to one side so that a narrow stream of light fell across the room, particles of dust sitting along the column of light like distant galaxies in space. Kazuo's eyes instinctively followed the beam of light falling into the far corner of the room, and he was surprised to find the shadow of a person flattened against the far wall. He pulled open the curtain a little more and Alexandra's body appeared before him, much to his surprise, her features set as if in stone; she might well have been a mannequin.

Alexandra did not appear to acknowledge Kazuo's presence, but, perhaps as a result of the beam of light now throwing itself across the living room, she rocked her torso, and then stood up and walked over to the main wall. Kazuo found himself captivated by the back of her head, the chestnut and grey hair lying side by side, as conflicting as life and death. She paused for a few moments in front of the crowded hieroglyphics, and then drew a symbol between two diagrams that had been completed earlier that day. She walked past Kazuo once again and returned to her chair. Kazuo stood motionless for a while and then stepped slowly toward her, his movements muffled by the thick rug partially covering the wooden floorboards. He stopped in front of the chair and waved his hands in front of her eyes, clicking his fingers to try and elicit some reaction. Alexandra seemed to have returned to her trance, and her whole body assumed an opacity of such intensity that Kazuo's immediate thoughts were that he was standing in front of the living dead.

Kazuo acknowledged that he should probably call Nathan, but their recent exchange had annoyed him and he felt his ego rising under his skin like an emerging bruise.

"Don't go there," he said to himself, but it was a little too late, his pride had been jabbed between the ribs and he was simply irritated. He looked back at Alexandra once again and snapped his fingers in front of her face, this time almost touching her.

"My name is Kazuo," he said quietly, "and I need to ask you some questions, Alexandra. It is Alexandra, isn't it? I need to know about the prophets, where they are, you can talk to them in your mind, I know that, you must tell me where they are hiding, they are in danger and I need to help them."

Kazuo paused and stood up straight to stretch his back. There had been no response from Alexandra and still no acknowledgment that he was even in the room with her. He walked over to the main wall and paused in front of the mass of symbols, none of which made any sense to him. He glanced at his watch and shrugged off his coat before he threw it over the back of a chair. He rubbed the bottom of his jaw in quiet contemplation, the odd whisker catching against his fingertips as he ran his mind over his situation. He knew that he was going to kill this woman, but he also knew that Nathan would be disappointed if he was unable to glean any information about the prophets. Just as he knew that, he also knew that he was unlikely to succeed in this task as the target was a vegetable. Unless she had some sort of condition that might pass in time, there would be little he could do.

Perhaps she is heavily drugged, he pondered. *You only have to look at her, she is completely fucked up, so I need to get her somewhere where we can observe her, where we can take time to apply whatever pressure is needed.*

Kazuo had already calculated in his mind that a second person must live here, a friend or a carer? There was simply no way that the creature in the chair would have kept the place clean, let alone install a steel door with a keypad.

And why the keypad? he mused. *Because the other person knows that Alexandra is special, so she must know about the program or at least something, so she, too, has to be eliminated, but not until we have also spoken with her.*

He acknowledged a problem though — getting Alexandra out in daylight might be tricky, the neighbours would obviously know her, there might be a scene, and Nathan had always said, "No scenes related to anything about this project will be tolerated, just remember that in the field, or we will no longer require your services." Which they all knew to mean something a little more drastic than simple retirement.

"Veasna is dead," a voice said suddenly, from the chair in front of him. "You killed him. You should never have taken him there, to that place. You condemned him to death."

Kazuo found it momentarily hard to breathe, as if an invisible force had grabbed him by the scruff of his neck and pulled him to the darkest depths, so deep that the pressure squeezed his lungs and a cold sweat broke out across his skin as if he had been retrieved from a watery grave. A layer of clamminess surrounded him like another skin. He took a step toward Alexandra who now seemed to see him for the first time.

She raised her index finger slowly and pointed toward him. "You," she said simply. "I can read your thoughts, your mind, you killed him, the one you loved, your pretty Veasna."

Kazuo's mind flashed to images of the cult, the young boy, barely a man, his lover, lying in a pool of his own blood, a clumsy assortment of ropes tied around his ankles and wrists.

"You should never have taken him there," Alexandra repeated. "You killed him."

Alexandra's torso swayed toward Kazuo who remained glued to the floor, his arms hanging by his sides like a weary boxer, his shoulders slumped forward in raw defeat. He seemed to have exchanged bodies with Alexandra and was now rooted in a trance, his mind jumbled with orders and commands, images slapping him across his face as they swept past him like racing cars spinning around a circuit. Alexandra stood up from her chair and stepped into the space between them, her index finger moving up and down in the small arc in front of his face. A small growl emerged from Kazuo's mouth and his body momentarily contorted as if he was about to have a stroke. His eyes focused on the finger wagging in front of his eyes and he snatched at it, pushing it into his mouth and biting through the bone and cartilage below the knuckle, the bloody stump of the finger spraying blood across the floor between them. Alexandra sank back into her chair and Kazuo fainted, plunging to his knees before falling sideways, the finger falling from his mouth onto the cheap rug.

It started to rain, the drops of water smearing grime across the windowpanes, the muted patter of water against glass like fingers across the skin of a drum.

Something must have roused Kazuo from whatever trance he had succumbed to. He glanced at his watch, he had been unconscious for over an hour. He wiped his fingers across his mouth and could feel dry, encrusted blood around the corners of his mouth and on his chin. He pulled himself up against the side of the sofa and stumbled toward the kitchen where he spat into the sink, a tiny splinter of bone swirling within a bloody whirlpool in the plughole. He retched before taking a deep breath, clutching at a cloth next to the sink, which he wiped across his face and forehead. He leaned back into the sink and ran his tongue under the cold water, spitting once more into the plughole, desperately trying to shake life back into his face.

After a few more moments to gather himself, Kazuo walked back toward the living area, an uneasy sixth sense shrouding him with trepidation. Alexandra had slumped back into her chair where she still sat, her chin resting on the top of her chest. A line of blood ran from her index finger onto her skirt and then finally down the chair leg, a twisting line of her mortality, like ivy, gathering in a small pool by the side of the chair. She was dead, and Kazuo sensed this immediately; he did not need to check her pulse or lift her head back. Even in death, her persona still leapt at him from the chair, as if she had left a latent force in the room to goad him as her spirit had fled her tattered corpse. Kazuo sensed anxiety creeping across his skin, a plague of distortion crushing his psyche and consuming his rationale in greedy mouthfuls. He could feel his strength draining once again as he stumbled to get to the door, the need for fresh air subsuming all professional precedence. He bounced against the walls as he fought his way down the stairs, eventually falling into the street like a drunk and stumbling toward Broadway.

He had left his coat with Alexandra's dead body.

2065, New York, The Relay

No sooner had Brian boarded the subway than he found himself regretting his cowardly withdrawal. He rubbed his eyes, a heavy fatigue closing around him like thick molasses, the last few days finally catching up with him. He felt as if he was at the back of the pack, straining to keep pace with events. He closed his eyes momentarily and drifted into an uncomfortable sleep.

A dream filtered through the shuddering subway train. In his dream, Brian found himself on an athletics track that, on reflection, looked like the old athletics track at his junior school. It was a simple track surrounding the cricket pitch, and appeared during those brief summer months when the weather forecasters teased the ever optimistic English that they were going to have a sweltering summer. However, although the track was the same, it appeared that the athletes were grown men, an assortment of faces that Brian had encountered during his life; he recognized an old school friend and a couple of patients from his practice. Brian felt uncomfortable in his running kit, and, for some reason, he had to run barefoot as opposed to in running spikes. The sun had yet to lift the thick dew from the grass, so another competitor warned him not to slip as he started.

These details were comparatively irrelevant compared to the aim of the relay, so to speak, or at least what the competitors had to do before handing over the baton after their respective 100 metres. The aim of the race was still to cross the line in first place, but at each handover station, women had been positioned on all fours and competitors had to perform anal sex with the women in their lanes before they could hand over the batons to allow the race to continue. When Brian arrived at his starting position at the end of the first bend, he found a huge man standing in the adjacent lane, a Goliath with legs like tree trunks and running spikes glistening in the damp grass like sharpened stilettos. The man had a steely glint in his eye and offered Brian his hand as they limbered up in their starting positions.

"Hi, I'm Brian," the man said cheerfully. Brian was intimidated and he became even more agitated when he realized that the other Brian had a huge erection pushing against his running shorts, literally straining at the bit.

"Are you allowed to run like that, with that?" Brian asked him, rather sheepishly.

"Guess so." The man grinned. "Means I'll be able to fuck my girlfriend as soon as I get to the end of the straight, you'll be ages otherwise."

"I didn't know that you were allowed to bring your own girlfriend," Brian said.

"Oh yes," the man said cheerfully, "wives or girlfriends, it's in the rules."

Brian considered his dilemma for some time and even tried to conjure up sexual images, desperately trying to work his way to an erection, but he was concerned about the spectators and knew that his mother was watching, although none of that made any sense. Before he had time to pile any further woe on his predicament, the starting pistol was fired and the anchor runner quickly came into view around the first bend. Moments later, as can only happen in dreams, Brian found himself neck and neck with the other Brian, the man's penis stretched out in front of him as they tore down the back straight, Brian's feet slipping occasionally as he fought for traction. They arrived at the end of the straight where Brian was appalled to see Jan, his Jan, crouching on all fours in the other lane and another Jan, the same Jan, a twin, in a similar position in his lane.

As he arrived at the end of the straight, the other Brian lowered his running shorts with a fluid movement and, in a seamless move, pushed himself into his wife's arse, his huge penis somehow accommodated by her, an enormous groan echoing around the stadium. Brian, on the other hand, stood in limbo, his right hand pushed inside his shorts, desperately trying to rouse himself for action. It was not long before the other Brian screamed in ecstasy, his semen falling across her back and onto the grass, the baton handed over, and the race continued. Brian remained rooted to the spot, the other members of his relay team screaming across the track at him to "do something, do something!" His Jan, the one in his lane, had a quizzical look on her face and was chatting to the other Jan. He caught the odd word.

"What did that feel like?" she asked. "He looked huge, did it hurt?"

And then the subway car screeched at Brian and he woke up. On waking, Brian reflected how such an incredible volume of detail could pass through his subconscious psyche during just one stop on the subway. He shook his head slowly.

"Fuck," he said to himself, "what a mess."

Brian decided against Times Square but chose instead to wander down Fifth Avenue toward the Rockefeller Center. He walked past the huge statue of Atlas and then found himself in the Lower Plaza area where the gilded statue of Prometheus bringing fire to mankind dominated the sunken area in front of 30 Rockefeller Plaza. Brian seemed to recall that Prometheus was a Titan and a brother to Atlas. He found himself reminiscing about Latin lessons at school, and his mind naturally returned to his dream and his school athletics track. He scratched inside his mind for the relevant Greek mythology that relates to Prometheus, and memories of stuffy classrooms began to filter back through his mind.

Do we reminisce when we are unhappy? he wondered.

He seemed to remember that Prometheus fought with Zeus, who had hidden fire from mankind. Or at least Prometheus stole the fire back, for which he was punished, chained to a rock in the Caucasus where his liver was eaten by an eagle every day only to be regenerated by night, a sign of his immortality, until eventually rescued by Hercules who slayed the eagle. He also remembered that Zeus sent Pandora in revenge, a woman fashioned by Hephaestus out of clay and brought to life by the four winds, with all the goddesses of Olympus assembled to adorn her. Brian remembered something he had learned at school, a quote from Hesiod, "From her is the race of women and female kind, of her is the deadly race and tribe of women who live amongst mortal men to their great trouble, no helpmeets in hateful poverty, but only in wealth." So Pandora carried a jar with her from which "evils, harsh pain and troublesome diseases which give men death" were released on mankind. Pandora shut the lid of the jar too late to contain all the evil plights that escaped, but hope remained in the jar.

My God, Brian thought, *have you become my Pandora, Jan, surely not?*

A little dramatic, don't you think? he said to himself.

But what of hope, and why am I thinking about these things now, today, why these Greek legends, these half-god, half-man Titans, and how on Earth can I remember that quote from Hesiod after all these years? Perhaps I have found myself here to remind myself that I am in the wrong place, he said. *What about Valeriya's last morsel of hope, what of that? Perhaps I am the only thing left at the bottom of her jar, and yet here I am running away from her daughter.*

K had been tracking Brian since leaving the subway, and, to her, it looked as if someone had turned a switch back on in her target's mind. He looked as if he was heading back in her direction, back toward the subway. She turned away slowly and picked up a magazine from a newsstand. Brian passed her and K turned to follow him. She stayed about 15 metres behind him, but such precaution was unnecessary; Brian was hardly trained in counter-espionage and his mind was focused elsewhere. K was just about to head back down into the subway when her telephone buzzed. It was Kazuo.

"What, be quick," she said to him, "I'm about to go underground."

"I am in a bad way, a bad state," Kazuo whispered. "I need your help, please."

K had never heard Kazuo talk like this or ever ask for anything, let alone her help. She glanced up at Brian's back as he took the steps in twos.

We have the tracking device in the book, it can wait.

"Where are you?" she asked Kazuo, as she raised an arm to hail a cab.

As agreed when they last spoke, Ruth waited for Sophia just outside the main hospital entrance and the two women fell in step with each other. It was a frosty atmosphere given what was about to occur, and a latent friction filled the space between them as they hurried north toward Sophia's apartment.

"How long did you say this might take?" Ruth asked, trying to muster some friendship into her voice. It might not have been an odd choice of words if they were ordering a pizza, but given the circumstances, Ruth's clumsiness personified her inability to relax in

Sophia's presence, that she felt inadequate and somehow out of her depth.

Sophia glanced briefly at Ruth and simply responded, "My place is just in the next block."

The two women walked in silence for the next few hundred metres before Sophia indicated that they must cross over Broadway to reach her street. As the two women approached the front of the building, a man walked past them in great haste and up the steps in front of them. He pushed his finger against the buzzer, an impatience inherent in the way that he stamped his feet on the doorstep and repeatedly pushed the buzzer. The two women stopped just behind him and Sophia could see that he was ringing her doorbell.

"Excuse me," she asked, "who are you, what do you want?"

He turned to find himself confronted by the two women.

"Who are you?" he replied. "I'm just calling on the person in this flat," he said, pointing at the buzzer.

"You mean me," said Sophia, "that's my apartment."

The man looked momentarily confused, his expectations not being met.

"Alexandra?" he said, looking a little helpless. Sophia was naturally wary of this stranger, but she pushed past him and opened the door quickly.

"Whoever you are," she said quickly, "I don't want to stand out here all day, come inside and you can explain who you are. Alexandra is my mother, which you might have worked out if you really knew my mother."

"My name is Brian, and I don't know your mother," he said quickly. "I know her mother, Valeriya."

The name made Sophia stop on the stairway and she turned back toward the man.

"What's going on?" Ruth asked, her mood further disrupted by the appearance of this stranger.

"Let's talk inside," Sophia replied. "This is very weird."

As soon as Sophia reached the third floor, waves of fear swept through her like a bitter wind. The steel door to the apartment was ajar and she instinctively realized that something was wrong. She stepped over the threshold, fear and adrenaline coursing through her body. She noticed immediately that a stream of natural light fell across what was usually a dark room, that her mother's eyes could not bear sunlight, her physiological state now so at odds with her surroundings. The light caught the hieroglyphics on the main wall of the living room, in this case a corridor of Sanskrit scribbled onto the paint.

She knew before she even glanced to one side that her mother was dead; she could no longer sense her spirit, the huge psychological presence she had known since birth. She looked at the motionless body for some time, her mind piecing together the puzzle before her. Brian and Ruth followed her into the room but also stopped in their tracks. Brian immediately noticed the index finger on the worn rug, the finely balanced tip in such contrast to the tattered and bloody stump, and he was reminded of his dream, the strange vet with the cat's paw. Ruth pushed past Sophia and knelt next to the body, her natural medical instincts prevailing, her fingertips searching for a pulse.

"Don't bother," Sophia said, her voice edged with ice, "she's dead, gone."

"I'll call the police," said Ruth quietly, fishing in her bag for her cell phone. "We shouldn't touch anything."

"Don't call anyone," Sophia shouted. "I reckon we have a few minutes to get out of here alive, trust me on this one."

Brian moved over to stand next to Ruth, placing a hand under her armpit and helping her back to her feet.

"She's right," he said quietly to her, "we need to get out of here."

"Who are you?" Ruth asked, confusion and fear spreading across her features.

"It doesn't matter now," Brian said quickly. "We need to get away from this place."

Sophia appeared in the small hallway, a holdall clutched in front of her.

"What's that?" Brian asked. "Where are you going?"

"It's my grab sack," she replied quickly. "I'm going to another safe house, I have a car in a lock-up garage two blocks away. You," she said looking directly at Brian, "you're coming with me, I need answers. You," she said looking at Ruth, "make your mind up quickly, coming with me or not?"

"And what if I don't choose to come with you?" Brian said quietly.

"Then I will shoot you now, here, so choose."

Brian could not see a gun anywhere visible but had no doubt that the creature in front of him was as capable as she seemed determined.

"Ruth, wake up!" Sophia raised her voice. "What are you doing, coming or going back to the hospital?"

Ruth still looked in shock, her wide eyes moving from Sophia's face to the body in the chair, the bloody finger on the rug and the hieroglyphics on the wall. She was incapable of making a decision.

"You're coming with us," Sophia said decisively, "or you'll be dead one way or another without me."

"Wait," Brian said momentarily, "that coat, a man's coat, does that belong here?"

"No," Sophia replied, "let's take it with us. Now, you two, wait outside for me, I'll be two minutes."

Brian retrieved the coat from where Kazuo had thrown it over a chair and ushered Ruth into the corridor.

"What are you doing?" he called over his shoulder toward the heavy steel door.

"Covering tracks!" Sophia called toward the landing. "Get out and start walking north on Broadway, I'll catch up." Brian and Ruth made their way to the head of the stairs and quickly found themselves back on the street. Sophia threw her holdall into the corridor and then went back inside the apartment.

Fuck, she said, *where is that damn cat? Must be outside, I guess.*

She moved into the kitchen and retrieved a plastic container from under the sink. Unscrewing the top, she moved back into the living room and doused the curtains and soft furnishings with petrol, finally pausing by her mother to pour the last few remnants across her clothing.

"Sorry, Mum," she whispered, kissing Alexandra's head, "but you taught me well." Sophia lit a match and ignited one of the old, threadbare curtains that caught fire immediately. She pulled the steel door behind her and ran for the stairs.

Unbeknown to Sophia, the cat had been asleep on a small pile of linen stored next to hot water pipes adjacent to the boiler. As the flames engulfed the small apartment, the cat wrinkled its nose and pushed open the door of its habitual hiding place, stretched briefly, and then trotted quickly into the living room where the flames were creeping toward the worn rug. The cat poked its head with curiosity into the corridor then, and on seeing the door closed and no one there, the cat returned to the living room and rubbed its flanks twice on the legs of Alexandra's chair. The cat then walked tentatively onto the worn rug and paused next to Alexandra's finger, running its nose along its length. The flames caught the edge of the rug with a hiss, which startled the cat. The cat glanced over its shoulder at Alexandra in her chair and picked up the finger in its mouth before jumping lightly into Alexandra's lap. The cat curled up in a puddle of petrol with Alexandra's finger, to wait.

Had the cat been able to see through the thick smoke surrounding the unlikely pair in their makeshift funeral pyre, the cat would have noticed that someone had left a book on the chair where Kazuo's coat had been thrown. Had the cat been able to read, it would have noticed that the book was entitled *The Origin of Consciousness in the Breakdown of the Bicameral Mind.*

2065, Cuzco, Peru,
Between Fermina's Breasts

Augusto Garcia sat on the small balcony of a coffee shop and cast his eyes across the Avenida del Sol to the entrance of the Cathedral of Santo Domingo, which dominated the Plaza de Armas, the central square in Cuzco. He envisaged the scene inside as the faint echoes of the Catholic Mass drifted across the square and climbed the first storey to his perch where his coffee steamed in the mid-morning chill. The thin, dry air of Cuzco buffeted against his thick jacket, with an occasional shiver causing him to hunch his shoulders toward his ears. His mind flickered like a candle between thoughts of the woman he loved, crouched in abeyant prayer within the cavernous walls of the Gothic Renaissance monstrosity, and the jumble of words that buzzed inside his head like angry hornets, their relentless torment synonymous with his tortuous existence.

It was like his own internal tinnitus, but instead of a ringing sound, his perpetual noise was whispering voices, scattered texts and ancient dialects whipping around inside his mind like a phalanx of whirlpools. They seemed to get worse as the months and years passed by, as he slipped into his forties and now his fifties. What had been a blessing, a saintly gift, had become an affliction, a curse that he bore bravely but which he drowned in alcohol each evening, the only poultice that seemed to stem the tide of madness and that numbed his brain long enough for him to find momentary peace in sleep.

Rather like Valeriya in some ways, Augusto had been on the run since the prophets made their collective escape in 2048, some five years after their incarceration following their staged self-sacrifice in 2043. After a number of years of wandering, Augusto, as he now called himself, had returned to Cuzco, a location he had fallen in love with during his time as a prophet. His incarceration, and the toll on his body inflicted by the relentless voices, meant that he was unrecognizable to the masses as the same man who had healed so many over those few years between the ages of 25 and 33. Augusto had been named Francisco at birth, the name intended to arouse memories of the famous Spanish saint, Francis Xavier, an association that was meant to kick in when Francisco started preaching, as his main target was to be the Americas, particularly South America, a relative fortress for the Catholic Church in a sea of agnosticism.

Augusto sipped gingerly at his coffee and cast his eyes across the Plaza de Armas, small groups of tourists gathering in noisy pockets around the capital of the Inca Empire despite the early hour. He thought about Fermina Marquez who would probably have been the first in the queue for confession that morning and one of the last to leave her knees at the end of the service, her faith shining from her like a bright star, the immovable certainty in her life. Augusto had no idea anymore where he sat with all of this religious mumbo jumbo; his mind had been playing tricks with him for so long that all he could really fathom was that he, like the other prophets, was a living paradox. On the one hand, literally in terms of the one side of his brain, his mind still received an endless stream of messages, voices, inner Gods with lists of instructions in numerous languages and dialects. In his early days, he had never questioned these voices, the other side of his brain, his introspective side, simply confirming that he was special, and therefore that further introspection or explanation was unnecessary, even if he had been capable of such mind manipulation.

Augusto and his fellow prophets had had no need to question these inner Gods and no time to introspect, that was until their destiny had been ambushed. When their road to self-sacrifice had dissolved into confusion, the three mavericks plunged into despair — from prophet to prisoner overnight, from salvation to cynicism, or at least an emerging cynicism, an ability to question, to reason, finally, to introspect.

What the architects of the program did not know, which, even then, they acknowledged, hence their decision to keep the prophets alive and under observation, was quite where this bizarre mixture of DNA, these neurological hybrids might end up by way of physiology, even by way of sanity. They had not been expecting an Alexandra, that much was certain. What they did underestimate was the brain's ability to rewire itself, rather like its ability to recalibrate after a major stroke or injury in the same way that researchers had made such progress in constraint-induced movement therapy. This process, this neuroplasticity of the brain, showed a very different picture to that envisaged by Valeriya, a process in which the brain can reorganize itself as a result of environmental demands or severe trauma such as a stroke or even a limb amputation. Such were not the cases for Augusto and the other prophets, but, nevertheless, their trauma had been psychologically extreme, so their captivity eventually kick-started the rewiring process, albeit slowly and albeit without giving them the ability to shut down the constant streams of inner torment. So, while in captivity, they had begun to reason, to send messages to each other telepathically, endless questions, the answers to which might help unravel their collective confusion, their clinical demise.

And so, some 22 years later, Augusto still sat in a state of inner conflict. He knew that they had been manipulated, that there was a greater design at work, he knew that they had been in great danger, that they were still in great danger, but he was not quite sure why. Perhaps most importantly, he knew that they had agreed a pact amongst themselves, that if they escaped, none should show their true selves, that they should hide in the farthest corners of the planet, anonymous, low profiles and, above all, no miracles, no healing of the sick which might lead their betrayers to find them. This had been their agreement before their escape and, thus far, for many different reasons, each had abided by that pact as time and circumstance gradually began to assuage their collective passion to find the truth or unravel the grand design.

Augusto unbuttoned the top of his quilted jacket and waved toward the waiter, a cousin of Fermina's, who winked back at him and, a few minutes later, pushed another cup of coffee under Augusto's nose.

How weird life is, Augusto thought. The unanswered questions, the years of captivity, then hiding and on the run for so long — all this friction could not compete with what he had found in Cuzco, in the burning eyes of his beloved Fermina. She was the most simple of women, a woman who could not speak multiple languages, whose approach to life and destiny was one-dimensional by comparison but whose well of compassion had quickly eclipsed his desire to unravel that grand design. Her love for him had eroded that inherent curiosity, so much so that, subconsciously, he had chosen peace over ongoing conflict and despair. Were it not for his voices, his life would have been perfect.

Augusto remembered the day he had first seen Fermina. It was not long after his arrival in Cuzco when he earned his money through gambling, a cheat, as he found it easy to read the cards and even easier to read his opponents. Telepathy did have its upside, and the gambling had proved a lifesaver for him as he moved around in hiding and was in such contrast to his former life that it had become a useful prop for obscurity. At the time, Fermina had worked as a waitress in the bar where Augusto made most of his money. She kept a low profile despite the attention she received from some of the other players and rarely spoke. Augusto had arrived in Cuzco a virgin, despite his 51 years, and had never imagined that sex or a romantic relationship would ever form part of his life. The architects had intentionally suppressed the prophets' sexual urges to enhance their spiritual purity, but these had, over time, re-emerged as their brains fought to recalibrate.

Fermina was taller than most women from the Cuzco Province, and her features told a story of mixed lineage somewhere in her family's history. She shared her skin colour with her compatriots, a skin tone that at times resembled the dark red pigmentation of okra pods, but any other similarities were far more subtle. She was at least a head taller than most, in some cases more so, and her facial features were more refined as if a stranger from India or even Ethiopia had paused in Cuzco to draw breath and drink the Peruvian cacoa or sample its artisanal chocolate.

It's her eyes, Augusto had said to himself one evening, *they are simply the darkest eyes I have ever seen, sparkling nuggets of coal, an opaque density which challenged anyone who held her gaze for too long. Or was it her hair*, he wondered, *her thick mane of dark curls falling to her waist?*

For her part, Fermina had remained a spinster, her independence as daunting to most suitors as her eyes. Besides, she found men weak and often thought that she should have become a nun, to have spent her days and weeks in the convent of St. Dominic, but then she would have found the other nuns supercilious and she had little time for chastity, a concept so absurd to her despite her strong Catholic heritage.

Augusto had been visiting the bar where Fermina worked for over six months before she woke up one morning and decided that she wanted to fuck him. He later learned those had been her exact words as she applied a thin layer of eye shadow in front of the small, cheap mirror that hung in her cramped bathroom.

"I will fuck you today, strange man," she said to her reflection.

Yes, she confirmed to herself after lunch, *there is something special about this man, he does not look like a gambler, he does not act like a drinker, he is like a wounded animal, a stray dog far from home, and I will fuck him tonight, when he has finished playing his stupid cards.*

Like most things in life, Fermina approached her desires that evening with a calm, full-frontal assault. She waited until the poker game had reached its climax and she was collecting empty glasses from amongst the players. Augusto had moved away from the playing table and was staring into space, subconsciously caressing a tumbler of whisky in his right hand, moving the tip of his index finger around the rim. The effects of the alcohol were slowly working their way into his brain, throwing mufflers across the voices that gradually waned as the whisky worked its magic.

"I have a troublesome neighbour," she said simply, as she paused beside him at the bar, "will you walk me home, please?"

Her directness caught Augusto off guard and he found himself clearing his throat, colour rising across his face like a purple birthmark. He wiped a nervous hand across his lower jaw.

"Yes, of course," he said sheepishly. "Whenever you are ready, perhaps I should wait outside, to avoid any embarrassment for you?"

"If you like," she said simply and disappeared into the small stockroom behind the bar.

Augusto waited outside in the cobbled alleyway, and, some 15 minutes later, Fermina emerged from a side door, pulling a warm shawl around her shoulders.

"Thank you for waiting," she said, and slipped an arm within his as they moved into the cold night, a blanket of stars throwing a canopy of fireflies across the clear sky. She said no more to him until she steered him down a small alleyway close to the Plaza Regocijo and then stopped in front of an old, two-storey building. Up until then, there had only been the echo from their footsteps bouncing up and down the ancient bricks and mortar lining their path.

"Will you come up, please?" she asked. "I want to make love with you tonight."

As she murmured these words, Fermina turned to face him to ensure that he could see her eyes, sparkling flints of dark fire that cut a thread of determination across her features.

Despite his confusion, Augusto met her gaze evenly and spoke quietly. "I have never been with a woman," he whispered, "and I am old now to start, so to speak, I will come with you if you are patient with me, patient and gentle."

Fermina squeezed his arm through his thick jacket and then took his hand, which she raised to her mouth, brushing her lips across his fingertips.

"You are safe here, Augusto," she whispered, "with me."

Fermina led him to the second-floor landing where she opened the door to her tiny apartment and pulled him gently behind her. The room was shrouded in shadows and Augusto thought that he could smell the faint aroma of sandalwood. From a candle perhaps, he had said to himself. Fermina threw her shawl across the back of a chair and snapped on a small lamp, a corner of the room jumping to life. She helped Augusto remove his coat, which she also threw over the back of the same chair.

"Say nothing," she said quietly. Augusto felt as if he had been nailed to the floor, his breath catching in short bursts as she moved away from him toward the only bedroom. Almost as if she had forgotten to fetch something, she returned and stood in front of him. "This way," she said, and took his hand once again.

Augusto found himself standing at the foot of her bed and watched as she removed her jewellery, which she placed in a small basket on her dressing table. She pulled off her sheepskin boots and threw her socks into the corner where they were swallowed by the darkness. Fermina returned and stood in front of him, momentarily looking into his eyes before she pulled his shirt over his head and then gently undid his belt buckle, pulling his trousers down around his ankles before doing the same with his underwear. She stood up and slowly manoeuvred him onto the bed, pushing a second pillow behind his head.

"You must watch me," she said quietly, "and relax."

Fermina stood at the end of the bed and slipped out of her thick skirt before slowly unbuttoning the white blouse she always wore for work. Augusto found himself transfixed by her fingers as she quickly released the clasp of her bra and he found excitement surging through him as she momentarily touched one of her breasts. She moved over him and ran her nails across the base of his stomach, her fingers catching in the tight curls below his navel. Her thick hair fell across him as she took him in her mouth, and he reached out a hand to touch the back of her head as it moved back and forth.

She paused momentarily and looked up at him. “Is that okay?” she whispered.

He dared not attempt to speak but closed his eyes and nodded slowly. She moved her face up to his and kissed him slowly around his mouth, her tongue tracing tiny circles against his lips until she gently pushed her tongue into his mouth, his tongue slowly responding to hers as he felt her breath quicken. Moments later, she moved away from his mouth and gathered her breasts in both her hands, cupping them around his penis, which she moved in and out between them. Augusto dared not touch her but began to feel his body tense as he watched what to him was the most erotic thing he could imagine. Fermina could feel his excitement and began to murmur quietly, increasing her tempo as she felt his body contort as he moved toward his orgasm. She kept moving as he lost control, his semen falling across her breasts and onto her stomach, her hand subconsciously moving between her thighs where she began to rub herself frantically, eventually falling against him as she had her own orgasm. Silence fell between them except for their heavy breathing, which subsided after a few minutes, a layer of perspiration shining in the shadows between them. Augusto slowly brought his hand to the back of her head and stroked her hair, small tears rolling silently down his face.

Augusto sipped at his coffee once again as he contemplated the wonder of that memory, brushing it across his mind like a paintbrush, other memories pushing for attention. The sum of their four years together were personified by her compassion that night, by their deep love for one another, a mutual contentment that surpassed anything and everything he had ever known, something he would do everything and anything to protect and sustain. He pursed his lips suddenly as another memory pushed itself to the front of his mind, a concern that teased him like a needle goads a splinter, a darker episode still sitting in his mind like a stubborn, uninvited guest.

The episode had taken place recently, only three months earlier. On the occasion in question, Augusto had woken with a start in the middle of the night, engulfed by panic as if he had woken from a nightmare, a clammy sweat covering his chest and arms. He sat up in bed and rubbed at his perspiration with the duvet, a chill descending around him like a curse. He could smell his own fear and something else, something that clawed within his mind like a caged animal. He glanced down at Fermina, who was still asleep, her thick hair lying across her back like layers of woven silk. Like a goddess at rest, he had thought to himself. His hand was drawn to the back of her head where it hovered like a hummingbird. He could feel his hand shaking as he moved it across her scalp, the tumour crouching against her cranium like a predator, its teeth bared, saliva dripping like poison into her veins. He remained motionless for a while before lying down once again, tears gathering around the corners of his eyes as indecision dug into his psyche in repeated stabbing motions.

We swore a pact, he said, *but that was long ago and before this life, before this real life.*

Unbeknown to Augusto, and in typical Fermina fashion, she had been suffering from severe headaches and vomiting for some time and had eventually decided to seek medical advice. A visit to the local doctor resulted in a referral to the main hospital in Cuzco and an eventual scan. The tumour was a form of brain cancer, the consultant told her quietly, the worst type in fact, glioblastoma multiforme. She accepted the results with her usual stoicism.

"Can you write that down for me?" she had requested.

The consultant told her that even with aggressive multimodality treatments, which might include radiation, chemotherapy, or surgical excision, her chances of survival were minimal.

"You might live for another nine months, Miss Marquez," he said quietly. "I am sorry. You must decide whether you wish to undergo treatment. It's a balance of quality of life, you must reflect for a few days."

Fermina had wept briefly on the way home, a short interlude on the bus, before she dried her tears and resolved to put her life or death in the hands of God. The thought of returning to the hospital filled her with dread, she might as well have been constrained in a cell. She decided not to tell Augusto, not yet anyway.

For his part, Augusto woke the next morning and took the early train to Machu Picchu where he spent the day walking amongst the ruins, and even climbed the mountain Huayna Picchu, overlooking the ancient city, in the hope that he might find clarity through the fresh air and exertion. He did. In the early hours of the following morning, Augusto moved quietly from their bed, and, with one of Fermina's shawls wrapped around his shoulders against the biting chill, he moved his hands across her body. He whispered to the shadows, realigning her chakras, her energy, the tumour pulled from her like a cork from a bottle, her sickness swallowed by the night, consumed by Augusto's vibrations. The process took 45 minutes, by the end of which Augusto was exhausted. He rubbed tears from his eyes as he crawled back into bed and fell into a deep sleep; such had been his focus, he could not know that Fermina had woken during the process but, engulfed by a sixth sense of sorts, had remained motionless beneath his healing hands.

In the morning, she felt it was better not to mention the episode.

That had been three months ago, Augusto reflected, as he caught sight of the worshippers leaving the cathedral. He placed some money next to the coffee cup and hurried down to the Plaza de Armas where he crossed the street and skipped up the few steps to the main cathedral entrance, a familiar tingle in his stomach that he often felt whenever he had not seen Fermina for a couple of hours. He slipped his arm through hers as she emerged into the bright light.

"So," he said, smiling at her, "breakfast?" She smiled at his mood and he felt a shard of her sunlight carve into him. "I hope that you confessed all of your sins, this morning," he teased her, "all of your wickedness."

"You are my only wickedness, my beloved Augusto," she said quietly, and kissed him lightly on the cheek. "Vamos!"

Fermina had, as Augusto suspected, been the first in the queue for confession that morning. She knew Father Bonifacio well; they had been childhood sweethearts at some stage, and he was, oddly enough, remarkably similar to Augusto in age and appearance, although their two lives had taken different paths, and mutual similarities were limited to the physiological space.

They even have similar cute, trimmed goatee beards, she thought to herself as she climbed into the confessional box. But then Bonifacio had turned into a dull, old priest while Augusto was just, well, Augusto, her love, her gift from God. When he had blessed her at the end of her confession, Fermina asked if she could share something with him, something she had to share with someone. She told him about her sickness — she even pronounced glioblastoma multiforme correctly — she told him about Augusto that night, her subsequent return to the hospital, the consultant's disbelief following her second scan, her renewed energy, and…

"It was a miracle, Father," she said quietly, "but also a secret, my secret, please."

Father Bonifacio thought about Fermina later that day as he sat on his balcony where he habitually drank a glass of brandy before bed. To date, his life as a priest had been distinguished by mediocrity. After some time, but not perhaps as much as he might have taken to fully reflect on Fermina's incredible story or her wish for her secret to remain just that, he reached for his telephone and called a number in Rome.

"I wish to report a miracle," he said to the operator in the Vatican.

2065, New York, Three Blind Mice, Three Heads of Cerberus

It took the unlikely trio about 90 minutes to reach what Sophia had referred to as her other safe house, an equally nondescript building with basement parking where Sophia left the car. The apartment was off Manhattan Island, just off Grand Central and close to LaGuardia Airport on the edge of Queens. She closed the door behind her and quickly drew the curtains.

"I'll get some supplies a bit later, but first, you, Mister English, I need some answers, and then I'll deal with you, Ruth, as I promised, and then you can go back to your life."

Ruth had not spoken since leaving Broadway and she looked tired and drawn. Sophia boiled some hot water and made a pot of tea, which she placed on the small central table. The place was a little dusty but was obviously visited from time to time to keep things ready in case of just such an emergency.

"What happened back there, at your apartment?" Brian asked quietly.

"I burned it down," Sophia said simply.

"No, I meant before that," Brian continued. "What happened to your mother? Not just today but before. She looked extraordinary, like two people living in one body."

"I'll get to that if you need to know," Sophia snapped back at him, "but first, you, how did you find me, how did you know Alexandra's mother?"

"Okay," said Brian, "I'll tell you, but I also want some answers, it seems my life is also in danger now."

"You are lucky to be alive now," Sophia murmured, a whisper of revenge curling around the corners of her mouth. "So I want your story now, all of it, and it better be convincing."

Brian scoffed momentarily. "Or what, you'll shoot me down here, like a dog, just like that?"

"Not like a dog, no," Sophia responded with icy intent. "I like animals. Now, let's hear it."

Brian sighed and shrugged his shoulders. "Okay, well, it is all so crazy that it would be hard to make up. My name is Brian, I am English, and I am, or was, a dentist…"

For the next 40 minutes or so, Brian recounted his last few days. He began with the dental convention and his personal crisis, although he did not go into graphic detail. He recalled winning in the casino and losing his wallet, followed by his incredible coincidence with Valeriya, her subsequent story, and then that fateful morning, finding her body, events that brought him to where he was today.

"So, hang on," Sophia interrupted him, "my grandmother who, incidentally, I never met, and I don't even think that she knew about me, she just meets you in a bar and sets you on this incredible mission, to find the prophets through my mother and reveal this dreadful conspiracy to the world. Bit of a tall order for a dentist, wouldn't you say?" Sophia was shaking her head, a mixture of anger and disbelief crossing her features.

"Yes," said Brian, "a very tall order. She told me that they were closing in on her; she was afraid, I suppose, perhaps I was a last resort. I was, am, anonymous, foreign, at the end of an emotional tether, and suddenly very rich. She must have been hoping that I would get more from your mother, from Alexandra. I am sorry about your mother, and your grandmother," he added.

"So they must have followed you here," Sophia said quietly. "They were watching all the time. They have been waiting to find my mother for a very long time." Sophia left her chair and walked around the room for a few moments, desperately searching for something, a hidden clue.

"I don't think that they followed me here," Brian said, his mind also searching the previous day's events for something out of the ordinary.

"Of course they fucking did," Sophia snapped back across the room. "You naive imbecile, do you really think that your meeting with Valeriya, all that passed between you, and now my mother's death, can you really think that these events were just coincidences? Fuck, you have no idea what we are dealing with here.

These people run the planet, moron, did you not listen to anything Valeriya said?"

Brian was humiliated, his blood rising to his cheeks. Sophia's mind was bristling, prowling; she pointed at Brian.

"You had a book when we met you outside the apartment, where is it?"

Brian looked confused, he could not link the threads. "Um, I don't know," he replied. "I must have left it in your apartment."

"Where did it come from?" Sophia asked. "And why did you have it with you in the first place?"

Brian cast his mind back to the moment when he retrieved the coat, taking the book from under his arm and placing it on the chair.

"Valeriya left it for me to find," he said. "It was a clue, I thought that Alexandra would find something in there."

Sophia buried her head in her hands for a moment. "No, Brian, no, *they* left it there, thinking perhaps that you might find it. That's how they work, they can pre-empt the mind, your mind, any mind, it's what they do." She paused. "Well, at least we know how they found us. There will have been a tracking device in there, I am certain."

Brian considered the facts for a moment, they seemed plausible; he slumped back in his chair, an acknowledgment that he had inadvertently played a part in Alexandra's death.

"I don't know what to say," he said. An uncomfortable silence closed in around the three strangers.

"Do me a favour, Brian," Sophia said quietly. "Go and buy some groceries, be at least one hour, no fucking questions, just do it."

Brian could feel his temper beginning to rise.

This precocious little brat, he thought. *Insults, orders, more fucking insults. Fuck you, I will leave and that will be that, you stupid little stuck-up cow. I have had my fill of freaks*, he told himself. *Even a confrontation with Jan is preferable to this bullshit.*

"And come back, Brian, please," Sophia said gently as he opened the front door. "The freak needs your help."

No sooner had Brian closed the door of the apartment than Sophia turned her attention to Ruth, a savage look of determination etched across her face.

"Right," she said, "let's deal with you, quickly, then you can leave. I have lots to do."

"I can go anyway," Ruth said, defeat and bewilderment clouding her features.

"That's hardly the woman I met a few days ago," Sophia responded. "Where's the bohemian, where's that aggression, where's the cunt in you?"

Ruth attempted a smile but instead her eyes moistened around their corners and she raised her hands in hopelessness.

"I don't know what to think anymore," she said. "Your mother, Brian's story, these people chasing you, killers. What's next?"

"That," Sophia said simply, pointing at Ruth's breast. "Let's deal with that quickly, come."

Sophia led Ruth by her hand into a small adjoining bedroom where the curtains were also drawn, the late afternoon light creeping around their edges, the bustle of the city muted by the murmur of an archaic radiator.

"Lie down," Sophia said, "and try to relax."

Ruth lay on the bed, facing the ceiling. She could see what looked like a watermark above her head, and she imagined water dripping through the ceiling at some stage in the sorry life of this dilapidated place. She closed her eyes.

"Don't look at me," Sophia said simply.

Ruth kept her eyes closed, aware only of occasional murmuring from Sophia, indiscernible words whispered above her as Sophia moved adjacent to the bed. She thought about the images from the CCTV cameras and the bizarre events that had brought her to this place. She drifted into sleep. Images filled her mind as she slept, and she found herself in a burning building, which she recognized as the apartment they had just left. She was in a rocking chair, opposite Alexandra, and the two women were surrounded by encroaching flames. Alexandra was smiling across the small space between them, sometimes pausing to focus on something in her lap. Ruth leaned forward in her chair and noticed that Alexandra was knitting from a tight ball of wool sitting in her lap. As she finished a line and her knitting needles clicked like high heels on a marble floor, Ruth noticed that the line of wool was in fact a thick hair, the origin of which lay across the floor between them. As she followed its course, she discovered it to be her own elephant hair, running from somewhere inside her shirt, under the light material and then onto the floor. Alexandra seemed oblivious to the fire and was intent on her handiwork.

"What are you doing?" she asked.

"Repairs." Alexandra smiled back at her. "Look," she said, raising her hands from her lap. Despite the smoke, which had begun to cloud the space between them, Ruth could see that Alexandra was not knitting a garment, she was knitting her missing finger back on in its rightful place, the elephant hair used for the crude stitching. “See, dear,” Alexandra whispered, “we are connected now.” Alexandra raised her hand to her mouth and bit through the elephant hair. “There,” she said, admiring her handiwork, “all done, good as new!”

Ruth thought that she could hear a cat purring somewhere in the room as smoke filled her eyes, and she woke up. Sophia was standing at the end of the bed, sweat glistening across her face, running off her cheeks.

“Did you have a cat in your apartment?” Ruth asked.

Sophia nodded, but did not speak.

“I thought so,” Ruth whispered. “Don’t know why, but I did.”

“You are safe now,” Sophia said. “It’s done, and you might want to sleep for a while.”

“No, I don’t. Thank you, Sophia. Now I want to help.”

Brian detected a subtle change in the atmosphere when he returned to the apartment, his arms full of shopping bags. The aggression between the two women seemed to have dissipated and he could hear someone running a bath. He unpacked the shopping as best he could and opened a bottle of red wine, which he poured into three tumblers as he was unable to find any wine glasses. He could hear Ruth and Sophia talking in the bathroom, so he decided to sit quietly and wait for them to finish. The two women emerged after about 15 minutes, and the three sat quietly around the small Formica-top table, a throwback from the turn of the century or even the latter part of the previous century. Time seemed to have stagnated in this apartment and Brian felt as if he was momentarily in a time warp of his own.

"So, now what?" he eventually said, his question delivered to the four walls of the apartment as much as to the two women in front of him. "Alexandra is dead, now what do we do?"

Ruth glanced over at Sophia, and Brian imagined that the two women must have been discussing this very topic in the bathroom.

"Well, I think I had better fill in a few blanks first, and then we can devise a strategy, or we can all simply run away."

"Go on." Brian gestured with his wine glass.

"Well," Sophia sighed, "where do I begin?" She paused and took a small sip from her glass of wine. "Okay, let's see, given what Brian has told us about his encounter with Valeriya, this is my take on events. Firstly, there is a program to control population explosion through self-sacrifice centres, that much is obvious, and it has worked pretty well so far. The manipulators, if we can call them that, created the three prophets to advocate self-sacrifice. Now, my grandmother had a role in this, but I don't know if she knew the whole story, there's something missing; her role, as I understand it from my mother, was to dabble with the brain, in the way that the two sides of the brain interact, so that the prophets themselves would believe that they were receiving messages from a God or Gods. What is not clear, however, is where the

DNA came from to create these prophets, as my opinion is that it was not wholly human." Sophia paused and let what she had just said percolate through the room. The other two looked a little dumbfounded.

"You see," she went on, "it's all very well creating prophets and dabbling with the brain, surgically, but that does not account for the extraordinary mental and physical powers the prophets demonstrated or even my abilities, a generation on."

"Well, how do you account for those?" Brian asked gently.

"Well, as you now know, my mother was a twin, an unexpected addition to the program, and that embryo was stolen by my grandmother and developed separately. She told me that the architects of the program were unaware of the fourth until it was too late. They would obviously have destroyed the fourth child as all plans had been predicated on three prophets, not four. Now, the reason I spoke of a DNA that is not wholly human is as a result of what happened to my mother — you two saw her body, its deformed development, her insanity. My belief is whatever was mixed with human DNA is so much more powerful and advanced than us that the creators were not really sure exactly what might happen over time, hence their decision to keep the other prophets alive and under observation, that is until they escaped. So, irrespective of whatever went on by way of brain manipulation, the whole corpus callosum bit, it's in the raw material, it's in the DNA that our answers lie. Basically, where did it come from, whose is it?"

Ruth was about to ask a question but Sophia raised her hand.

"Sorry, let me just add something," she said quickly. "You see I am different, the next generation, so my DNA is diluted further, it's less toxic, if that's the right word, so I have many of the same gifts. I can heal, do telepathy, and all sorts of other things, but the main advantage I have is that no one has fucked with my brain, so I can think through these things logically."

"So," Ruth asked, "do you think the other prophets are like your mother, in the way they have developed? Or perhaps their bodies have been able to carry this strain of DNA without falling apart?"

"I don't know," Sophia responded. "Perhaps her twin is the same as her, I have no idea. I can probably find them, telepathically, but there is an inherent danger in that, as the creators will also be looking hard, they will have been looking for many years. They will also know that my mother was not alone; whoever left that coat will have realized that she lived with someone and they will quickly find out that I exist, and they will want to dispose of me very quickly. They will also assume that I have inherited some of my mother's powers. So, it's a bit of a race."

An uneasy silence fell amongst the three musketeers.

"Here's what I think needs to be done," Sophia added, "if you two have the stomach for it?" She looked at Brian and Ruth who both held her gaze and nodded in agreement.

"Okay, well, three things that I can think of. Firstly, there is this missing link, the whole DNA issue. Where is it from? If it's not entirely human, then how can that have been hidden from mankind? So, that's research, rooting around, something you can do, Ruth, here, in New York, our 'foot on the ground' so to speak. You can go back to work, lay low, and feed us information."

These ideas filtered into Ruth's mind and she nodded slowly, deep in thought.

"The second major task is to find the prophets. I can hone in on them telepathically, but someone will have to go and close the loop, literally, pick them up. Someone anonymous, rich — I think we know who that is," she said smiling at Brian. "Lucky you, Brian, you wanted to travel, to get away from whatever has happened to you, privately."

Brian scoffed. "I am sure you know," he said. "You seem to be able to read minds."

"Only if I choose," Sophia responded quickly, "and emotions are stored in a very discreet part of the mind and I prefer not to go there."

"So, what will you do?" Ruth asked, pulling the conversation back into focus.

"I will also work on the bigger question," Sophia said, "but the practical end of what you are doing, Ruth. I need to find the people who started this — they will still be around somewhere, old, yes, but alive. I can feel them; as much as they look, I can feel them looking, so I need that confrontation. It's as important as Brian finding the products of the program, the prophets themselves. I will try and get answers from the beginning so that we can pre-empt and outflank them."

The other two nodded; a three-pronged attack sounded constructive.

"So," Sophia added, "we need to split up, we need your money, Brian, or some of it at least, and we must agree on a communications protocol that is foolproof, and we must apply it with ruthless discipline."

"In that case," said Brian, "I'm going to open another bottle of wine."

The room was silent. Neither Ruth nor Sophia had any concept of British humour.

2065, Eugenics and Chromosomal Chronology

"What the fuck is going on?" Nathan hissed, his voice edged with such menace that K half expected the head of a cobra to strike at her from the receiver.

"I'm not sure yet," she replied, trying to keep her voice steady. "The woman, Alexandra, is dead, but something happened in there, to Kazuo. I still can't get much sense out of him, it's as if she has put a spell on him. He is sleeping now, so I'll see what he says when he wakes up."

"Give it to me in English, can you?" Nathan continued. "I spoke to him when he was in there, he flashed the pictures to me."

"Yes, Nathan, I know, I saw them too." K paused. "Something happened afterwards. He told me that the woman, Alexandra, was like two people in one body, old and new living together, parts of the body regenerating, parts dying." She paused while Nathan digested this information.

"Go on," he said quietly.

"Well, from what I can gather, she was in a trance, insane, then she seemed to attack Kazuo and then she died, just sat back in her chair and died — shut down, as if someone turned off the switch."

K decided not to tell Nathan about the finger, at least not until she got more sense from Kazuo. Nathan said nothing and K tried to imagine the scene at the other end of the telephone.

She decided to continue. "There's another thing, it looks as if someone else lives with her, a helper, a carer, we don't know, but one thing is certain, she was not alone and she or they were worried about security, so we assume that the other person knows about the program. We've also lost the tracking device but it has served its purpose."

There was another pregnant pause and K decided that she had said enough. There were loose ends that needed to be clipped and cauterized, but she preferred to let Nathan take the lead. She waited.

"Okay," he said finally, "let's see. The way I see things, we need to find the helper and question her before we neutralize her. Then, there is the Englishman, he has fulfilled his role, so we can get rid of him quickly. No need to delay there. He knows some of the story but not so much, so, please, tidy up that loose end before he goes anywhere else, is that clear? In New York, please."

"Yes, Nathan," she replied, "very clear. That should not be difficult."

"Okay, you've got three days," Nathan continued. "Then I need you back here for a briefing, and then I need you both in South America, something's come up, very significant, we hope."

"Oh?" K murmured.

"Yes, oh," Nathan continued, and K detected excitement in his voice. "There has been a report of a miracle. I have a photo, it's not very clear but it could be one of them, so I need you down there quickly to verify and to do the necessary. So, be quick with your housekeeping at your end, and I will see you here before the weekend, is that clear?"

Nathan did not wait for K to respond, the line simply went dead. She was used to his mannerisms. She walked quietly into the adjoining room and took a quick look at Kazuo who still seemed to be in a deep sleep. She frowned to herself. This was very unlike him, a man who seemed to prowl even when asleep, a man who seemed immune to physiological discomforts, a man who would normally float above the flotsam and jetsam of life, an impervious stone, literally rock solid. Yet here she found him — asleep, disturbed.

Spooked, she said. *He has been spooked by Alexandra in some way or another.*

She sat down opposite him and watched his eyelids flutter and twitch; he looked a bit like a dog, she told herself, a bulldog dreaming, chasing rabbits in its sleep. She smiled at the analogy and decided to let him sleep a little longer.

"Then we can go hunting," she whispered to the silence, "hunting the English."

Spooks, now that's a good word, she thought. *We all have our spooks, that's for sure.*

K had been correct in her assessment; Kazuo was dreaming. Sadly, he was not dreaming of chasing rabbits. His dream took him back in time, and it began with familiar images, images that initially caressed him like a light breeze. The dream began as others had, a recurring one he used to have frequently but which had slowly diluted in time, but not so much that he did not recognize the images as they pushed into his sleep, a familiar beginning at least. In fact, he recognized the places and faces, and he felt as if he was coming home, momentarily anyway.

It was in the early days of the cult. He and Veasna were two neophytes embodying hope, shrouded by love for one another. The religious movement was pushing back barriers, an emerging beacon of light contiguous with other such movements creeping across the face of the planet like a plague. Religion had become addictive gossip as word of the prophets filtered through historical precedence and language. He and Veasna embraced the heady potion of love and hope like a couple of hippies, as their fellow beings were subsumed by revision, and the cynicism of the agnostics was overwhelmed by demonstrable facts, by substantiated, scientific proof that the miracles were just what they were, miraculous. In those early days, Kazuo and Veasna would sneak away from the small settlement at dusk, an idyllic walk to the beach where they would swim and then lie together on the sand where they would sometimes make love.

So, Kazuo's dream began as it had before, the familiar walk, the setting sun just visible across the curve of the horizon, the salt from the ocean mingling with the sand as they touched each other in the dusk. As before, in some versions of this dream, Kazuo would move behind Veasna, pulling him back toward him, pushing into him, the thrill and excitement of seeing himself moving in and out of his lover sometimes too much to bear, and he would awake before climaxing. So, his dream followed that pattern; he slowly adjusted the position of his lover so that he could push into him and run his hands across his thighs and back. In this dream, Kazuo found comfort as they rocked backward and forward together, and his excitement built; he looked for his familiar source of arousal, to see the head of his penis entering the young man, but on this occasion, as Kazuo looked down, his mind filled with horror, his psyche overwhelmed by a bilious raw. His penis had been replaced by Alexandra's index finger, the bloody stump somehow attached to his lower belly in place of his penis, the gnarled fingertip with its broken nail pushing in and out of his beloved Veasna, the young, unblemished skin invaded by withered age. Kazuo started to panic — he desperately wanted to withdraw from his young lover. He couldn't bear to imagine what might happen if he reached an orgasm. Kazuo fought to leave his dream, to leave that beach, to leave that memory.

As K worried about Kazuo, the band of three pulled together the bones of a plan in the small safe house that had become a temporary sanctuary for Sophia. Brian had returned to the hotel during the evening and checked out immediately, laying an elaborate trail of taxi rides in the early hours to guarantee that he had not been followed before returning to the safe house where he curled up on the couch. Ruth also left the safe house that same evening, the general consensus being that she was probably still anonymous, that she could continue a normal life while they gathered information. Brian woke early, a sense of unease surrounding him like an extra blanket. He awoke to find Sophia sitting in the adjacent chair, a cup of coffee steaming next to her, and a second cup that she pushed across the cheap table toward him. She attempted a half smile, and he noticed a fragility that he had not noticed the previous day.

"I wasn't sure if you would come back yesterday," she said, "but I'm glad you did." She lowered her eyes and reached for her coffee, a much needed prop.

My God, she looks young, Brian thought. *A young hybrid with the orchid eyes of a wild animal.*

But he was unable to recall what animal, if any, had orchid-coloured eyes. He wondered if there was such a creature.

"Nor was I," he said, raising his eyebrows and reaching for the coffee. He stole another quick look at Sophia. She was dressed in chocolate-coloured silk pyjamas with cream piping, and he could sense the shape of her body beneath the light fabric, a body personified by youth, a flat, hard body, like a flat, hard pebble on a perspiring beach. He imagined picking her up and skimming her across the incoming tide. He found himself in momentary envy of her youth, of her vibrancy.

Did I waste too many years? he wondered.

"It did occur to me that I am probably condemned to death, as anybody seems to be who is connected with this project."

"Yes, I can tell you that you are," she said. "I have lived with this all my life, I can sense their power and influence even if I cannot touch it, not yet anyway."

"What happened yesterday, when I was out?" he said, changing the subject. "What happened between you and Ruth? You seem an unlikely pair."

"We were thrown together, through error, through my stupidity."

"So, what happened?" Brian persisted.

"She had breast cancer," Sophia continued, as if she was talking about a common cold. "I took it away while you were out."

"You took it away," Brian said with incredulity. "What does that mean?"

"I don't really want to discuss that now," she said quickly. "Let's just say that she was sick and I made her better, I can do that, you know that."

Brian shrugged. "Okay, but it's pretty incredible for us mere mortals." He smiled. "So, am I sick, you know, anything growing in me that I don't know about?"

Sophia uncrossed her legs and ran her fingers through her hair. "No, Brian," she said, as if she was talking to a small child, "your issues are a little harder to cure — sadness, a deep melancholy, regret, the normal stuff, I suppose, when people get to your age."

"Fuck," Brian chuckled, "wish I hadn't asked."

"Anyway," Sophia continued, her tone suddenly businesslike, "what I did not mention to you yesterday, or to Ruth as she doesn't really need to know where you are, is that I think I know where one of the prophets might be. You see, well, I think you know that I have inherited some of these telepathic powers from my mother."

Brian nodded.

"Well, I have taught myself to scan that spectrum for signals, for similar energy sources to mine in the hope of connecting with the prophets. I have been doing it for years but have never received anything back, it was always as if the switches at the other end had been turned off. That was until a few months ago when something happened in Peru, a huge surge of energy, my guess is a miracle."

Sophia paused while Brian digested this information. He nodded for her to continue.

"You need to get down there while I try to establish contact with whoever it is. If you get to Peru and wait, I'll hopefully have something for you over the next few days, a more exact location."

"How do you know it's Peru?" Brian asked. It seemed odd to him that he had also thought of bunking off to Peru to drop out and sit on the beach while he tried to reconcile his thoughts concerning Jan.

"I have no idea," Sophia said calmly. "I just sort of know."

"Good enough for me," Brian said smiling. "I'll start to make some travel plans after breakfast."

Ruth woke the next day in her apartment and wondered if she had been having a dream; the previous day's events scored across her mind like an ancient text. She felt as if her body had undergone an overhaul, and she could feel health and energy literally bursting out of her skin as if she had experienced a spiritual release. She bounced out of bed like a child on Christmas morning eager to explore her stocking and found herself humming rock ballads under the shower. It was a Saturday, and although weekends were often irrelevant to her hospital routine, this Saturday was a day off for her, and she planned to spend the day in the main branch of the New York Public Library, to launch into her research as soon as she could. When she finished her shower and had dried herself off, she lay down on the chilly tiles of her bathroom floor and began to move her fingers across her right breast.

"Where are you, my little axillary tail," she murmured. "Ah, there you are, now, Mister Lump, you were here or hereabouts."

Her fingers worked their way up to her armpit and then back down across her breast until she arrived back at the areola around her nipple. A tear ran from the corner of her right eye and was absorbed by her hair, which lay bunched on the tile floor.

My God. I have been touched by a god of sorts, literally. It truly is a miracle.

Ruth lay where she was for some time, breathing deeply, enjoying the vibrancy surrounding her like a second skin. She ran her fingers slowly across her skin, occasionally pausing on a small bump or blemish to tease her fingertips.

Fuck, she thought after a few minutes, *I feel like a new woman, I feel as if I need to breed.*

She could feel a growing anticipation between her thighs and moved her fingers below her navel where they hovered for a few seconds. Her mind wandered toward her last lover, and she touched the very tip of her clitoris with her forefinger, eager to push a finger inside herself.

Wait, you, she said to herself, tapping her finger against her clitoris as if she was scolding a small child. *There's work to be done, lives to be saved, I'll get to you later, it's payback time for now! What was that Sophia said?* she asked herself. *Where's the cunt in you, or something like that?* She smiled as she stood up. *Should have been, Where's the sopping wet cunt in you?*

Given her tenacity, it did not take Ruth long to realize that a few hours each day in one of the branches of the New York Public Library was unlikely to break the back of the huge amount of information she needed to wade through in the hope of coming up with something vaguely tangible. By the end of the weekend, she felt so overwhelmed that she decided to take a week's leave to devote herself to her research full-time. She waited outside the library in the mornings and was still there in the evening when the curator had to force her out. She had divided her research into three main areas, the first being DNA and what might or might not have occurred to enable the creation of these so-called prophets. The second was linked to DNA and involved the genomic evolutionary tree. The third was to see if she could find any link between the first two topics and anything recorded historically, anything that might make sense of the whole subject or at least provide a logical explanation. She had also made arrangements for a holographic portal the three could use when in different locations, and so, after ten days of research, it was into this encrypted space that she reported to Sophia and Brian. The former was still in New York, the latter waiting patiently in Lima while Sophia trawled the energy waves for signs of the other prophets.

“Well,” she began, “it’s hard to know where to begin, but I’ll give you the main points of interest which I’ve come up with and one or two possible conclusions.”

“Can you keep it in English, please,” Brian interjected. “I seem to remember Valeriya using words that I could barely pronounce.”

“I’ll try,” Ruth added. “Some of it is pretty hard to follow, and I am also just a novice in this field, so, here goes.”

Ruth paused momentarily and then leapt in.

“Well, as I think you know, I started with DNA, as it seems to me that the prophets have a different, ‘stronger’ DNA to us, which enables them to use far more of their brains than the ten percent we do, and enables them to operate at a different frequency; we know this as a result of their healings, the miracles, and have even seen it first-hand with you, Sophia. From what we discussed together, I am pretty sure that the program devised by Valeriya involved some sort of DNA cloning, certainly a cloning with a far superior DNA to ours to create the prophets as we know them. My guess is that the physiological effects of this potent and possibly toxic mixture were too much for Alexandra to bear, her body that is, and, in her case, complications may have arisen as a result of the cell dividing to create the twins.”

She let this initial statement drift across the airways and then continued.

“So, the next thing I wanted to find out was whether there was any precedent for this, so I delved a little deeper into the human DNA. Now, within the DNA of *Hominidae*, which are basically humans, orangutans, gorillas and chimpanzees, all groups have twenty-four pairs of chromosomes except for *Homo sapiens*, which only have twenty-three as a result of an end-to-end fusion of two ancestral chromosomes. In us humans, it's chromosome two which shows this characteristic, basically that it fused at some point in history, most probably as a result of breeding."

She paused and was not surprised to hear Brian's voice.

"Hang on," he said quickly, "so all the *Hominidae* share the same DNA but we have one less pair of chromosomes?"

"Essentially, yes, so, within what is known as the vertical evolutionary tree, the chronology of evolutionary events, the chimpanzee has nearly identical DNA sequences to human chromosome two, but in the case of the chimpanzee, they are found in two separate chromosomes as is the case with the more distant gorilla and orangutan."

There was a worrying silence and Ruth wondered if she was losing her audience.

"Let me put it this way, it's within our chromosome two that scientists believe lies the answers to the main differences between us and other similar species, as it's within chromosome two that we evolved distinct genes which relate to our cognitive behaviour, our metabolism, cranial features, and our rib cage, for example."

"So," Sophia interjected, "you think that the answer to the superior DNA lies within chromosome two, essentially?"

Ruth paused as she considered how to explain the next part.

"Yes, I do, but we need to dig into the next layer down within our DNA, so to speak, which involves our genes."

"Okay, I'm still with you," Brian muttered, "just."

"Good," she continued, "so, each chromosome contains many genes which are the basic physical and functional units of heredity and variations between organisms. So, as an example, the human genome contains about thirty thousand genes, compared to about thirteen thousand six hundred for a fruit fly or about nineteen thousand for a worm, just to put us in perspective. And, within these sequences, research has shown that there is very little unique about the human gene sequencing; in fact it is about ninety-nine percent similar to the chimpanzee and seventy percent similar to the mouse, for example. And, within this paradigm, over ninety-nine percent of our DNA is similar to that of Neanderthal man. However, and this is where it gets interesting, when tracing the vertical evolutionary record contained in the human genome, scientists encountered an enigma in that they found two hundred and twenty-three genes that don't have the requisite predecessors on the genomic evolutionary tree, genes, for example, that are completely missing in the invertebrate stage."

Ruth paused once again.

"So, in English, if you look at evolution, you can trace the lineage of genes through the invertebrate stage to vertebrates such as mice or chimpanzees, and finally to humans. But, within this process, these two hundred and twenty-three other genes have appeared from somewhere else, from somewhere that does not follow the normal and scientifically proven chronology of events as they relate to evolution."

"So, there was an event, something happened?" Sophia asked.

"Exactly," Ruth said. "An event occurred quite recently in evolutionary terms whereby humans received these genes horizontally, not vertically by the accepted evolutionary Tree of Life, and these genes might account for man's extraordinary advantage over his fellow creatures."

"But you said that we share ninety-nine percent of our DNA with chimpanzees," Brian stated, his mind clearly wrestling with the subject.

"Yes, I did," Ruth said, "but consider this, we humans have about thirty thousand genes, of which two hundred and twenty-three are unaccounted for by way of evolution. Now, two hundred and twenty-three might not sound like much when compared to a total of thirty thousand, but if you consider that the difference in DNA between us and a chimpanzee is only one percent, and one percent of thirty thousand is three hundred, so those two hundred and twenty-three genes are actually two-thirds of the difference between us and a chimpanzee. So, those two hundred and twenty-three genes now start to look very significant, and, what's more, research also shows us that the functions these genes perform through their proteins relate to important physiological and psychiatric abilities, one might argue they are responsible for the huge differential between us and a chimpanzee."

"So, where do they think that the two hundred and twenty-three genes came from?" Sophia asked innocently.

"Well, the scientific explanation is what they refer to as a horizontal insertion of bacteria, although it is not clear whether the transfer was from bacteria to human or vice versa, but either way, if it was from man to bacteria, where did man acquire those genes in the first place?"

"Hang on," Brian interrupted, "can you just recap for a second, I'm a little lost."

"Sure," Ruth said, "so, within our DNA, there is an anomaly with chromosome two, it's been fused through breeding, possibly, for example, between *Homo erectus* and Neanderthal man or, and I'll come to this in a minute, perhaps through another event. As of now, there is no clear conclusion as to what bred with what, just supposition that a breeding event took place which accounts for the fusion in chromosome two and the fact that *Homo sapiens* have one less chromosome pair than the other hominids. More importantly, despite the near identical DNA we share with other species through evolution, we humans have two hundred and twenty-three genes which do not follow the vertical Tree of Life but which were received horizontally, somehow, and which scientists refer to as a sideways insertion of genetic material. It's through this insertion that some explain man's vast intellectual advantage over other species, what has been referred to as the missing link when discussing Darwin's theories in his *Origin of Species*."

"Where are you going with this?" Sophia asked.

"Well," Ruth continued, "the main question that came out of my research obviously relates to this event, this horizontal transfer, and given the ability you have, Sophia, and having seen what the prophets were able to achieve, my feeling is that this event might have been a cloning, an intentional cloning, not some haphazard or random transfer of bacteria, and that those capable of such an event perhaps four hundred thousand years ago would certainly be capable of engineering another such event fifty years ago to create the prophets, that is if they were still around."

There was a deafening silence.

"Okay, consider another angle," Ruth said. "If such an event took place, a cloning, and if this cloning accounts for the fusion seen in chromosome two, that might explain some of the illnesses and diseases we all suffer from and those which relate to genes located on chromosome two. Diseases such as autism, infantile-onset ascending hereditary spastic paralysis, certain diabetes, certain cancers, dementia, to mention but a few, my point being that such a cloning might have upset, literally, the natural order of things. To put it simply, should we get all these illnesses? Is it just about diet and environment or have we been fucked with somewhere along the evolutionary way?"

"Ah," murmured Brian, "that's an explanation I can get to grips with!"

"Take another analogy, what if something like this did take place and they then decided to add further, alien DNA to this already cloned species, would they really know just how potent or how toxic the mixture would be? That would account for the prophets' extraordinary powers, of course, but it might also account for Alexandra's extraordinary physiological state. Perhaps her human body, the evolutionary bit, the pure bit, so to speak, was not able to cope with this hybrid mixture? Nor, for that matter, could her brain. I would love to find her other half, the other twin, to see what she's like. Furthermore, Valeriya told Brian that the prophets did not self-sacrifice, that the masters of the program, the architects, wanted to keep them under observation. Why would they do that if not to see what long-term effects such a cloning might have?"

"Wow, there is some logic in all of this," Brian said, as the three of them settled into a reflective pause.

Sophia was the first to speak. "So, you must have more, Ruth, you obviously have a theory as to why or how this happened?"

"There is more," Ruth said. "Almost too much to fathom in such a short period. Every time I turn over a stone, there's another deluge of possibilities, far more than just science. I had to go a little offline, so to speak."

"Try us," Brian chuckled, "I have nothing much to do down here."

2065, Metamorphoses, Mind and Matter

Brian had been waiting in Lima for over a week and was finding it increasingly hard to relax. His sleep was punctuated by mysterious dreams, the forces of good and evil battling in his subconscious state, their collisions played out through familiar characters — Jan, the landlord at his local pub, characters from school and university whom he had not considered for many years, all thrown together in a maelstrom of different scenarios. He was fascinated by some of what Ruth had tried to explain — baffled, yes, bewildered, but fascinated nonetheless.

"Look," she had said, "we are dealing with extraordinary events so we need to think with open minds … and we need to go back a long way." There had been a brief pause while she composed herself.

“Anyway,” she had continued, “the big challenge for me was not only figuring out where this horizontal injection of bacteria came from but also to consider different subjects in history, those who have obviously been blessed with superior DNA or at least the ability to access their full DNA capacity. This is where it gets complicated, as this is where science, spirituality, mysticism, and mythology merge into the unknown.”

“I need it in English,” Brian had quipped.

“That’s harder than you think,” she had murmured, as much to herself as to the others. “Okay, when you really start to dig, and the further one goes back, inevitably interpretation is compounded by lost languages but also trying to situate those languages in time and space. Sorry.” She had paused. “I am not being very clear.”

“Take your time, Ruth,” Sophia had said softly.

“Okay, put simply, there is no question in my mind that evolution has either been designed by a spiritual force far greater than we will ever comprehend, a God or multiple Gods, or the other option is the alien theory, which might account for our genetic manipulation. Under scenario one, the fundamental question is all about a mind-before-matter cosmos, the origins of human consciousness, so to speak, whereas scenario two has a more scientific explanation, albeit one that might suggest that the bacteria came from elsewhere in space. The irony is that the farther one looks back, the more blurred the canvas. For example, on the alien theory side, have either of you heard of the Sumerian tablets?”

There had been silence across the airwaves.

“Thought not, nor had I. Well, the Sumerians were an ancient culture that originated in Mesopotamia, now modern-day Iraq, somewhere between the period 6,000 and 4,000 BC. During the latter part of the last century, there were numerous archaeological finds of what are now referred to as the Sumerian tablets, some of which can be found in places such as the British Museum and which date back to the same period, pretty obvious I know. What is extraordinary about the tablets is that they tell a very similar story to the Bible, the Old Testament; in fact, many argue that the Old Testament is in fact a synopsis of sorts of the same story told by the Sumerian tablets. So, whereas some might have believed that the Old Testament is perhaps part myth, the Sumerian tablets tell us that these events actually took place, including, most spectacularly, the creation of mankind through a cloning type of event. Quite a lot was written on the subject by someone called Zecharia Sitchin who died in 2010 and who spent many years translating the tablets. The trouble is, he lost quite a lot of credibility through what some felt was mistranslation and trying to squeeze his alien theories out of the tablets."

"So, how come we have never heard of all of this stuff?" Brian had asked.

"Well, it's hard to tell, really," Ruth had said. "As I say, some of his ideas were dismissed by scientists and academics on account of flawed methodology and translations. You can imagine what the main religious institutions would have made of all of this — God's chosen race actually not quite the divine intervention we have been made to believe but a cloning event of sorts."

"Sure," Sophia had added, "but cloned by who or what?"

"Well, the story told by the tablets goes as follows. Unbelievable as it may sound, the tablets tell us that approximately four hundred and fifty thousand years ago, the Earth was visited by a race referred to as the Annunaki who came in search of gold. According to the story, they came to Earth to mine gold and obviously created colonies amongst what would have been whichever species of man existed at that time, possibly Neanderthal man, *Homo erectus*, I am not sure which. So, over a period of time, the colonials, so to speak, the rank and file of the Annunaki, became frustrated at their collective lot, fought amongst one another, and mutinied over dissatisfaction with their working conditions. The tablets tell us that the Annunaki were referred to as the Elohim in Genesis, literally 'those who from Heaven to Earth came' — the Gods. Their solution to their dilemma on planet Earth was to create primitive workers, a slave species essentially, to do the mining for them. Their chief scientist, someone called Enki, suggested that they use their knowledge of genetic engineering to create this primitive worker from the existing hominids on the planet. The quote from the tablets is 'the being that we need already exists; all that we have to do is put our mark on him.' So, the project was approved, and, as echoed in the Bible, the tablets tell us 'let us fashion the Adam,' a process which was led by Enki and their chief medical officer, someone called Ninharsag, who, after much trial and error, held up the perfect model. This was the prototype Adamu, literally translated as 'worker' in a scene depicted on one of the ancient Sumerian cylinder seals."

Ruth had paused to let the information sink in. There was not much feedback from either Sophia or Brian.

"So, what you are saying," Brian eventually said, "is that the horizontal insertion of bacteria you referred to earlier was in fact a cloning process, a genetic engineering, performed by the Annunaki?"

"Yes, I'm not saying this is true, it's just one option. What is true is that the Gods' interference with man's evolution is referred to throughout history and in all cultures. The Book of Enoch, for example, also talks about fallen angels and a giant race born to those who had mated with the angels or Gods, the Nephilim or Titans in Greek and Roman mythology. The fundamental question is whether the 'manipulators' simply have an alien origin and agenda or whether they are the spiritual Gods recorded throughout history, literally the Gods of Olympus."

The lines had fallen silent.

"That's a little more than a fundamental question," Sophia had whispered. "It's rather defining."

"I'm not sure I get you," Brian had said.

"What I mean is simply this," Sophia had continued, "if this was an alien event, then we might imagine that we are dealing with the remnants of that race, those left here, perhaps, to manipulate, something one-dimensional. If there is a more spiritual explanation, then we are dealing with entirely different forces, both good and evil."

There had been a long silence before Brian asked, "You said something earlier, Ruth, about others with superior DNA?"

"Yes, well it's a sort of an addendum but I am not sure it gives us any answers. You see, when you look at mankind's development, historically, there has been a series of incredible individuals, individuals who have literally changed the course of history. Jesus Christ, of course, but others at key points in the movement of the constellations, Pythagoras, the Buddha, Mohammed, Alexander the Great, and so the list goes on."

"What's your point, Ruth?" Sophia had cut in rather bluntly.

"I thought that might help answer our dilemma but it doesn't really," Ruth had said quietly. "I suppose that I didn't know that there had been others with similar healing powers to Jesus, for example. The trouble is that we are trying to answer questions that have baffled the greatest of minds for centuries…" Her voice had reduced to almost a whisper.

Brian had broken the silence. "Okay, what if, for example, the Annunaki story is real, irrespective of where they are now? What if they are still here, and still manipulating us but in a much more subtle way, those whom Valeriya described as the manipulators, those who effectively control the planet, those who decided that if the planet is to survive to meet their long-term gains, then population control was seen as an imperative, hence the project, the prophets, where we find ourselves today? What if there are those amongst us who have that superior DNA, or more of it, a breed within a breed so to speak, who perhaps know that they have it, and it gives them the edge over the rest of us? They rule by proxy, from the shadows, they sit behind all those conspiracy theories and play with humanity. Surely, if we find the prophets, maybe we'll find the answer to that question?"

"I doubt it," Sophia had cut in. "Remember that Valeriya told you that the prophets had to believe, they had to be convincing, credible, so they won't know the full picture and certainly won't be conscious of their DNA."

"So how do we know if these people, these manipulators, are conscious of their own abilities, so to speak?" Brian had asked.

Sophia had scoffed with some cynicism. "I would have though that was pretty fucking obvious," she said quietly. "Their efforts to kill Valeriya and my mother are sufficient evidence, it's very meticulous and very conscious. So, as well as finding the prophets, we also need to find the source, both ends of the puzzle need to be ratified. I am probably the only one that can do that part, I'm just not quite sure where to begin. That's all we can do for now, the question of origin, these alien or spiritual Gods, well, we'll just have to wait and see. I am not sure which is worse."

2065, Death Speaks, Amid Semen

Kazuo and K sat quietly in the small atrium that dominated Nathan's private residence in Vienna. Despite their familiarity with these surroundings, the pair looked uncomfortable, particularly Kazuo who had still not regained his composure since his encounter with Alexandra. K was also worried about her companion — it was as if his outer skin had been peeled off, his energy skinned from him like an animal to reveal a pallid and plagued inner fabric, something that might burst at any point to reveal a gangrenous soul. The pair shifted uneasily like a couple of truant children outside the headmaster's study. The sound of a small bell crept out from under one of the thick, mahogany doors, and the pair stood up abruptly and followed the sound of the bell into the room. Nathan was seated by the fireplace where the flames threw shadows across the room like ghostly replicas. He pointed toward two upright chairs opposite him and the pair sat down, somewhat awkwardly, not quite sure what tirade of recrimination they might expect.

"So," Nathan said quietly, "the Englishman eluded you and the scent has gone?"

K cleared her throat and was about to provide an explanation but Nathan raised his hand, the wrinkles around his wrists bunching like creased linen.

"You need to understand," he continued, "that this will not be as easy or straightforward as we might imagine, not because this Englishman, this Brian McCarthy fellow, has suddenly become a superhero, he is more of an irritant, but because parts of the puzzle are highly perceptive and intelligent. Some of that — what shall we call it? — let's just say that some of that intuitive DNA will rub off on those around them. So, it is frustrating that we have lost the scent for now but there are strange events occurring which we need to tend to. The pace or tempo is quickening; the stakes have trebled, quadrupled even."

Nathan let his words circulate, their resonance mingling with the heavy, leather-bound volumes lining the bookshelves around three corners of the room.

"I also see that this experience has left its mark on you, Kazuo," Nathan continued. "Perhaps better to learn this unpleasant lesson now so that you can prepare for your next encounter, as I am not, truly, in a confident enough position to tell you what beast you might encounter next, what type of Frankenstein you might confront during the next round."

The door to the study opened and a butler appeared with a tray of tea, which he placed on a small table next to Nathan. The butler moved around the back of Nathan's chair and prepared to pour but Nathan waved him away.

"I'll be mother, thank you, you are excused."

The austere servant clenched his jaw momentarily and left the room. Nathan took some time to pour the tea and K noticed that his hands were steady as he passed a cup to each of them. The silence hung between them like carcasses in an abattoir.

"Now," Nathan continued, "here is what I have for you both, our next chapter together, possibly our last chapter together, that would be a good epitaph for me were this to prove to be so."

Nathan took a delicate sip from his teacup before continuing, "I have summarized the following from what we know and from certain energy fields that we can detect at work. The woman, Alexandra, was mad, yes, destroyed internally and externally, because, well, just because, leave it at that, and she is dead now, so, some progress. However, the three prophets remain at large and we must assume that they are in a state that might fluctuate between perfect sanity or something similar to that encountered by Kazuo in New York."

Kazuo leaned forward in his chair to offer a comment but Nathan raised his hand.

"Let me finish," he said quietly. "Now, my supposition is that the carer in that apartment was probably more than just that, possibly a daughter, given what some preliminary investigations have uncovered since the building was destroyed by fire. The police questioned neighbours who confirmed there was a relative of some sort. And we must also assume that this possible daughter is aware of the program, and who knows what hereditary traits she might have within her. That is to be determined and will be in time. We must also ask ourselves if the Englishman and this daughter have joined forces, an unlikely pair, maybe, but it's possible nevertheless."

Nathan paused and K said very quietly, "We also assume this to be the case."

Nathan looked up at the pair in front of him, over the rim of his teacup, almost as if he had forgotten that there were others in the room, lost in his own soliloquy. He murmured something to himself and replaced his cup on the tray.

"Now," he said, "let me tell you what has been happening and where, and what I would like you to do. The first thing to report is that we have picked up a considerable increase in telepathic activity over the last few days. Sadly, our resources are feeble in comparison to whoever is concocting these messages, but they do seem to be one way. That is to say that certain energy fields are being thrown across the curvature of the Earth but are falling on fallow ground or, simply, I should say, falling into space, dropping into the deep oceans, not, as we might fear, bouncing back off similar physiological receivers. However, two significant events have occurred; the first is a report of a miracle from a priest in Cuzco, Peru, by a man who carries a similar physical profile to the prophet Francisco and who might be about the right age. Kazuo, I want you to go there, verify if this is the case, and kill him. Oh, and kill the person who reported the miracle — a woman, one Fermina Marquez, his lover. This should be a simple enough assignment.

"Now, the second event is a little odd to fathom but might be significant given what you found in New York. Since these telepathic releases have been firing across the electromagnetic spectrum, we have received reports from a contact in Thailand. These are reports of a woman who has been in the care of a monastery, a woman who has been in a coma for over ten years but who woke from her coma some days ago, the dates coinciding with these energy strikes, a woman who has since been scribbling strange texts and talking in unintelligible tongues. My initial thoughts are that this could be the other twin, the other half of Alexandra. I want you to look, K, and, of course, make a judgment accordingly."

K nodded across the small space between them. Nathan picked up his cup and saucer but then replaced it, as if he had overlooked something.

"One other thing," he added, "en route to Thailand, you are to visit England, masquerade as a policewoman, we will make those arrangements, of course, and visit this Englishman's wife. He will undoubtedly contact her at some point, so she may provide us with a lead. You can play the concerned detective and perhaps throw in something about Interpol, missing people, something like that, you know the score."

K nodded once again as Nathan reached for his cup. He turned his gaze toward the fireplace and was momentarily lost in the fire's energy, the wood shifting autonomously as the flames leapt and parried like fencing adversaries. Nathan looked back at the two Ks as if to say *why are you still here?*

The pair stood up and Kazuo cleared his throat. "Nathan," he said, "we normally work together; we will be many miles apart on this next phase."

Nathan considered this point for a moment and stood up slowly, his long, elderly limbs unwinding from the armchair like an old serpent. He took a step forward so that he was facing Kazuo and placed a hand on his shoulder.

"Yes, my friend," he said with some affection, "but these tasks are within your gift, and besides, I can only entrust these final, decisive acts to my most trusted." He turned to face the fire and the two Ks left the room.

Far off in Cuzco, Augusto Garcia glanced at his watch in the half-light, the small, luminous dials telling him that it was, as he already knew, still the small hours of the morning, just after three to be precise. The previous week had been one of turmoil for him as he had wrestled with a torrent, a barrage of psychological babble that superseded his normal voices. There was a new voice, a shrill, nervous voice that swept through his consciousness and entered his dreams, a relentless voice that the alcohol seemed unable to abate, a voice unlike any he had encountered for many years. Over the years he had always been able to pull a blanket across his telepathic space, a poultice which had formed a metaphorical mucous, a temporary cast around this potential injury.

He glanced at Fermina across the small bedroom from where he sat by the window as a darkness enveloped him. A sixth sense told him what he already knew, that his recent miracle, that recent gesture of love and kindness was already a curse, not for Fermina, not for her health anyway, but for their life together. It told him that to keep her safe, he would have to leave her or, as sure as he was of his love for her, he was sure that the ricochet from his energy discharge would burst back into their lives like a destructive phoenix. He could smell the pack of descending wolves as strongly as he could smell his own fear. He glanced once more at Fermina, her soft scent filling the air like a drug, his drug, his addiction, the only one not worthy of repentance. He lay down next to her once more and watched the small dials move through the early hours as dawn emerged across the hills around Cuzco.

Fermina woke early as usual to find her lover gazing at her. A slow smile swept across her features like a light aria, and she reached over to squeeze his hand.

"Are you working today?" he whispered.

"Yes," she yawned, "and what will my wicked gambler be doing?"

"Walking in the hills," he replied, "and then gambling, wickedly."

"Mmnnn," she smiled through her drowsiness, "wait here."

Fermina left the bed and he heard her splashing water onto her face and then her toothbrush before she came back and lay beside him.

"Look," she said gently, "no, feel," and she took his hand and moved it under her nightdress. "Can you feel how wet I am? I want you to fuck me before I go to work and then I will smell you on my skin, inside me all day, every time I go to the bathroom I will smell you inside me. Maybe I will never shower again. What would you say to that, my beloved?"

Augusto smiled and moved his hand against her thighs.

"Never again might be dramatic," he said with a smile, "but never again today is a start."

Fermina pulled her flimsy nightdress over her head and turned her body toward him, shifting her torso so that her legs moved across him and so that her breasts were just above his face, her skin blending with the faint morning sunlight that threw particles of dust into strands of focus. She reached in between her thighs and moved Augusto into her.

"Don't move," she whispered, "I am going to move you in me until I am ready."

Augusto raised his hands to touch her thighs but she caught them in hers and pushed them back onto the bed.

"My game," she whispered.

Augusto closed his eyes as she moved above him, her breasts moving slowly in front of his mouth, inches away. He could hear their mutual movements, the moisture between her thighs chaffing against his lower stomach as she pushed down on him. He opened his eyes momentarily to find her eyes closed, her teeth biting down hard on her lower lip, her forehead clenched in concentration as her excitement rose. She stopped moving and clenched her internal muscles around him, a small cry of pleasure creeping from the corners of her mouth as his orgasm moved inside her. He sensed tears around the corner of his eyes and blinked as they moved silently across his cheeks. She remained in that position for a few minutes before leaving him suddenly with a giggle. She stepped across to their chest of drawers and pulled out fresh underwear, pulling her panties on as quickly as she could.

"I want to keep it all in there," she said, smiling, "all day."

Augusto fell into a doze and only woke again when he heard the front door closing. He glanced toward his bedside table where he could smell the coffee she had left for him. There was a small note next to the cup, which he picked up and read.

"When I can't smell you anymore, I am coming back home for more!" she had written simply, in her bold handwriting. She signed it, "your beloved." He clutched the note to his chest as his mind told him what needed to be done, what he had decided that very morning. Two hours later, he settled into his seat in the airport departure lounge, a small duffle bag between his feet. He had not left a note for Fermina, no few words could even begin to describe his loss.

Jan had not seen Brenda in person since she had received the message from Brian that day, which she recalled was not so long ago, but seemed to belong to a different era. She had explained what had happened to Brenda and simply asked her to be patient, said that she had to reconcile certain things in her own mind, and, of course, between herself and Brian.

"But he's gone off somewhere," she had explained over the telephone. "Gone for a drive, he told me, that's hardly helpful."

"He'll resurface," Brenda had said gently. "Men and their egos, love, that's a problem."

"So, what do you suggest?" Jan had asked her.

"Nothing, just wait, he'll have to come home at some point, he probably just needs space, as you do, too, that's fine, you know where I am."

That conversation had taken place less than two weeks earlier, but it felt far off to Jan, almost as if recent events were happening to another person, like she was reading this sad story in a novel or watching events unfold on the big screen. On this day, however, Jan found herself outside Brenda's door once more; she had stayed away for almost two weeks but found herself in need of a friend, another's touch, or at least some support. She rang the doorbell unannounced and was surprised to find Brenda looking dishevelled, her eyes bloodshot, her mascara smeared across her cheeks. Although mid-morning, she was not dressed and looked as if she had barely slept. She stepped to one side to allow Jan to enter the apartment.

"My God," Jan said, "you've been crying. What's wrong, what's happened?"

Brenda sat down and attempted a smile. "Oh, nothing really, an old friend died yesterday, an old lover actually. There were things that had been said, things that had not been said, things that should have been said, but egos and events intervened, and then time passes, and then, suddenly, they are not there anyway, snatched from within our grasp. We are left wondering why we never made that extra effort, never took that conciliatory step, a step you can't take with the dead." She paused and wiped tears from her eyes. "Anyway, I was low last night and started to write a poem which only seems to have made things worse!"

A couple of sheaves of paper were laying on the table in front of her, which Jan picked up to read.

"What's it called?" she asked.

"Death Speaks," Brenda replied, attempting a smile. "Catchy, don't you think?"

Jan cast her eyes across the verses.

Death spoke to me today from her villa by the great lake,
A busy night of carnage resting gently on her brow,
Her religious sheen of hypocrisy creased by hope.
She raised a bejewelled finger from her lap
And scratched my conscience, a wound reopened,
A memory undone in the blink of mortality, my running sore.
I have been busier than you know, she smiled,
Whilst you chase your dreams, I have been harvesting,
Others' overripe fruit, their final breaths
Falling around my feet like dead apples,
Invested with disease from busy worms,
The innocent shackled to my purpose,
Fate drawing chalk marks in the sand, another casket.
You have not heard, have you, why would you,
Why should you, she sighed, as if a feigning propriety
Might forestall her shallow victory, another
Life crushed in abeyance, the eulogy forgotten,
Tears dried in time, tangled wreaths of wretched
Love rotting in dark corners, a whispered memory
Crouching in a tortured soul.

And so she spoke from her tangential recline,
Busier than you think, she mused,
Her soul sits in my palm now, your memories

Tainted by my haste to claim such a prize,
Unfinished business in your life
Snatched like candy from your guilt,
Your arrogance compromised as you sipped wine
And plotted riches, playing for time.

Perhaps you will weep now, she cackled,
Blood gathering like storm clouds in her scarlet eyes,
But you weep for yourself, swaddled by weakness,
Drowning in hypocrisy, you sob for shipwrecked memories,
You wail for inflicted pain, for lost years
When shallow reparation draws comfort from betrayal,
But you are too late, she lies with me now,
Silent, your lies casting shadows across your soul.
She has found peace, and I will wait for you my friend,

Suffer now as she did.

"It's beautiful," she said. "Sad but beautiful."

Brenda stood up and ran her fingers through her hair. "Well, make sure you don't make the same mistake with your Brian, whatever happens between you both," she said quietly.

"Come," said Jan, "let's get you cleaned up."

She led Brenda by the hand into her bedroom and pulled her clothes off, which she threw in the corner. She ran the water in the shower and then quickly undressed herself, easing Brenda into the shower cubicle where she gently manoeuvred her around the small space while she washed her hair and then soaped her down, rubbing a soft sponge across her back and shoulders, watching the bubbles gather like old memories around their feet. She kissed Brenda gently between her shoulder blades and then towelled her down before dressing once again. She wrapped a robe around Brenda and then sat her down in a chair, positioning herself opposite in another chair so that she could place Brenda's feet in her lap and apply nail polish. The two women had not spoken, but serenity had resurfaced in Brenda and the lines across her face had disappeared.

"So?" Brenda asked after a few minutes, her question addressed to the top of Jan's head, which was bowed over Brenda's feet. "So, what news from Brian?"

Jan raised her head briefly. "Nothing," she said simply. "He disappeared off the face of the planet, I don't know what to say, there's not much to say." A gentle silence fell between the two women. "But…" she said.

"What?" Brenda asked. "Something has happened, you didn't come over here to do my nails. Spit it out."

"Well, I did want to mention something," Jan continued. Brenda raised her eyebrows for her to continue. "Well, out of the blue yesterday, I had a visitor — a detective, she told me, from Interpol — a tall, gangly woman with a very slight limp."

"And?" Brenda urged her to continue.

"Well, she turned up out of the blue, hard to tell where she was from. She had a badge and all that, an ID, but wants to know where Brian is, have I heard from him, there are people worried about him, all that sort of thing. Apparently, she told me, he was in some way involved with a fire at an apartment in New York, caught on a CCTV image; she didn't say that he was in trouble, but it had been arson and they just wanted to question him. It all seemed very odd." She paused and dipped the small brush into the pot of nail polish.

"And?" Brenda urged her once again. "There's more."

"Well, I obviously told her that I thought that Brian was in Las Vegas, that I had not heard from him; I didn't tell her anything about our personal disaster."

"So, it's odd," said Brenda, "but not impossibly odd."

"I don't know," said Jan, "there was just something about her; I felt as if she was interrogating me, that she wanted to see if I knew something else, although I obviously don't know what that something else is. But there was a menace about her, a difference — it was almost as if she has another layer of skin, a cloak of violence or capacity for violence she carries with ease. I felt frightened by her. She left me numbers to call if I heard from Brian, she even hinted that Brian might be in danger — all very odd."

"So, then what?" Brenda asked.

"Nothing, she left. I felt as if I had been visited by a cold, icy wind, by something more than a mere detective from Interpol." Jan looked up into Brenda's face and smiled. "There, those toes look a lot better now." Brenda leaned forward and kissed Jan on her forehead. "And then, blow me down," Jan continued, "a few hours later he calls me, tells me that he's in Peru of all places but can't tell me why. And yet I had the strangest feeling that he is in danger, that there's something going on that he won't tell me. He started asking after me as if he might not see me again, very strange, very unsettling. I asked him when he was coming home, he said that he couldn't tell me, and then he starts banging on about financial arrangements, a large sum of money and where it was, and then I told him about the detective and he seemed to panic, and then the line went dead and that was that, nothing conclusive."

"So," Brenda asked, "did you tell this woman, this detective?"

"No, not yet," Jan said quietly. "I was not sure what to do so I came over here to paint your toes." Jan sighed and absentmindedly rubbed the instep of Brenda's right foot.

"What do you think I should do?" she asked Brenda.

2065, The Irony of Father Bonifacio

Fermina did not tell anyone that Augusto had disappeared into thin air. She wondered if she held her breath for as long as she could whether he might reappear and kiss the back of her neck as he always did or trace an imaginary picture across the palm of her hand with his fingers. She was used to him heading off into the hills, occasionally for one or two days, but never without leaving word. She played out certain scenarios in her mind and even looked under the bed and under their heavy wardrobe for the note he must have left. The small note that would tell her he was walking the Inca Trail for a few days, that he would be back by the end of the week, that she was his beloved, that she made him catch his breath and miss a heartbeat. Perhaps the note was left too close to the window, she told herself.

Yes, that's most likely, a gust of wind carried his note away, but he will return on a similar gust of wind, on another, similar gust to that which brought him into my life.

Despite this optimism, Fermina knew that he had removed his few belongings, belongings that were not needed for hiking in the mountains. This simple fact drove tears from her eyes as she lay in bed, and cut furrows of despair across her soul as if a giant plough had been pulled across her chest, slicing her rationale into deep, logical trenches.

Despite these undisputed facts, Fermina hung onto a stubborn, metaphorical candle and attended early morning Mass where she beseeched the Virgin Mary to intercede on her behalf, to restore the balance in her life. At work, her friends made enquiries after Augusto, which she brushed aside, her mouth attempting to form a smile as if to imply that all was well, that he was in such and such a place although she never actually said where that place might be. And so the first week passed and every day she tried to forget a little more about him, to drain him from her life like emptying a sink of cold dishwater. But these efforts proved fruitless, and despair settled across her forehead like an old record stuck in a groove, the needle catching at her mind with remorseless predictability. Besides, that particular, metaphorical sink was blocked; some things are not meant to be washed away, to dilute in grubby drains, her memories were too fresh and raw, and too original to be fraudulent; something had happened, she knew instinctively, just as she knew that Augusto was not an ordinary man, she had always known that.

After a week or so, Fermina bumped into Father Bonifacio after Mass. Although he might have lost that sheen that fell across his early years in life, the tenderness he held for Fermina had never diminished, and it was not difficult for him to detect a deep sadness in her, crouching around her movements like glue, confining her spirit, which had retreated under her skin. When he asked her how she was, she simply shook her head and tears welled behind her eyes. He looked around for Augusto who normally appeared by her side after Mass but he was nowhere to be seen. He offered to come and see her later that day, during the late morning, and she nodded without saying anything, a crease of hope passing across her features like a shadow.

It was probably only the shadow of false hope at best, but it might be enough to sustain her during the long hours of Sunday morning when she normally wandered the streets with Augusto, occasionally stopping to chat with friends or drink coffee on the café balconies around the Plaza de Armas. On this Sunday, she walked home alone, the cobbled streets echoing her footsteps, reminding her of her loneliness, of her solitude. It was odd, some of the narrow streets in Cuzco held strange memories for her, memories of their collective footsteps echoing up the walls and into the shadows only to return like bubbles of oxygen rising to the surface. Somehow, her footsteps sounded brittle today, sharp and unkind, even their solitary echo reminded her of her deep sadness instead of cosseting her in their usual embrace.

When Fermina arrived home, she paused outside her door to find her keys but then realized that the door was open, a shaft of light squeezing itself between the door and its frame. Although an oversight, this was hardly unusual in Cuzco where the local inhabitants often left their doors open and people came and went as they pleased. That said, Fermina was sure that she had closed the door when she left for Mass, and she felt her heart jump inside her jacket, a surge of hope that her beloved man had returned, that she would find him gazing out of their window across the city, which dropped away dramatically from their small, second-floor bedroom balcony.

Her pace quickened and she pushed at the door, calling his name as she stepped over the threshold. She moved into the small living room, which was empty, and glanced into the kitchen, half expecting to see a steaming kettle on their small stove. She felt the threads of panic and despair tugging at the back of her mind as she rushed toward the bedroom door, her last hope of finding Augusto at home. As she entered the room, she momentarily caught sight of the side of a hand — a blunt, heavy hand that looked more like the sort of short axe that an Apache might have used to scalp his foe. The blow struck her across the back of her neck and she was vaguely aware of the same hand catching her as she lost consciousness.

Kazuo lay Fermina on the bed and walked methodically back to the front door, which he closed quietly. He then ignited the gas stove and put a small kettle on to heat, noting where the gas bottle was stored on a small ledge outside the kitchen window.

This place is still medieval, he thought, as he checked the few kitchen cupboards and opened a few drawers in the living room.

About 20 minutes later, while Kazuo watched on, Fermina regained consciousness and found herself facing the open window of the bedroom. A stretch of heavy tape had been flattened across her mouth, and she was having a hard time breathing through her nose. Her arms had been pulled around the back of the wooden chair and tied individually by her wrists. She could wiggle her fingers but the ropes around her wrists were rigid. Kazuo had tied her feet together and these were also secured to the bottom of the chair; her scope for any lateral movement was minimal, although she could move her head from side to side, but he saw her wince as this only exacerbated the pain she still felt from the heavy blow. Kazuo had positioned her in front of the bedroom window so that she had a good view of part of the city sprawled before her like a sleeping animal, the beast slowly waking from the excesses of Saturday night.

She would only be able to hear noises coming from the kitchen and the opening and closing of drawers. Kazuo caught sight of her struggling to pivot her position, trying to catch a glimpse of her assailant, but he had taped her torso to the chair with heavy, insulating tape. This had been Kazuo's intent, to create fear and uncertainty, to let the woman see all that was familiar to her, her home, the streets where she grew up, but to deny her sight of him. He would question her from behind and remain anonymous; she might see his hands occasionally, but that would be all. Besides, he was not expecting this to last very long. She looked average; she would not be very hard to crack even if that proved necessary. Her lover might return at any minute and save him the bother of breaking her body and her will.

Kazuo had found a few rudimentary items in one of the kitchen cupboards and set these up on a small side table behind Fermina. He arranged things as if he was planning a tea party, and Fermina's discomfort and fear grew as she listened to his footsteps moving back and forth from the kitchen to the bedroom, his shoes occasionally murmuring to the floorboards as he padded this way and that, like an enclosed lion pacing in front of the bars of its cage.

Kazuo spoke only rudimentary Spanish, but he was confident that he would only need a few questions to ascertain the whereabouts of the target. He could then dispose of the woman quickly and get on with the main task at hand. He shifted the small table that was positioned behind Fermina to one side and then stepped toward the back of the chair as if he was stepping in to punch a boxing bag in the gym. He delivered two short jabs to her lower back through the openings in the back of the chair, below her shoulder blades, and felt two of her ribs crack under his onslaught. The blows were so sudden and so heavy that Fermina's body momentarily shut down in shock before she had time to catch her breath and before the pain brought vomit into her mouth, which she tried to swallow but which then rose again in her throat and into her nasal passages.

Kazuo reached around the front of her face and removed the tape, allowing her to vomit onto the floor in front of her. He picked up a damp cloth from the small table and wiped her mouth and nose, almost as if he was tending to a small child who had dribbled food onto its bib. He wiped her mouth with great care and gentleness, knowing that such extreme violence followed by care and attention would only confuse the woman and, ultimately, add to her insecurity and fear. He walked methodically back into the kitchen and ran warm water over the cloth to rinse off the vomit before returning to the back of Fermina's chair where he wiped her forehead briefly and then the back of her neck.

He pushed the blurred image of Augusto, which he had received from Nathan, in front of her face.

"This is your lover, yes?" he asked.

Fermina could still barely breathe and Kazuo had no doubt her ribs cried out in agony as she fought to regain her composure. She shook her head, her mind fighting to align her thoughts with any sort of rationale. Kazuo took a step back behind the chair and delivered another blow to her right side, in exactly the same place as his first. The unbearable pain sent a spasm through Fermina and she lost consciousness. Kazuo lifted her head off her chest and quickly examined her face. He was annoyed with himself; he had hit her too hard and now he would have to wait for a few moments. He walked back into the kitchen and poured hot water over a tea bag he had found in the cupboard above the sink. He noticed a small blackboard and chalk to the right of the cooker with a short list of groceries, and, in one corner, someone had outlined a love-heart in red chalk. He looked around for the red chalk but could only see white chalk. He was not sure what he might have done had he found the red chalk, but it was irrelevant as was her list of groceries; she would not be visiting the shops again.

Kazuo took his tea back into the bedroom and sat down behind Fermina, occasionally sipping from the cup as the bustle of Cuzco filtered through the open window. He would have preferred sugar with his tea but had not found any in the cupboard. After a few more minutes, he heard Fermina groan as she regained consciousness. He put his cup to one side and moved the image in front of her face once again.

"Where is he?" he asked quietly. "Is he coming home today, where is he?" he repeated.

Fermina shook her head slowly. "I don't know," she whispered. "Please, don't hurt me, I don't know."

"I have already hurt you, Miss Fermina Marquez," Kazuo said, his words uttered close to the side of her head, "and I will continue to do so unless you tell me where he is."

"What has he done to you?" she asked innocently. "Why are you looking for him?"

Kazuo did not want a protracted conversation so he replaced the tape across her mouth with a sigh.

"It's a simple question," he said to her, "very simple. Just tell me where he is, if he is coming home today, and then we can make you better, get you to a doctor."

It might have been his rudimentary Spanish that led Kazuo to choose those particular words, but those five words, "get you to a doctor," struck a dramatic chord in Fermina.

As his words filtered through her misery, a second voice took up her cause, a voice of reason and logic that told her in no uncertainty what she already knew. There would be no doctor, this man with hands like sledgehammers was a professional, her life would end shortly, and she must get to that point with some dignity and do whatever was necessary to protect her beloved Augusto.

Your life is over, she told herself. *You have nothing to bargain with so don't bargain, close down and pray, retreat inside your memories, dissolve into your soul.*

Her tormentor did not seem to notice that his victim had undergone a metamorphosis, and he was still busy behind Fermina. He sounded heavy and squat, solid, like a railway sleeper, she thought to herself, but also light on his feet; she had no experience of such things, but she could smell the inherent violence he brought with him, his metaphorical briefcase full of raw extremes. She heard the hiss of the gas and found confusion and terror clouding her judgment once again as she pondered the source. She wondered if he had found the small, portable gas stove in one of the cupboards, the stove Augusto often carried on his hiking trips.

"Now," he said to the back of her head, "the same question, where is this man? I won't hit you again, I promise."

Fermina felt him grip one of her hands behind the chair and then an excruciating, sharp pain as he gripped her index finger between a pair of pruning clippers and removed her finger below the knuckle. Fermina thought she would faint once again but her body stayed with her as she heard a tiny, light thump as the severed finger fell onto the wooden floor. White heat boiled against the wound and cauterized the bleeding. She screamed in agony but her cries were muffled by the tape across her mouth.

"Are you ready to talk now?" he asked the back of her head. "Or shall we take another?"

Fermina nodded in desperation and she caught a glimpse of his hand in front of her face as he removed the tape.

"So, where is he and will he be home soon?" he asked once more.

And then a strange thing happened to Fermina as she prepared to answer his question. The sun, which had slowly risen across the Cuzco sky since her return from early morning Mass, caught the edge of the tarnished metal window frame so that it momentarily lit up like a mirror, and she caught his reflection behind her — his small table of accessories, his cup of tea, the way his head sat on his broad shoulders like a pumpkin.

That's better, now I see you, she said to herself. *I am not frightened of you anymore, and perhaps you are not quite as clever as you think you are.*

"He left," she said simply, "so, no, he will not be coming home."

Kazuo wrinkled his brow and glanced at the back of her head once again. He was surprised at her sudden composure and felt as if he had been disenfranchised, that a third dimension had suddenly changed the order of events, that he was no longer the master of ceremonies. He pushed the tape back across her mouth and grabbed at her hand once again, fumbling with her fingers until he managed to get her middle finger between the crude blades and severed a second finger. Fermina lost consciousness before the finger arrived on the wooden floorboards, and so she did not scream internally as he ran the blue flame of the tiny gas stove across the bloody stump to stem the flow of blood. Kazuo stood up in frustration and walked around to the front of the chair, pausing to lift her head from her chest. He shook his head in disgust, as much in himself as in anything else.

Kazuo's predatory senses returned seconds later as he heard footsteps on the short flight of stairs outside the front door, footsteps that were obviously moving toward the second-floor landing. He moved out of the bedroom, closing the door quietly and then lifted the catch on the front door to enable any visitor to enter without a key. He returned to the bedroom where he shrank into a corner by the door to the bathroom. He heard a knock on the door and the shuffling of feet. A second knock followed and then a voice called Fermina's name.

"It's me," the voice called again and then Kazuo heard a hand on the door handle and the heels of what sounded like smart, office shoes on the floorboards.

"Fermina," the voice called once again and Kazuo could imagine the visitor peering into the kitchen, "it's me, hello, anyone home?"

Kazuo crouched in the shadows as he heard a hand on the bedroom door, and then the door was pushed open gingerly, with some apprehension, and a man with a neat little goatee entered the bedroom. It took him a few moments to focus and to comprehend the scene before him, the back of Fermina's head, her arms and legs bound, the small table to one side of the chair, the gas stove burning in isolation. He stopped in his tracks, frozen by confusion, and Kazuo could practically see the tentacles of fear sliding across his skin; he fumbled for his spectacles, his hands shaking. After what seemed like minutes but was only one or two seconds, this man crossed the distance between the bedroom door and Fermina, grabbing at the back of the chair to pull her around to face him. As he did so, Kazuo struck him viciously across the back of his neck and he crumpled like a rag doll.

Kazuo nudged the man with the edge of his shoe and then tore off a strip of tape that he bound across his mouth. He glanced down at the man at his feet and picked up the image of Augusto he had left on the small table. He noted the similar features, the apposite age, the small goatee. The man in the photograph was not wearing spectacles but that did not mean much. He rummaged in the man's pockets but only found a few coins. Kazuo glanced at his watch and decided that he had spent long enough in Fermina's home; the job was done. He quickly untied her ropes and lifted her onto the bed; he placed her two severed fingers next to her hands.

He moved the chair back to the kitchen and returned the few items to where they belonged. He then moved the man's body from the floor onto the bed so that the two looked like lovers enjoying each other on a long Sunday morning. He then moved back into the kitchen and removed the pipe from the back of the gas cooker; he nodded in satisfaction as the smell of gas immediately filtered into the enclosed space. Kazuo picked up an old magazine from a table in the living room and shoved it into the top of the toaster, forcing down the internal element so that it burned red. He left the house quickly, knowing that he might only have one minute before the magazine caught alight and ignited the gas in the small kitchen. He walked quickly away from the steps and slipped into the shadows at the end of the cobbled street. Forty-five seconds, he noted, as an orange fireball burst across the Cuzco skyline. He nodded to himself with satisfaction and walked back toward the Plaza de Armas. He felt like something to eat.

Unbeknown to each other, Brian and Augusto Garcia were not far away from each other in Lima on the Monday morning when news of the gas explosion in Cuzco was reported in the inner pages of the *Peruvian Times*. The news did not even register with Brian, but Augusto felt the walls of desperation close around him as he read what to most would have been an innocuous article.

> *The calm and tranquility of Cuzco was rocked by a gas explosion yesterday morning when two people lost their lives in this tragic episode. Police investigating the incident reported finding a faulty gas pipe in the remains of the building where the couple, named as Fermina Marquez and Augusto Garcia, were found dead in the bedroom. A police investigation is ongoing and the Fire Department will submit a full report to the coroner...* And so the report continued.

Kazuo read the same article as he waited to board his flight from Cuzco to Lima. He nodded to himself with some satisfaction as his flight was announced over the intercom. He felt his phone vibrate in his jacket pocket and found K's face smiling at him.

"Well done," she said, "but don't get too comfortable, this Brian character is in Lima. I just got a call from his wife. We'll get you a hotel name and location over the next few hours, so you can finish that piece of work as well." Kazuo nodded at the screen. "I'm moving to Chiang Mai," she added, "so I'll contact you from there." Kazuo put the phone back in his inner pocket and pulled out his boarding tag.

2065, Chiang Mai, Thailand, The Monozygotic Twin

The prophet Parvati had been named after the Indian goddess known in Hindu teachings as the daughter of the Himalayas. After the prophets' escape, it was perhaps not a surprise that she spent some time in hiding in Tibet where she took the name Tara after the female Buddha Kwan Yin before moving to Thailand where she became a Buddhist nun. She took refuge in Chiang Mai where she was hopeful that the 300 Buddhist temples and millions of tourists each year would provide a safe backdrop for her to remain anonymous and secure. At the age of 45, Tara sat down outside the northern entrance to the ubosot at the temple of Wat Phra Singh in Chiang Mai and closed her eyes. Like her fellow prophets, she was constantly beset by voices and images but had managed to control aspects of what she now felt was a form of insanity through various forms of Buddhist meditation, particularly vipassana. She hoped to find prajna and thereby extinguish her afflictions, which was how she reflected on her powers, and bring about bodhi, her enlightenment or awakening.

When Tara sat down that day, it was simply because she felt a little dizzy and she asked one of her fellow nuns to fetch her some water. When she returned, Tara seemed to have fallen into a deep sleep and the other nuns were unable to wake her. What was even more bizarre was that Tara had fallen asleep sitting in an upright position with a straight back and neck, not completely rigid as in rigor mortis but seemingly in control of her neck and back muscles. The other nuns were able to call a tuk-tuk and move Tara back to their quarters where they sat her on some cushions and waited for her to wake up. When night fell and Tara was still asleep, they managed to get her into bed and kept watch over her during the night, two or three of her closer friends agreeing to share the watch and pray quietly for their companion.

A few more days passed in the same fashion, after which a medical examination took place. All those who examined Tara were able to surmise that she was asleep or in a coma, seemingly in no distress, and that basic medical care should be administered until she woke up. No medical explanation was forthcoming as to why she might have fallen into a coma. The nuns were given the option of caring for Tara in situ or installing her in one of the hospitals in Chiang Mai; not surprisingly, they decided on the former.

What some of the medical team failed to report to the nuns, but which eventually percolated through gossip and intrigue, was that although Tara was in good physical health, hers was a case of *dextrocardia*, a congenital defect in that her heart was situated on the right side of her body. In fact, if the doctors had performed further examinations, they would have realized that Tara's case was one of *situs inversus* or *situs transversus* in that all her major organs were reversed from their normal positions, a condition sometimes found in identical or mirrored twins.

As the days slipped into weeks and months, Tara remained asleep or in a coma and her care became an inherent part of life for the other nuns who kept a constant vigil over her. They maintained their vigil even during the small hours, should she wake up and wonder why she was still not sitting on the wooden bench outside the ubosot of Wat Phra Singh. However, what did start to change, as she entered her sixth year in a coma, was her appearance and some of her habitual movements. As in the case of Alexandra, Tara's body began an extraordinary metamorphosis and evolved into a harlequin of patterns like her twin sister — the old and new juxtapose, the new seemingly rejuvenating, like a snake shedding its skin, the old falling to decay, her skin hanging in folds like rags on beggars, portions of her hair vibrant and glossy, other parts grey and dull like a heavy, lifeless sea.

Were it possible, what would have been interesting, would be to have placed the two women side by side, for, just as Tara's organs were reversed, so her physiological condition was in reverse to that of her sister. Where Alexandra's right breast was withered like dried fruit, so Tara's was like that of a younger woman and vice versa. Where Alexandra's index finger on her right hand was crooked and decayed, so was the case with Tara but on her left hand. The two women were literally mirror images of one another.

Tara remained in this state of limbo until events began to unfold in New York and elsewhere. Sophia's bursts of telepathic energy initially failed to reach the sleeping harlequin whose internal switches seemed to have been shut down since that fateful day in 2055. However, as Sophia persevered, so it was as if a small army of inquisitive ants had invaded her senses, prising open drawers and cupboards, clearing out small compartments in her mind to see if there was anything left of value, any hope left at the bottom of Pandora's jar.

Sophia's bursts of energy began to have an impact. Shards of communication, like shards of light, struck receptors that sent signals to her brain, a brain cauterized by an unknown toxic force that was manufactured by a certain chromosome, a genetic defect as a result of a perverse, rampant DNA that had run amok inside her mind like a rabid dog, tearing her psyche to pieces, so that shutdown had become the only option. Nevertheless, as Sophia fought to communicate, so the neurotransmitters struggled to life, harassed by those ants that never slept, cajoled from their slumber and pulled into line like a slovenly platoon of recruits.

Over the course of the initial few days, Tara's carers began to notice changes in her facial movements, particularly her eyes, which jumped and flickered as if that same army of ants was busy running back and forth behind her eyelids, rummaging, spring cleaning. On the third day, she opened her eyes for a few minutes, but this event went unnoticed by the other nuns who were deep in meditation. After a week of receiving Sophia's voices, Tara sat up in the middle of the night and opened her eyes, peering around her slowly to determine where she might be. She cast her eyes across her body and rubbed her arms and shoulders, pinching life into her skin as she wiggled her toes.

Her sentinel remained unaware of Tara's resurgence and had fallen asleep at the bottom of Tara's bed where the nuns had set up a bench where her carers could read or meditate. By the time the other nun awoke, Tara had covered the walls of her small ward with hieroglyphics and ancient texts, and then returned to her bed, closing her eyes once more in a comatose state. Over the next few days, this became her routine, bursts of wild activity followed by a return to a comatose state.

The medical team, which routinely checked on Tara, visited with a sense of urgency but left as confused as when they had arrived.

"She will probably settle into consciousness at some stage," was all that the team leader could surmise. One of his team was more fascinated by the images scrawled across the walls and took some discreet pictures during his second visit, images that slowly dripped into the network, eventually appearing in Nathan's study where he placed them juxtapose to Alexandra's hieroglyphics, which Kazuo had sent through that day. The images were similar in many cases, identical in many ways but with one extraordinary exception, which took him some time to work out. Whereas Alexandra's images and texts could be read conventionally as with any normal language or dialect, to interpret Tara's images, Nathan had to hold them in front of a mirror. Despite this anomaly, which he was unable to fathom, Nathan knew instinctively that he had located Parvati.

Brian had become increasingly frustrated as he waited in Lima and even more concerned after his brief conversation with Jan, a sudden realization that his participation in events could also endanger his life as far afield as sleepy Salisbury. It had been a strange conversation, he reflected, neither broaching the subject of her text message or his response, his decision to "go for a drive," or the vast void that had opened between them in such a seamless fashion. Perhaps, on another day, they would have got that far in conversation, but Brian had simply rung off when Jan had mentioned the detective from Interpol.

He cast his mind back to his departure from their town house in Salisbury, that certain familiarity that comes with time and habit. He glanced down at the coffee cup in front of him, the name of the hotel emblazoned on its side, the Country Club Lima.

That's the odd thing, he thought, *if I open a cupboard at home I can tell you exactly where the coffee cups will be, where the glasses are stored, where the knives and forks sit and in which drawer. I can tell you where my socks live, where certain tools are stored in the garage, which photograph was taken where and when, every inch stored in subconscious familiarity.*

Yes, he thought, he felt that he was drawing close to that enigma, to some sort of definition of his dislocation from events or a realignment with another set of events, a more dramatic turn of events, certainly, but simply another set in time and space.

The thing is, he said to himself, *the thing is that the whole routine and habit thing is good and bad; it lulls us, blunts us, conditions us, it even erodes us, and then we fail to see what was once so clearly in front of us. I can tell you where my socks live, sure. I can tell you which wine glass Jan prefers for red or white wine. I can tell you all these things; at some stage I could tell you what turned her on, what areas of her body made her more excited than others, whether being on top or perhaps behind her excited different parts of her cunt; and I will use that word now, because someone else has been inside your cunt and that makes it redundant to me. So, all that routine, all those socks, cups, saucers, big knives, small forks, dessert spoons, all that knowledge which makes home feel safe ... and the missing link is what?* he mused sardonically. *The missing link is that I knew no routine with my wife's arse, that would seem to be the issue here.*

Brian looked up as a few faces passed him in the hotel foyer. Something took a short stab at his memory, a small surgical incision, but he knew not what; the image had disappeared as fast as it had appeared.

I was thinking about routine and habitual arses, he reminded himself.

Actually, you were just torturing yourself, he mocked.

Brian finished his coffee and returned to his room to prepare for a short, holographic session with Ruth and Sophia. He felt redundant and anxiety throbbed inside his mind like the thump of an old tune he could not quite remember.

"So, what news?" he said as soon as the three came online, eager to hear some progress.

"Not much for your end, Brian," Sophia said quickly. "I'm sorry, I still can't get a receptor, I'm close, I know that, but it's gone very quiet." There was a pause. "But I am travelling tonight," she added, "I have been receiving some very strong energy sources from the Far East, from Thailand; I know I'll be able to hone in on the source if I am a bit closer."

"What do you think it is?" Ruth asked. "Or who to be more precise?"

"I think it's my mother's twin," Sophia said. "I am sure in fact, the messages are jumbled, they are not directional, but I get the same spikes as I used to get when my mother would go into one of her hieroglyphic spins, it's just a bit weaker."

"So what am I supposed to do?" Brian asked with some frustration. "I seem to be wasting my time here and I'm worried about my family. You know that my wife had a visitor; it's obviously them."

There was a long silence at the other end of the line.

"Well?" he asked, his angst bubbling like lava in the space between them.

"You need to sit tight, Brian," Sophia said, an edge creeping into her voice, an edge conveying an order as opposed to a request. "We know that one of the prophets is close to you. There is a dormant signal, almost as if the radio has been turned on but it's not transmitting, but even in that state, I can detect a presence."

Brian sighed but said nothing.

"I have something for you, Brian," Ruth piped up, "but I'm not sure you're going to like it."

"No shit," said Brian sarcastically. "What is it?"

"Well, it's hard to describe, really, and I'm not sure you'll get this; in fact I'm not sure that I get it." She paused. "I think that danger is very close to you, very close." The line went quiet.

"Is that it?" he asked. "I thought that we were all in danger, so is this dangerous danger or dangerous, dangerous danger?" His attempt at some light humour was lost on the two women.

"Yes," Ruth continued, "but it's linked to Alexandra, a dream I've had and some sort of connection with her killer. I sort of received a message, I know it's weird but I did nevertheless, and the message was for you, not for me."

"So, what was the message, for fuck's sake?" Brian asked, his language symbiotic with a slither of fear that ran across his skin and left its mark like a slug leaving a trace of its slime.

"That was it, I'm afraid," Ruth continued, "but be careful, please." The line between the three fell silent.

"Look, I've got to go," Sophia said, breaking the deadlock, "I need to get ready. Brian," she added, "please be patient and vigilant; I also feel a sixth sense around you, very close to you." And then the line went dead.

Brian sat on the edge of his bed and peered out at the rooftops of Lima. A heavy mist had descended on the city from the Pacific and a thick layer of cloud gave a sense of confinement, the city with its back to the sea, pushed toward the ocean by the range of mountains to the east, squashed between immovable masses of such different textures. Something was very wrong, Brian knew this, he had seen something, recently, that very day, but it skipped across his memory like an elusive bird, moving from branch to branch, flower to flower, but never remaining in any one place long enough to allow him to gain focus.

"What are you?" he screamed to himself.

Brian closed his eyes in the hope that his mind might also skip freely; perhaps by doing so, he might suddenly find himself on the same branch as that elusive bird, pushing his beak into the same flower. He reflected on their recent holographic conference call, the stilted energy that sat between them like a heavily pregnant woman, awkward, cumbersome, even clumsy under such heavy but important baggage. He imagined Sophia in her constricted space, her safe house, urgently throwing a few things into a holdall. It was there, he said to himself, in that space, literally her space, where he was trying to get to. And then his mind and memory opened simultaneously. He had alighted on the same, tenuous branch as that elusive bird; it had been behind Sophia, still thrown over the back of a chair, the coat he had retrieved from Alexandra's apartment. He had caught that same coat, that exact colour and cut, in his periphery vision in the lobby before he came upstairs. Like a train of camels crossing a distant sand dune, eclipsed by the sun, his mind had registered an image but it had not had enough time to decipher or unpack what it had seen.

He sat up with a start.

Fuck, he said to himself. What were the chances of such similar coats in such different places? What sort of man buys two coats that are exactly the same? A grey man, he told himself, a methodical man who pays scant regard to fashion statements, a man who likes to disappear into shadows, a man driven by practical expediency. A man who thinks nothing of cutting off someone's fingers.

"My God," he whispered under his breath. *The hunter is literally on my doorstep. Alexandra's killer is downstairs, hunting me, not hunting, he has found me, my guillotine has been raised.*

For the first time in his life, Brian felt real fear. Up to now, it had been a tangential adventure, someone else's game, a game at arm's length, at finger's length?

Not anymore, he told himself, *there is someone downstairs who has every intention of killing me in a short while and who, in that field of expertise, is my better by an unquantifiable factor. I am, to him at least, already a dead man walking.*

For the first time since that fateful text message, Brian wished that he could sit down in a boring conference hall and listen to some idiot talk about dental floss.

2065, Chiang Mai, A Cavity

K left the Imperial Mae Ping hotel in Chiang Mai and decided to wander the streets for a few hours until the late afternoon. Despite the beauty and splendour of the historical city, K found it hard to relax in any conventional way and had never been comfortable in the role of a tourist. She had already carried out a reconnaissance of her target area and was confident that she could easily enter the nun's quarters in the middle of the afternoon when the number of tourists seemed to be at its maximum, dispatch Parvati, and then decide what to do with her time as soon as the job was done.

That was her problem, really, or one of her problems, what to do with her time? She thought about the colossal amount of work she had done for Nathan, over ten years of loyal, well-paid service, and the huge bank balance sitting untouched in various accounts around the globe. For the most part, she shunned contact with fellow human beings and preferred to find comfort and relaxation in books. What had Hemingway said? "There is no friend as loyal as a book." She liked that quote as much as she liked Hemingway and her small "lock up and go" apartments were both lined with bookshelves stacked to the ceilings with a variety of authors; it had to be fiction, though. Historical accounts or biographies held little interest to her, as they were as distorted and as manipulated as reality itself. She knew that first-hand having worked for the DNA conscious for so long, although her knowledge of their internal initiatives and secrets was circumspect, a factor she had never dared to question.

K found herself outside Wat Chiang Man, the oldest Buddhist temple in Chiang Mai, and thought that she could kill at least a couple of hours in the late morning. She tagged along with a group touring the historic site.

"King Mengrai founded the city of Chiang Mai (meaning 'new city') in 1296," said the guide, "and it succeeded Chiang Rai as capital of the Lanna kingdom. The ruler was known as the Chao. The city was surrounded by a moat and a defensive wall…" and so the guide continued.

K's mind was elsewhere, hopping between her colleague in Lima and her own forthcoming task. She was still worried about Kazuo; yes, he was back on track in as much as he had executed his task in Cuzco with typical skill and alacrity, but the incident in the apartment in New York had left an undeniable mark on him, more than that, a deep scar. He had bitten someone's finger off, for God's sake, hardly an acknowledged annex to the assassin's field guide. So, she knew that there were strange powers at work and had resolved to perform a quick, clinical kill and then leave the city before regrouping in Europe. With two prophets dead, and the Englishman's death imminent, there might be a strategic pause while they waited to see if a third prophet emerged. There had been rumours a number of years ago suggesting a man who resembled the third prophet had committed suicide, but the body had been cremated before she and Kazuo had managed to get to it. That was a while ago, she reflected, at least eight years ago.

So, she thought, *I guess that we'll just have to wait and see, to see whether Nathan feels that the job is done. Perhaps the cantankerous old bastard can drop dead then, perhaps he will feel that he can relax, that his life's most crucial project can now run its course into the future.*

On the other side of the world, it was still about midnight and Brian was trying to form a plan wherein he could somehow get out of the hotel without being seen by the man in the grey coat. He wondered if he could perhaps turn the tides on his adversary, not to confront him physically but at least to outflank him and disappear while he sought help or advice from the others. He was frightened to leave his room or even to order room service in case his tracker was waiting for him in the corridor or had already made some arrangement with the hotel staff. What Brian did know, however, was that if he stayed where he was, it was simply a question of time before the man got bored and came up to his room.

He must know which room I am in, Brian told himself, *so he will come in the early hours, perhaps around four in the morning when the hotel is probably at its quietest.*

If he stayed like this, a rabbit frozen in the headlights, he might as well just go down to the lobby and present himself to his killer. He thought about obvious things like fire escapes or the back stairs and decided that he would have to take the risk and chance his luck, his one, slim advantage being that the man who was hunting him did not know that Brian had made a connection between the two coats and identified him as the same man. So, a dentist versus a trained assassin, but at least Brian had something in his favour, or so he thought.

For his part, Kazuo might have been scarred by his confrontation with Alexandra in New York, but he was still a consummate professional and, as such, had picked up on the flicker of "something" that had crossed Brian's features as he walked across the hotel lobby. He had been wearing dark sunglasses and knew that Brian would not have been expecting him to have been looking directly at him, why would he? So, when Brian went upstairs to his room, Kazuo sat in the hotel lobby to unpack and reassemble the events of the last few days.

There are no such things as coincidences, he reminded himself, *not in this line of work. The Englishman saw something and his mind will eventually drop whatever it is into his lap; that's how the mind works.*

He knew that it might take a tangential event to stimulate this or, perhaps, just time, but he would get there. So he must consider himself compromised; but how, why, what had he overlooked?

So Kazuo sat and his mind wandered, like a hummingbird he hovered over events, adjacent to events, dipping his beak deeply into every source of nectar, clearing his senses before moving on to another flower, another source of inspiration. And just as Brian had done, he reconstructed the previous days, the events in Alexandra's apartment, rolling up the sleeves of his shirt, spitting bone into her cheap kitchen sink. He sat with an untouched cup of coffee in front of him for almost one hour, and then the obvious link dropped from the sky and made him grimace with disgust in himself; it had been so obvious. The answer was literally in front of his face, or, more precisely, thrown over the back of the chair next to him. He picked up his cold cup of coffee and sipped at the rim gingerly, as if he might burn his tongue, before replacing the cup on the saucer.

He needed to get the Englishman away from the hotel; that much he knew. The hotel security was extremely tight and there were cameras in all public areas.

What will he do, he asked himself, *if he has really made the connection? Will he run, sit tight, or try to gain an upper hand?*

The logical choice should be one of the former, Kazuo told himself, but this Englishman had already surprised them. There were still parts of the puzzle that would play out, but Kazuo decided to try an experiment. He called his driver, who was dozing in the hotel car park, and spoke to him briefly when the young man arrived in the lobby. He gave his instructions and left the man wearing his coat and with his sunglasses perched on his head. Kazuo went outside and decided to wait in the car, curious to see what might play out over the next few hours.

Brian waited until just after three in the morning and then gathered his key belongings together in a small rucksack, which he strapped to his back. He had paid for an extra day when he booked into the hotel and had no qualms about leaving his clothes and a suitcase behind, his mind focused more on survival than housekeeping. He stepped quietly into the corridor outside his room, made his way to the two-storey flight of stairs that served as the fire escape, and made his way down to the ground floor. The stairs brought Brian out at the back of the hotel and into the beautiful gardens, parts of which were illuminated by bright spotlights. He crouched down in the shadows of a huge palm tree and tried to bring his breathing under control. He glanced up at the back of the hotel, most of which was shrouded in darkness with the exception of one or two rooms where the lights were still burning. He could hear the dull hum of a television broadcast and the familiar signature theme of a world news channel.

"Man found chopped to pieces in Lima," he said to himself. "British dentist found dead in hotel room … The Lord Lucan of dentistry emerges in Peru, suicide suspected."

Brian could feel his heart jumping under his jacket, his pulse skipping ahead of him, out of control.

Now what? You do have choices.

K had done her best to disguise herself as a Buddhist nun and had even shaved her head that morning in her hotel room. Dressed in traditional robes, she made her way to the ubosot at the temple of Wat Phra Singh and waited patiently, not far from the small bench where Tara had fallen into a coma so many years earlier. After about 20 minutes, she tagged along with a small group of nuns as they emerged from the northern entrance of the ubosot and made their way slowly toward the living quarters where she knew Parvati was under care. Once inside the monastic courtyard, she slipped away from behind the group and made her way down a short flight of stairs in accordance with the information she had received.

Parvati had been cared for in one of the lower levels of the monastery where the days were cooler, particularly during the summer months when daytime temperatures reached as high as 36 degrees Celsius. K sensed the subtle change in temperature as she moved quietly into the lower corridor, just as she sensed a change in her own tempo, a quickening of her pulse, a thin layer of perspiration covering her skin like body armour as she prepared for battle. She counted the rooms as she moved silently down the corridor and glanced into the room where she knew she would find Parvati, a quick look to confirm that her directional senses were tuned, that the directions had been correct.

The door was a few inches open and K caught sight of a bed, some rudimentary medical equipment, and the bowed head of another nun who seemed to be reading or in meditation at the end of Parvati's bed. K slipped into a small alcove beyond the room and waited in the shadows. She knew that during the late afternoon there would be a pause in Parvati's care as the nuns changed over, ate their evening meal, and prayed. This small window of opportunity was all that she needed to slip into the room and perform her task. Yes, she could do it now, but that would mean killing another nun and things might start to get a little messy. She preferred to have time to make good her escape.

Brian wished that he had considered his choices more carefully before he left his hotel room, not because leaving his room was a choice he regretted, rather he now found himself out of immediate danger and with, perhaps, more choices than he had a few hours ago. And he was struggling with these choices, that much he acknowledged, mainly because he had no clear view of an end state, because he could not imagine an end to this game. He was unable to see a scenario in which their small, intrepid band could outwit this overpowering machine that lived in shadows and pulled invisible strings. They had never even discussed a real plan to reveal the prophets' existence to the world; how did they hope to achieve this before being snuffed out like dying candles?

Brian tried to pull himself back to reality, to the here and now. The here and now was what? Run and keep running, or perhaps try and gain an upper hand, keep his killer under some sort of surveillance until he could liaise with the others, until Sophia confirmed the presence of the twin or the other prophet supposedly close by.

Despite any real logic to his thoughts, Brian's curiosity and fear grappled with each other, almost like a wringing of hands. He found himself, almost unconsciously, moving through the garden at the back of the hotel until he found himself by the swimming pool, which was accessed through the main atrium. The atrium, in turn, was linked to the front of the hotel and a set of steps leading down to the street and parking area, the colonial entrance dominated by two huge palm trees and two pairs of majestic street lanterns.

Brian glanced through the double doors separating the pool from the atrium and tried to focus on the other end of the lobby where a number of ornate armchairs sat around a marble fireplace. Despite the half-light and a few members of staff passing within his field of vision, Brian could see the profile of a man with his back to him, at an angle to the reception desk and main entrance. He could not see the man's face or whether he was reading or dozing, but he recognized the coat and knew instinctively that this man was waiting for him, waiting to kill him or capture him, did that make much difference? Brian glanced at his watch and decided to wait for a few moments, shifting his weight from one side to another as he balanced on his haunches.

After what can only have been one or two minutes, Brian sensed a change in body language in the man in the chair who sat up abruptly and held a receiver to his ear. He stood up quickly and, waving toward the reception desk, passed through the main revolving doors and made his way toward the set of stone steps down to the streets. Giving little thought to a plan, Brian went back to the side of the hotel and ran across the lawn to the front of the hotel where the long lawns ran adjacent to the street behind high, stone walls. Brian clambered up the side of the wall and peered down into the street, his heart pumping with fear and adrenaline. The man wearing the coat was moving away slowly, to his right, his shadow drifting in and out of the small pools of street lighting.

Kazuo had told his driver to leave the hotel and to make his way on foot through the San Isidro district toward the city centre and that he would pick him up in 15 minutes. He stood in the shadows on the edge of the golf course, which faced the hotel, and tracked the driver as he descended the steps and moved off toward the commercial centre of the city. A wry smile crossed his features as he saw a shadow drop into the street at the base of the garden wall away to his right-hand side. He waited to see which way the shadow would turn, what levels of bravery, curiosity, or stupidity would come to the fore.

He was fascinated to see the Englishman turn to his right and cautiously follow his driver, some 100 metres behind him. Kazuo moved quickly back to his car and drove back around the hotel in a counter-clockwise direction, eventually moving adjacent to the two men on foot until he passed them on parallel side streets, pulling ahead a few blocks where he parked and moved toward a point where he could find a suitable ambush site.

At just after 4:30 p.m., the nun attending to Parvati glanced at her watch, peered across at her patient who had not moved throughout her shift, and then left the room. K heard the door squeak and glanced along the corridor at the back of the retreating nun. As soon as she heard her soft footsteps on the stone stairs, K left the alcove and slipped into the room. She moved close to the bed and glanced down at her victim who seemed to be in a deep sleep.

How weird, she said to herself, *it's almost identical to the scene in New York, the same tapestry of life and death cast across her skin.*

She picked up a chair and positioned it to one side of the bed and then flicked open a small camera device that she balanced on the chair.

The small device emitted a barely audible bleep and Nathan stirred in his deep armchair in front of his log fire in Vienna, an image of the small room in Chiang Mai appearing like a ghostly spirit across his ceiling.

In Lima, Kazuo felt a vibration in his pocket and flipped open his screen while he waited in his ambush position. No words were exchanged between the three. Kazuo glanced from the screen and then back down the street. His driver had passed him just over a minute ago and he could hear Brian's footsteps drawing closer. He closed the screen quickly, the faraway images burrowing under his skin, an indescribable fear passing through his body like a plague. His senses took him back to New York, so much so that he could taste bone and blood in his mouth; he could see the finger falling onto the cheap rug before he himself had collapsed.

Stepping from the shadows, Kazuo wrapped his hand across Brian's face as he passed his ambush position. One hand closed around his mouth, the other smashed into his rib cage. The air was driven from Brian's lungs in an agonizing assault that left him on his knees. Kazuo struck him once again from behind, his heavy hands, like axe blows, breaking multiple ribs as Brian desperately tried to crawl away from the assault, gasping for air. Kazuo's huge hands wrapped around the back of his neck, one around his throat, the other moving to the top of his forehead so that he could rotate Brian's head and neck in opposite directions and finish him quickly.

Brian had not recovered from the first blow and his body had gone limp, a vague consciousness that his little game of bravery had come to an end, that his dull life had come to such an exciting but abrupt finale. No drawn-out retirement, no self-sacrifice for him. He could feel the huge power within the hands of this man, that his head was about to be crushed or his neck pulled from his torso like pulling a weed from a flower bed.

As Kazuo broke Brian's body with his blows, K moved around the far side of the bed from where she had positioned the camera and pulled out a small pistol. She deftly slipped on a silencing device and took one pace away from Parvati's torso, extending her arms before firing five rounds in quick succession into her chest.

Nathan watched with deep satisfaction as the body kicked and jumped under the bullets; he snapped off the image and took a deep sigh.

As the bullets smashed into Parvati's body, Kazuo's body contorted as if he had been electrocuted. Pulses of energy tore into his aorta, a series of five acute heart attacks exploding within him just as he began to rotate Brian's neck.

Brian felt the vices loosen around his neck and heard the heavy thud of Kazuo's body behind him, like the distant echo of a heavy anchor reaching the seabed. He crawled a few feet away from the body, confusion and fear competing with pain and relief.

2065, The Living Dead, Perhaps

Two weeks later, the living and the dead gathered in their different corners of the globe.

With Nathan's tacit assistance, K moved Kazuo's body back to Vienna where arrangements were made for a discreet, private service. His personal papers were filed with Nathan's attorney who was given instructions to dispose of his assets in accordance with a short will he had prepared some ten years earlier and which he had never changed. The will was as impersonal as his life had been and K found herself alone at the short cremation, her tall, willowy figure standing upright in the front aisle, her shaven head more reminiscent of a scarecrow than an elegant, hired killer.

She waited outside the back of the building and watched the dark plume of smoke curl up into the autumnal sky as the dead were ferried in every 15 minutes, the bereaved in various shapes and forms, the dead, finally unburdened. She waited for 30 minutes until a man, who looked as if he was closely related to a stick insect, emerged with a small urn of ashes and placed it ceremoniously between her hands, his features cast in stone, his cheekbones the colour of ashen flints, a rather daft bowler hat perched on his head as if it had nowhere else to be. He nodded solemnly and she looked through him as if to say, you fucking idiot, why the drama, why the theatrical costume, my friend has simply gone back to where he came from, simply in a different form of energy.

K had been bereft of any real sentiment for much of her life, but she did resolve to indulge herself for a few moments before a scheduled meeting with Nathan. Kazuo had few luxuries in life that she was aware of, but much of their time had been spent together in unusual circumstances, waiting in dark corners, skulking in the world's flotsam and jetsam. Kazuo's only whim would be to order coffee while his mind worked within him, coffee that was normally only touched after an hour or so and then treated with such reverence despite its, by then, tepid and pallid character. So she took a taxi back to the centre of Vienna and selected a nondescript café close to Josefsplatz where she ordered herself a brandy and an espresso for Kazuo. She took perverse pleasure in stipulating a double as opposed to a single espresso when asked which she would prefer and propped the small urn next to her as she sipped at her brandy and watched the hustle and bustle of other peoples' lives passing in front of her.

Kazuo's autopsy had revealed a massive cardiac arrest and had given an approximate time of death. Nathan had procured some CCTV footage from the police showing the events unfold in the early hours of the morning. It showed two solitary figures walking through the San Isidro suburb of Lima, the second figure engulfed by a squat figure, beaten to submission, and then, at the ultimate point of delivery, the man, whose hands appeared to be working on a chopping board, contorted in sudden agony and collapsed, leaving his victim to crawl a few feet away before stumbling into the darkness.

K had studied the image and the time of recording, which she matched with the images that had been sent through to Nathan as she pumped five bullets into Parvati's torso. Despite the 12-hour time difference between their respective locations, K knew, before even checking, that his time of death was at exactly the same moment. The thought sent a shiver down her spine and she took a gulp of her brandy; there were forces at work she could not describe and she was relieved that the episode was finally over. She glanced at the urn and its espresso, which was cooling down in front of her.

What a strange life we lead, or some of us do anyway, she reflected. *A whole life can be defined or distorted by singular events, exponential events that override the conscious and the conscience, and drive us to an irreversible course of action.*

"We were similar in that way," she murmured to Kazuo.

You with your dear Vaesna, in my case with the stream of animals who fucked and sodomized me out of adolescence into a sterile numbness which I will never escape from.

After one hour exactly, K rose to her feet and left the urn with its tepid cup of coffee.

"I am sorry about Kazuo," Nathan said quietly, his back to K who was standing in his study, waiting for an invitation to be seated. She said nothing. "I did not know that he had a heart condition," he continued.

K remained silent and said nothing about the simultaneous timings; what would be the point? Nathan pointed at a chair close to the fire and K sat down.

"Your hair looks different," he said with a smile, "not sure it's really you, though," he chuckled, "makes you look like a refugee."

K smiled at Nathan and accepted a glass of brandy he had poured for her. He sat down with a deep sigh and looked into the flames. K could not remember a time when she had ever been in his study without a burning fire.

"So," he continued after a few moments of reflection, "I think that we can pause for a while unless you feel differently?" K nodded her head slowly. "Valeriya is dead, Alexandra is dead, as are Francisco and Parvati." He coughed and cleared his throat. "We have never really known much about the third prophet's whereabouts. You'll remember your trip to Lagos a few years ago, that we thought we might have found him but you both arrived too late, not your fault of course, just circumstances, events, as always." His voice tailed off.

"So, anyway, without a living prophet, what can they do? What can this carer person or daughter individual do without a champion; what can this ridiculous Englishman do without a cause? Not much."

"So you don't want me to find him, to kill him?" K asked. Nathan smiled and reached over to pat her on her knee.

"No, dear," he said simply, "he has had a good battering. He will run home with his tail between his legs and, besides, we know where he is, where his wife lives; we can always pay a visit if necessity calls."

"So, now what?" K asked, a sudden loneliness surrounding her like a bubble.

"We can afford to wait," Nathan said with a smile. "We have won this small victory unless the third prophet still lives, but I have my doubts; the little evidence we have suggests that he did indeed die in Lagos in 2057."

Nathan stood up, a signal for K to leave.

"So, we wait and watch as always, but I feel as if I might sleep better now, I feel as if the job is finally done, so you must rest too, K, take a break, you deserve it."

K attempted to smile at Nathan; she didn't want a break. She placed her half-finished glass of brandy on the mantelpiece above the burning fireplace and left the room.

Following the murder of Fermina and a second person unknown to him, Augusto Garcia left Lima and made his way to Quito where he thought that he might be safer for a while. He found a small room in a rundown part of the city and spent his days lying on a filthy cot and his nights gambling, piles of banknotes accumulating in his wardrobe and under the thin, bug-ridden mattress. There had been one of two huge outlets of energy before he left Lima, one in particular he was unable to fathom, and he had done his best to switch off his own internal energy fields, to subdue them under an alcoholic mucous that he succumbed to each evening. The mucous was a bandage when he was conscious, but it did not stem the tide when he slept, when the uncontrollable parts of his DNA ran amok, his genetic defects crashing into one another like a bespoke hadron collider.

Augusto had no idea what to do next. His instincts were to run and keep running, to remain anonymous, as he had been when he met Fermina, but this time to stay anonymous. He had no idea exactly what had happened, but he did know that his undoing, ultimately her death, had been as a result of his decision to cure her that night. The irony was laughable; by saving her, somehow he had condemned her. Was that event the energy outlet by which they found him? Could it be as simple as that, a homing beacon of that magnitude?

The other feeling that now surrounded him like quicksand was one of unbearable sadness, not so much guilt, but utter and complete despair. He was literally drowning. He knew instinctively that those few years with Fermina were more than most feel over a lifetime, a deep contentment and peace in another's presence, no pretence, no egos, a depth of transparency and honesty that perhaps only comes with age, forged from loneliness, perhaps, shaped even by independence, or non-dependence might make better sense. They had simply been as one in those emotional spaces where freedom also resides; that had been their secret, even if they had stumbled across it subconsciously.

Another feeling also lay submerged within Augusto, quelled in the early hours as he drank but which rose in his throat like vomit when he awoke. It was anger and frustration, a directionless rage, a rage that needed a mentor and a focus, and revenge, as much without purpose or direction as his rage, but these feelings sat in his gut and twisted his intestines into grotesque shapes. His mind remained a jumble but he knew two things: Fermina had been murdered because of him, because of his special powers, and those responsible for those special powers believed him to be dead. So, on that basis, a revenge of sorts might be feasible. But he had no idea where to start.

It was a few weeks before the three heads of Cerberus finally convened over the airwaves. On that fateful night, Brian had crawled away into the shadows, barely able to walk, and had got onto the first bus that passed him by, a bus that took him to the central bus terminal in Lima where he boarded another bus for Callao, the country's first port about 11 kilometres outside Lima. He found a small guest house in the Cantolao district where he collapsed in agony for the rest of that morning. In the afternoon, he found a hospital where he waited for X-rays, feigning a biking accident to explain the heavy bruising that covered his lower back and upper chest on one side.

"You have five broken ribs," the radiologist said with a smile, "but no perforation of the lungs, which is a plus, so no biking for six weeks or so. You'll need something for the pain and to help you sleep. I'll get you an appointment with the doctor."

Brian made a rather lame case to the woman who managed the guest house and so, for the next two weeks, she and her daughter prepared meals for Brian, which he took in his room, and they even brought him newspapers and magazines. After two weeks, he was able to start walking a little more freely, although the pain was still acute when he walked up a flight of stairs or sneezed, something he desperately tried to avoid.

He slept for many hours each day and his strength gradually began to return. So did his dreams, which were a jumble of distorted images, the protagonists from his last few weeks jumbled together in disarray, a huge, anonymous dentist with bear-like hands tending to Alexandra's mouth, her upper jaw a pristine white, her lower teeth black and in decay, Jan wagging her finger at him across the small kitchen table in their home, chastising him about not coming home or something like that; he was unsure, the dream had been elusive. He was relieved that he had not had to endure another dream that featured the other Brian.

He remained tormented by events near the hotel, in the early hours, when that man's ruthless strength reminded Brian of his own mortality, just how out of his depth he actually was when confronted by these manipulators who would stop at nothing. What had Valeriya been thinking? Yes, true, out of his depth.

But she did find your wallet, he told himself, *surely there are no such things as coincidences?*

In Brian's most recurring dream over those two weeks, when the heavy painkillers threw a blanket across his pain, he found himself apprehensive, fearful over his arrival back at home, desperate to find his feet, desperate for a lifeline from Jan, to prove his worthiness or their mutual worth in her eyes. In his dream, he arrived home to an empty house, his wife somewhere, who knows where, it did not seem important. Although the house seemed familiar, Brian became increasingly anxious as he moved around this familiar space. Each drawer, each cupboard was where it should be, the furniture was as he remembered, but their contents had been rearranged. He tried to make himself a cup of tea but could no longer find the cups and saucers, the drawers filled with rows of neatly severed fingers. He decided to take a shower but found another's clothing hanging in his wardrobe, his presence somehow usurped, substituted. His final frustration was in his appearance as he moved about his familiar space, desperate to make himself presentable before his wife returned. He could feel the man's hands around his head and neck, squeezing, crushing, and every time he checked his appearance in the mirror before her arrival home, he found his head cocked at a grotesque angle, twisted at 90 degrees, his skin blotchy where the man's fingers had dug into his skin, like a chef kneading dough, the structure of his skull realigned behind the outer fabric. A monster.

"So," Sophia asked him, "what happened, where have you been?"

"You were right, Ruth," Brian began, "I was in danger. The man who killed Alexandra was here, in Lima. The odd thing was that I recognized him from his coat, the exact same coat which he left in Alexandra's apartment. He was following me, well, he found me, clearly."

Brian explained what had happened that night, his injuries, and his slow, ongoing recuperation.

"My God," exclaimed Ruth, "that's incredible. It's almost unbelievable. It's just fucking unbelievable." The line went quiet for a moment.

"So?" Brian asked. "What happened in Thailand, Sophia?"

He could see Sophia shaking her head. "Just as incredible," she said. "Probably more so. Ruth knows what has happened but I'll tell you anyway."

Brian noticed lines of fatigue across her face; she looked like a woman who had seen a ghost.

"Well, as you know, I had received an energy source from Thailand, so I made my way to Bangkok where the signal grew even stronger, a huge spike in activity that led me to Chiang Mai. It was simply the strongest source of energy imaginable."

Sophia removed her spectacles and wiped her eyes, her emotions suddenly rushing from the corners of her eyes.

"Anyway, I seemed to know exactly where to go and I walked into this monastery, completely unchallenged, and found myself in a room filled with hieroglyphics, but they were in reverse, almost like reading the sign on the front of an ambulance, everything is in reverse, but I could read it, partly because of my mother, partly because of me, I suppose."

Sophia paused and wiped her forearm across the underside of her nose where her tears had gathered.

"Well, I instinctively knew that my mother's twin had been here but I also knew that something terrible had happened. I showed the nuns a photograph of my mother, the way in which she evolved, the old and the new, so to speak. They showed me pictures of their friend, their patient; they are the same, identical. The nuns do not seem to see what I see, that they are identical but mirrored, it's hard to see that when looking at a photograph. Their leader told me of events two days earlier, events which they found hard to recount, an unknown attacker in the late afternoon, an indescribable act, an unaccountable desecration of their holy space. Tara, as they call her, shot five times through the chest, assumed dead but not quite, close to death, but a miracle, for them anyway, perhaps not so for us."

Sophia paused but no longer tried to stem the tears that flowed freely down her cheeks.

"She's not dead, after that?" Brian asked quietly. "What happened?"

Sophia attempted a smile. "She is the mirror of my mother," she whispered, "in all ways. The bullets passed through the left side of her chest, a side which is an empty cavity. Her heart is on her right side; in fact, all her internal organs are the mirror of what we might consider to be typical or normal."

Silence fell between the three unlikely partners, partners in events that were simply too fantastic not to be true.

"So, she lives," Ruth continued for Sophia, "presumed dead, but she lives."

"My God," Brian added, "and they think she is dead?"

"There's more," Ruth added. "We have been digging further into South America, the energy surges which Sophia was receiving."

"Yes?" Brian asked eagerly.

"Well, we cannot be certain but Sophia thinks that there have also been incredible things taking place. She picked up on an event, a surge, as you know, and then I noticed something odd in the newspaper, a terrible tragedy, two people killed in a place called Cuzco, a gas explosion. Well, a few years ago, we had an intern here, at the hospital, from Peru. He and I had a thing, you know, anyway, that's irrelevant, so I called him. He did some digging for me and it appears that the dead couple were just that, a couple, the man, an Augusto Garcia, a drifter, he seems similar in age to what the prophets might be now, but that's not all. Wait for this; he pulls their medical records, the woman's and his, but he has none, this Augusto, he has never been sick, but her case is different, extraordinary, hers a case of a brain tumour, a death sentence, or should have been, but my friend tells me that she changed from one week to the next."

"Let me guess," Brian interrupted, "it vanished, miraculously!"

"Exactly," Ruth continued, "and one other odd thing. The police file is closed but my friend also managed to get a look at the coroner's report. So, yes, an accident, yes a gas explosion blah, blah, but one line struck him as odd, listen to this, 'although the deceased would have died instantly, their remains were sufficiently preserved to reflect their skeletal physiology. One factor puzzled the investigating officer in that in the case of the woman, identified as Fermina Marquez, two of her fingers seemed to have become separated from her hand during the fire, a result which the investigating officer finds hard to explain.' Ring a bell, amputated fingers?"

"So, murder, is that what you are saying?" Brian asked. "They found one of the other prophets?"

"Yes, but not quite so simple," Sophia interjected. "Those signals, those surges are still sitting on the airwaves. Whoever was killed by your man, we presume, it was not the person sending those signals nor the person who is still trying to muffle those signals. He seems to be further north now, maybe Ecuador, maybe Colombia, I can't tell, it's a bit mushy."

There was a long silence while each reflected on what they had just discussed. Eventually, Brian broke the silence. "So, what about Alexandra's twin, will she make it?"

"We think so," said Sophia, "but she seems as mad as my mother; she is at least evidence, evidence of their program, or the fact that the prophets still live."

"Maybe," Brian sighed, "but not much good if she's crazy."

"Well, we have her," Ruth interrupted. "She is alive, presumed dead."

"As might be this other prophet," added Sophia. "Now we have an edge, perhaps."

"So, now what?" Brian asked.

"I have a call to make," Sophia said, "and then we can discuss a strategy, our strategy." She paused, studying Brian's features across the huge expanse between them. "But perhaps you should go home, Brian; you look finished."

"I am frightened to go home," he said. "This is where all this started or ended for me, with a message from home."

2065, A Timely Resurrection

A day later, Sophia picked up Kazuo's coat and extracted the small camera device from his inside pocket. She had been waiting for such a time, when it might come in handy, and she also knew that there were no such things as coincidences. She flicked open the shutter and a small signal echoed across Nathan's study. Without thinking very carefully, his face appeared on the screen in front of her. It took him a while to configure his thoughts before he spoke.

"Ah," he said a little sheepishly, "I wondered who this might be. I don't believe in resurrections unless we arrange them ourselves."

Sophia said nothing but studied his face calmly.

"So, it's you," Nathan continued. "I knew your mother and your grandmother, for that matter. In a sense, we are related; I had a hand in your creation, did you know that?"

Sophia removed her spectacles so that he could see her orchid eyes.

He smiled. "Yes, I can see that you are also special, that you must have some of your mother's hereditary powers, poor Alexandra…" his voice tailed away. He waited for Sophia to speak but she offered nothing.

"You can come and find me, if you like, if it's revenge that you seek, my dear, but you know that the game is over, that you have no moving parts to speak of and, besides, I will die soon. Perhaps you wish to quicken my departure?" There was a pause. "Do you?" he asked. Nathan took a deep sigh. "You know, young lady, there are those who take life with forethought, fear, and introspection, and those who simply waste life in all and every degree. When you take life in either space without a mirror of the other, you can never judge. Think about that if you will."

Sophia touched the screen with her index finger and then closed the shutter. His image disappeared.

Iguana Books

iguanabooks.com

If you enjoyed *Moral Hazard*...
Look for other books coming soon from Iguana Books!

If you're a writer ...
Iguana Books is always looking for great new writers, in every genre. We produce primarily ebooks but, as you can see, we do the occasional print book as well. Visit us at iguanabooks.com to see what Iguana Books has to offer both emerging and established authors.

iguanabooks.com/publishing-with-iguana/

If you're looking for another good book ...
All Iguana Books books are available on our website. We pride ourselves on making sure that every Iguana book is a great read.

iguanabooks.com/bookstore/

Visit our bookstore today and support your favourite author.

www.ingramcontent.com/pod-product-compliance
Ingram Content Group UK Ltd.
Pitfield, Milton Keynes, MK11 3LW, UK
UKHW041632190726
13854UKWH00006B/2462